Kiss of the Virgin Queen

by

Sharon Buchbinder

Kiss of the Jinni Hunter Series

Kiss of the Virgin Queen

Cover Art by *Rae Monet, Inc. Design*

The Wild Rose Press, Inc.
PO Box 708
Adams Basin, NY 14410-0708
Visit us at www.thewildrosepress.com

Publishing History
First Black Rose Edition, 2015
Print ISBN 978-1-5092-0392-5
Digital ISBN 978-1-5092-0393-2

Kiss of the Jinni Hunter Series
Published in the United States of America

Arta Shahani stood at the curb

of the one-runway Summertown Airport, took a deep breath of clean air, and admired the pristine mountains. An eagle floated overhead, enjoying the updraft. He wished he could ride the wind with the bird, and watch the green vistas and mountains roll under him again. One of the hazards of living in the Washington D.C. area was he sometimes forgot the more remote, less populated portions of the country. No matter, once he was with Eliana, it didn't matter where he was. *"With thee, my love, hell itself were heaven..."*

He tapped his foot and jingled the change in his pocket and then stopped, suddenly self-aware of his mannerisms. Arta felt a flush of embarrassment dashed with a tinge of boyish anticipation. *Eliana.* All he had to do was *think* her name and crazy things came over him. His pulse raced, muscles tensed, blood rushed to all the wrong parts of his body. He knew the term for it, flight, fight, or f—

The sharp blast of a car horn interrupted his musings.

The object of his fascination sat in a black government sedan in front of him.

Eliana.

For a frozen moment, he stopped breathing. His stomach plummeted, and his pulse kicked into erratic beats. He couldn't stop staring at her. Her green eyes sparkled with humor, and a mischievous grin spread from one flushed cheek to the other. Just as lovely as the first time he met her and took her hand. A jolt of joy headed for his pants. That would never do. He placed his briefcase over his groin and waved.

Praise for Sharon Buchbinder

"Ms. Buchbinder weaves ancient secrets and modern mysteries into a beautifully written story that will keep you turning the pages."

~USA Today Bestselling Author, Roz Lee

~*~

"Sharon Buchbinder seamlessly blends ancient lore, intriguing, sexy characters, and a unique approach to the werewolf genre in a fast paced suspenseful plot that will leave you howling for more."

~Sharon Saracino, Author,
Undiscovered Angel, The Earthbound Series

~*~

"Sharon Buchbinder's writing grabs hold from the very first page and stays with you long after the last page has been read. Her skill in combining historical fact with suspenseful fiction creates an exciting and dramatic backdrop for her stories. Ms. Buchbinder's books are now on my must-buy list."

~Jennifer Lynne, bestselling author of
Gods of Love and Not Vanilla series

Dedications

This book is dedicated with love to my husband, Dale,
our son, Joshua, our daughter-in-law, Elyse,
and our grandson, Dexter.
They remind me every day
that the gift of a loving family is priceless.

~*~

It is also dedicated to my tireless and supportive editor,
Amanda Barnett,
who takes my lumps of coal and turns them into
diamonds.

~*~

And to Sharon Saracino, my patient critique partner,
who props me up and cheers me on
when words fail me.

Author's Note

Anyone who has read my previous novels knows that before I begin to write, I conduct extensive research and steep myself in the materials. This approach enables me to speak through the characters and narrative with rich and correct content. I also rely on subject matter experts and beta readers from diverse disciplines and cultural backgrounds who provide corrections and feedback to me before I submit a story for consideration for publication. I would be remiss if I did not thank my readers here, starting with my ever patient husband, Dale Buchbinder, who read every single draft of the story. My deep gratitude goes to the following people for their expertise and feedback: Deborah Barrett, Marta Bliese, John Darrin, Charlayne Elizabeth Denney, Hal Dorin, Karysa Faire, Tahereh Fazel, Joya Fields, Karen and Ken Giek, Nancy Greenwald, Sabrina Lemieux, Drs. Anisa and Ziad Mirza, Zee Monodee, Dr. Patricia Romero, Tina Rucci, Sharon Saracino, Tahmineh Shadkhoo, Dr. Jay Tobin, Robin Vandenbroeck, Beth White Werrell, Stephanie Williams, and Susan Willis. Big hugs to my brilliant editor, Amanda Barnett, who challenges me to polish my work until it shines.

This sequel to *The Kiss of the Silver Wolf* follows up on the origin of jinnis, or genies, who, like humans, can choose to be good or evil. I interwove jinni lore with the mesmerizing story of the Queen of Sheba and King Solomon, two heroic Biblical figures who, many say, had supernatural powers. I wondered how this three-thousand-year-old state affair between two super powers became embedded in our collective consciousness. I also wondered about the impact of this epic romance on our lives today, who the descendants of this royal romance might be, where they lived, and what they might be doing now. The importance of centuries-old hurts to contemporary events of today is evident in the daily news. Likewise, the Biblical storyline is important to the resolution of the contemporary portion of this book.

In my research, I discovered that despite the differences between and among cultures, four major religions, Judaism, Christianity, Ethiopian Coptic Christianity, and Islam, tell, retell, and revere the story of the Queen of Sheba and King Solomon. The Hebrew Bible, the Old Testament in the Christian Bible, contains the story in very short form, but repeats it in two places, in 1 Kings and in Chronicles, as if one telling was not enough. The repetition of the same tale in two places was a way to ensure the story would be found, told and retold, even if the books of the Bible were somehow separated from one another.

As the only foreign queen mentioned in the Bible who appears to be considered an equal to King Solomon, this mystery woman has been claimed by no less than three countries: Arabia and Yemen, where she is call Bilqis, Balqis, or Balkis, and Ethiopia, where she is known as Makeda. Her role in these stories has been interpreted by many scholars in multiple ways. The Queen of Sheba has been seen as a symbol of trade, as an example of nations converted to monotheism in a polytheist world, as a warning against foreign women and their wiles, and, finally, as a romance between a powerful king and an equally powerful queen.

Scholars who interpret the Queen of Sheba as a

symbol of trade point to the significant trade routes that ran through regions under the control of Israel. All trade routes had to be protected from bandits or the products would never reach the marketplace. Frankincense was so valuable that men who worked in the factories were required to strip and be searched before they left for the day to ensure they took none of the product home. This lightweight incense was prized all over the world and used in religious rituals throughout the Middle Eastern region, especially at funerals. The wealthier the individual, the more frankincense was used. Israel's territory lay between the region of production of frankincense and many destination ports. Without the protection of the King of Israel, other countries would not be able to thrive and survive. Was the Queen of Sheba merely a symbol of trade and the rest of the world showing its submission to the great and wise King Solomon?

Scholars who interpreted this story as a way of showing King Solomon's favor in the eyes of his Lord, and to underscore the significance of the need for monotheism in a world of multiple gods, point to archaeological evidence of multiple gods and goddesses still present in the time of King David and King Solomon. Archaeologists have found evidence that Asherah, the female goddess, was worshipped in the first and second temples of Jerusalem. Prophets and priests opposed to polytheism may have created the story of the Queen of Sheba's visit and conversion to monotheism as an example of what other nations should do. Was the Queen of Sheba merely a prop to provide a good role model for other nations?

Some stories about the Queen of Sheba have

indicated her origins were exotic and supernatural, with a mother who was a jinniyah, or genie. Other, darker stories demonize the Queen of Sheba and make her synonymous with Lilith, Adam's first wife, who left him to become a soul-sucking demon and baby killer. In early times, the war over which god would prevail was a very real one, and priests and priestesses of gods opposing one God were not well tolerated, even killed, on the road to monotheism. Foreign women became synonymous with foreign gods and evil ways. Solomon's tolerance of his multiple wives' religions was seen as a character flaw. Were these stories about the Queen of Sheba created to serve as a horrid example of foreign customs?

Finally, the romance between two great and powerful heads of state is irresistible. Many scholars offer strong support of a real love story. One of the strongest pieces of evidence is the use of the Hebrew word in the phrase "she came to him." There are many different words the scribe could have used, however, the one selected has a sexual meaning, used in the Hebrew Bible only in sexual situations. The romantic description of the meeting and their interactions, including such phrases as "she communed with him of all that was in her heart," "there was no more spirit in her," and "king Solomon gave unto the queen of Sheba all her desire, whatsoever she asked, beside that which Solomon gave her of his royal bounty," makes the reader wonder what he gave her, since she was wealthy, too. In fact, the largesse of her gifts of state is over the top, even for a visiting dignitary. Was it, in fact, a wedding dowry? If so, why did she leave and return to her own country with her servants? What happened?

Was this a love lost?

According to the Kebra Negast, the constitution and Holy Book of Ethiopia, Makeda, the Queen of Sheba from that nation, returned to her country with her servants and gifts only King Solomon could give to her: a signet ring, a child, and a Solomonic dynasty that endured to the last Ethiopian emperor, Haile Selassie I. For the purposes of this book, it is this story that I followed and brought to the twenty-first century via the African Diaspora.

The authenticity of the Queen of Sheba/King Solomon legend has been a subject of inquiry for many archaeological and Biblical scholars. Outside of materials written well after the tenth century before the common era (BCE), e.g., Kings 1-13 of the Hebrew Bible/Old Testament, Targum Sheni ("Second Targum", the second Book of Esther), the Ethiopian Kebra Negast or Glory of Kings, and the Holy Qu'aran, no written archeological evidence of King Solomon's existence has been found in Israel to date. Furthermore, no external chronologists, such as the Babylonians and Assyrians, recorded any stories about King Solomon, although they had written records about kings of Israel who followed him. Any timelines that exist have been scholars' estimates based on interpolation of times and names used in the Biblical era and extant sources, such as Babylonian and Assyrian records.

The past predicts our future and our family history and culture are intrinsic parts of our identity. Many families have oral histories and legends of connections to royalty. In this story, I follow one family's oral history through biblical and contemporary times. Join me on this epic paranormal journey into the past and present. Whatever your background or belief system, I hope you enjoy the story. If you are interested in the articles, books, movies, and other sources I used to research this novel, I would be happy to send you my list of references. Just email me at:

sharonbellbuchbinder@gmail.com

Happy reading!
Sharon Buchbinder

Prologue

> *No matter how far we are in the future,*
> *everything connects us to our past.*

Aksum, Ethiopia, 965 B.C.E.

Makeda clambered up the steep outcropping of rocks in pursuit of a white snake. She saw the creature sunning itself on a large boulder, its normally sleek shape enlarged in the center with a bulge the size of a rat, and she wanted him. After a big meal, the slithering would stop and he'd be easy to catch. As soon as she caught the snake, she'd shove him in Tamrin's face.

Stupid boy. How dare he say girls didn't know how to catch snakes in a tone used for speaking to babies? Even though he was twelve, two years older than she was, didn't she throw a spear farther, ride her horse harder, and catch more pheasants than he did? Fish practically threw themselves on her carved bone hooks.

In fact, Makeda ran faster, climbed higher, and hunted better than all the other children and many of the adults in Aksum. Hadn't she brought down a lioness when the predator attacked a woman in the market place? Everyone else had screamed and fled—the cowards. She, a mere *girl*, stood her ground and speared the big cat, saving the mother and her unborn child. Her actions proved to the men and boys she was a warrior in her own right, not just the king's daughter.

The only animals she didn't hunt were the red, long-legged wolves. She was five the first time she spotted the creatures. While riding out to hunt antelope with her father, a she-wolf surrounded by a litter of pups locked eyes with Makeda.

Frozen in time, it seemed as if the female whispered to her, "Go away. Leave me to raise my babies. Spare me and when your time comes, we will do the same for you and yours." At last, she had pulled away from the creature's penetrating gaze and caught her father watching her, his dark brown forehead creased in a worried expression.

"Why do you look at me in that way, *Baba*? Is something wrong?"

He reached over and felt Makeda's brow. "Are you not well, my daughter?"

She shook her head. "The wolf snared me with her eyes and spoke to me. Asked for mercy."

Her father's eyes grew as large as eggs, and he held up the palm of his right hand. "Stop. Say nothing more of this."

"Baba, what's wrong?" She had never seen her father afraid of anyone or anything. The supreme ruler feared nothing. Until that day.

His lips had thinned to a knife's edge. "Tell no one. Do you hear me?"

Baba had never spoken to her in such a harsh tone before. Tears rose in her eyes. She dared not speak for fear of choking on her words. Makeda nodded. They never mentioned the incident again. Now, despite the heat baking the stones beneath her feet, she shuddered at the memory. *Stop thinking about the wolves. Keep going.* A few more boulders to climb and she'd have the snake in her hand.

A sharp rock pricked her palm and a trickle of blood ran down her arm. Although at times, scraped, bruised, and covered in tiny cuts, her hands seldom scarred. Her father told Makeda her mother had healed the same way and the extra toe on each foot gave her special powers. *"My heart, you are my little goat."*

Tamrin shouted at her from below. The wind snatched his words and carried them into the clouds. She glanced over her shoulder, and the sight took her breath away. A shrub-strewn carpet of green grass broken up with craggy hills, a wandering river, and scrubby bushes stretched beneath her. This is why the Sun God rose each morning. To admire his handiwork.

"Nay! Come!" Tamrin's shout carried to her over a gust of wind. "Soon it will be sundown." She knew the rest. He ended everything with, "Your father will kill me and my family if I don't bring you back safely."

Where was all his boasting and blustering when it came to her father? Vanished like a rat in a hole. She dismissed his warning with a shake of her head, pulled herself over a ledge and headed upward, closer to the sun and the snake. Lazy beast. Sitting right in front of a large cleft, the snake hissed, as if to say, "Come get me."

Water gourd bouncing on her thigh, Makeda now stood on the boulder. Two more steps and she'd pounce. One, two—just as she reached for him, he turned his head, flicked his tongue, and slipped into the cave. She followed him into the darkness, deep into the grotto, her trusty feet feeling the way. Her eyes adjusted to the gloom. Aha! Right there on a big boulder. One more step and—

A soundless explosion of light dazzled Makeda. Blinded by its brilliance, she stumbled back. Cool and slick, the wet rock walls did little to help her keep her balance. She blinked, shook her head, and gasped. Where the snake had been, sat a giant. Even seated, the *ferhenjee*, this stranger with red skin the color of a young curly horned antelope, was twice her father's size. Mouth dry, heart hammering in her throat, her vision finally adjusted to the light.

The *ferhenjee* had a man's body with sparks circling his head like embers from a blazing fire. A prominent beak-shaped nose dominated his profile. He stared at her with eyes the same color of the morning sky. His gaze pinned her to the rock floor. Behind him, wings—too many to count, fluttered and stirred up a breeze. Her brow, once hot and sweaty, cooled.

Hands clenched into fists, her mind alternated between wanting to fight the creature, run away, or freeze in his sky colored stare. Immobility won.

He must be the Sun God, angry with me for climbing this high. "I only wanted to catch the snake."

The giant threw his head back and roared.

Released from his stare, Makeda fell to her knees and bowed her head. "Please don't kill me, Sun God. I'm sorry, I didn't mean to anger you."

"I'm not angry, child. I'm laughing." He chuckled. "Don't call me Sun God. It offends my King."

She jerked her head up. The *ferhenjee* was smiling. "Who are you? Are you from the stars? Who is your king? How did you get here?" She took a deep breath, prepared to ask more questions.

"Stop." His voice rumbled like the sound of a

rushing waterfall.

She bowed her head again. Maybe she should flatten herself on the floor of the cave to please him.

"No, Makeda, please remain standing."

Tremors shook her body and her teeth rattled. Just like she had heard the wolf's thoughts, he knew hers—and her name.

He sighed and wind gusted in the cavern. "I am Metatron, humble servant of the greatest of all gods. I bring a message for you."

She peeked up through strands of hair. "Me? Why me?"

"You have a majestic life ahead of you. Your son will rule a great kingdom."

Despite her fear, the notion of being a mother tickled her gut and tore huge gulps of laughter out of her throat. He had to be blind. She wasn't even a *woman* yet.

The creature stared at her. "You dare to laugh?"

"You don't understand. I'm never going to marry. I will never have children—"

The giant creature stood, and his head touched the top of the cave. Her voice caught in her throat. He looked like her father had the day she heard the wolf speak. He glowered at her.

"Hear me, Makeda. You will become the mother of a nation of kings. Go home and prepare yourself. Learn everything you can about love, honor, and becoming a wise and just ruler, so you can teach your son and his son."

She was terrified of this messenger and his god, but rules were rules. Her mother had been banished when she was a baby. Her father, the great king, forbid anyone to speak of her. No one ever mentioned her mother's name, for fear of being put to death.

She shook her head. "I'm sorry, whoever you are. I cannot rule my father's kingdom unless I am a virgin. It is forbidden for me to marry. I was born to rule. It is my destiny."

Sparks flew off him and the cave blazed with the light of day. Fear and awe filled her from head to toe when he grew larger and larger, filling up the space. One of his wings brushed her cheek, soft as the fuzz of a baby bird.

How could something so big have such a gentle touch?

"You are young and foolish. You will grow and learn. Above all else, you must seek wisdom. *That* is your destiny."

Chapter One

Summertown, West Virginia, U.S.A., Present Day

A picturesque flight over the Appalachian Mountains to Summertown, West Virginia gave Special Agent Eliana Solomon of the Homeland Security, Science and Technology Directorate, Anomaly Defense Division time to process the urgent report she'd received by email. Up until this week, the existence of werewolf packs had been concealed from the general population. Now reports of the secretive shape shifters exploded in her inbox. Where had this information been all this time? Had the government monitored them all along? If so, why had her boss, Bert Blackfeather, insisted on her obtaining proof of their existence, along with the jinnis? She'd pry an answer out of that closed mouth man—someday. Right now, she had a more pressing matter at hand.

Five days ago, three nine-year-old werewolf boys and their three eighteen-year-old sisters went on a birthday expedition in the heavily wooded state wildlife area and disappeared. By day, local human authorities, volunteers, and bloodhounds brought in from surrounding jurisdictions combed the forest, the hills, and caves. By night, pack members ran through the forest using their extraordinary senses—olfactory, visual, and auditory—to hunt for their missing kin.

Divers also explored the waterways, all to no avail. No clues to the kids' whereabouts had been found, not even a backpack—until two this morning.

A night security guard discovered the boys in the middle of the Adalwolf Winery parking lot. Slightly bruised and scratched up, but otherwise alive and well, in their human forms, the youngsters had no recollection of anything between arriving at the park and waking up in the parking lot with their back packs under their heads—their five-day-old lunches untouched.

Rushed to the ER and examined thoroughly, the boys displayed no evidence of physical abuse. The blank space in their minds where the memories should have been was inaccessible to parents and psychologists. If it weren't for the fact that the three older girls were still missing, the local authorities wouldn't continue to press the boys for information. Over time, their memories could return, but without ransom notes, calls or clues, the clock was running down for a successful search and rescue. The local police, state troopers, sheriff's office, and the West Virginia Bureau of Investigation feared the operation would soon become a search and recovery.

The plane touched down, bounced along the runway, and Eliana's cell began to vibrate.

"Solomon."

The gruff voice of her boss boomed in her ear. "New development in the case." Blackfeather paused. "A hiker found one of the missing girls in a culvert near an abandoned mine. Bites, claw marks. Throat ripped open. Damn thing nearly tore her head off."

She shuddered. "Black bear?"

"Based on the paw prints around the body, the first responders are saying these weren't bear bites. More like a dog—or wolf."

"Boss, aside from zoos and wild animal preserves, there are no wolves in the eastern U.S."

He sighed. "I stand corrected. Werewolf."

Her stomach lurched, and she gripped the armrest so hard her knuckles turned white. *Shit. Shit. Shit.* A werewolf attacking one of its own? Why? What the hell was going on?

"West Virginia Division of Homeland Security has a car waiting for you, fully loaded with everything you'll need for the investigation. Get to that scene." Her boss clicked off.

Bossy desk jockey.

A flush of shame rushed over her. He'd taken on the orphan Anomaly Defense Division of the Science and Technology Directorate that no one else wanted, along with a mission no one else supported or believed in. As abrupt and abrasive as he could be, the Gulf War veteran deserved credit for giving her the opportunity to pursue what everyone else thought was something out of the tales of *The Arabian Nights*: jinnis. With the needed proof of werewolves and jinnis from Project Aladdin, support surged into the division. A stable funding source made her jinni hunting work possible So far, it seemed wherever there were werewolves, there was jinni activity.

This case was no different. According to the report, relationships between the local humans and werewolves were more than cordial. They were so intermarried, almost everyone was family. A large non-denominational wedding facility placed Summertown on an international list of destination weddings, like Hawaii and Las Vegas, but specifically for werewolves. A thriving bed and breakfast trade supported the wedding industry, along with other leisure activities, such as biking, hiking, white-water rafting, and winery and sightseeing tours. Murder of a werewolf girl wasn't just bad for the family, it was bad for the town.

Eliana tugged her long sleeves down and pulled on a pair of black latex gloves the moment she climbed out of the car. Ten minutes and a rough hike down the rocky slope to the culvert later, she came upon a hushed crowd of crime techs and investigators.

Odd.

Normally there would be *some* chatter. Crime scene investigators needed to distance themselves emotionally from the victim. By calling everything, including the victim, "evidence" and following a strict checklist, they were able to wall themselves off, keep the normal human responses of shock, horror, grief, and anger at bay. The usual professional, calm exchange was completely absent, leaving an acoustic void in its place. A twig snapped beneath her foot, shattering the silence.

She took a deep breath. "Who's the lead?"

Round-eyed, a big man with high cheekbones and a dark blue jacket pointed at a tall red-haired female wearing a police uniform, a bright gold badge, and name tag that said "Chief Jane Novak."

Jane nodded at Eliana. "You are?"

"Agent Solomon. Homeland Security Science Directorate. Call me Eliana, please."

The cop snorted. "Your reputation precedes you, along with some not so subtle threats from your boss to cooperate with you—or else."

She repressed a groan. Bert meant well, but sometimes his heavy handedness with the locals put her in a tenuous position. No matter how she tried to reason with him, he always pulled the national security card. Yet, she couldn't apologize without appearing to undermine him.

"He wanted me to see the evidence as soon as possible, before any more decomposition set in. There are still two women missing. Much as I hate to say it, national security *could* be at stake."

Jane nodded. "I hear you. You can look, but don't touch. Follow right behind me. Don't even *think* of messing up my crime scene."

Eliana glanced overhead at the tree canopy, half-expecting a voyeur to be crouched on a limb, admiring his handiwork from afar. "I trust your team has panoramic videos and stills of every angle around the body and casts of the paw prints around her?"

Jane nodded. "Yes, but entrance and egress in an area this large is overwhelming. That's especially true when a werewolf may be involved."

Eliana marveled at the other woman's matter-of-fact tone. This wasn't her first time at the shape-shifter rodeo. Werewolves were nothing new to her, or her unnaturally quiet techs, it seemed. She gave a mental nod to the West Virginians for trading pitchforks for professionalism.

"We're trying to keep the crime scene intact as long as we can. At least until Mayor Schaeffer shows up." She shook her head. "Then we're screwed. Shifty Schaeffer loves to grandstand. I expect he'll be here with a reporter any time now."

Eliana took a deep breath, preparing for the worst while the other woman pulled back the blue tarp. Her boots-on-the-ground stint as a weapons expert in Iraq should have numbed her to the sight of bodies and the ravages of war. Still, tears stung her eyes. The girl was so young and beautiful—before her throat was ripped open.

Naked, except for the light fur on her body, it appeared *whatever* killed her attacked the girl while she attempted to shift into her wolf form. Bite marks and puncture wounds covered her body. A slash of scarlet replaced her throat. Eliana forced herself to crouch next to the remains. The smell of burnt matches singed her nostrils. *Jinni stink.* She stood and turned to the chief.

The victim was someone's daughter. "Does the family know?"

"Not yet." Jane's eyebrow quirked. "Well? Is it—"

"Jinnis?" Eliana shook her head. "Can't say. I need more evidence."

Jane gave her an incredulous look. "She's a werewolf. We're near an abandoned mine. You're the jinni hunter. I do my homework, too. It's like the case in Kentucky."

"What more do you need?"

"My own team of experts." She pulled out her cell.

The woman dropped the tarp back over the girl/wolf. "You might as well try sending up smoke signals. There's no service out here."

"Fabulous." She pocketed the useless phone. "Anything else I need to know?"

Static flared on Jane's radio, and a voice crackled. "Shaeffer's on his way down."

Novak bit her bottom lip and frowned. "Let me

keep this short and to the point. The Adalwolf family runs this town." She signaled to the techs to put the body in a waiting bag. "Lowell Adalwolf likes to keep his paws in everything. Rich, influential, protective of the pack. Some people—" she nodded at her techs "—are saying it may even be a rogue werewolf."

Just what she needed. An obstructive powerbroker. "Can't wait to meet him."

"Control freak, your regular, big, bad alpha wolf. Tight with the mayor. He'll insist on telling you the history of the pack and showing you his wine cellar. I'd go with you, because I want to see him squirm, but I need to notify the victim's parents." She sighed. "Some days, I hate my job."

Eliana knew just how she felt.

After a brief meeting with the mayor, who, as Novak predicted, spent more time grandstanding than speaking with her, she now stood in the chilly wine cellar and tugged at her jacket sleeves—wishing for a pair of warm gloves. Despite the cavern's bright fluorescent lighting and a giant wall hanging of workers harvesting grapes, her chest tightened. Werewolf politics, the scent of a jinni, and a subterranean vault sure to trigger her claustrophobia. *Could this day get much worse?* At least the elevator and emergency stairway were just a few steps away.

You can do this. Focus on the case.

"What can you tell me about the girls?"

The gray haired CEO, Lowell Adalwolf, raised his shaggy eyebrows and favored her with a piercing, green-eyed gaze as if sizing her up, searching for deficiencies.

Okay, two can play at this game. She stared back at

him. Yes, she was tall for a woman. Yes, her Ethiopian and Moroccan heritage gave her a permanent tan, and her thick black hair pulled back into an unruly ponytail needed a cut. *He* needed a good barber to trim those caterpillars over his eyes. But then again, he *was* a werewolf.

"You need to understand who we are and where we come from before you can start grilling people. When we decided to leave Livonia in the early 1600s, we settled in these hills. They reminded us of home. The pristine land and waterways were filled with wildlife, perfect for our people. We became model citizens, even fought in the Revolutionary War. The coal mining industry took off in West Virginia. Our pack owned the land and the coal beneath it, and we prospered. Over the centuries, however, we noticed the wildlife disappearing, and our hunts became sparse."

He shook his head, and Eliana had a sudden image of him in wolf form, large, proud, and gray. She blinked and the vision disappeared. She shivered and looked at the glowing red exit sign for the tenth time. "And?"

"There was a falling out in our pack. I'll spare you the gory details of our civil war. The death toll was high. Too high." He sighed and passed a hand over his creased face. "My faction won the money and the property. We followed the guidelines for closing mines and land reclamation, stopped up the deeper coring tunnels, and kept this one to remind us of where we've been and what we sacrificed."

A fresh crop of goosebumps erupted at the thought of a full-scale intra-pack war with werewolves tearing at each other's necks. And at the thought of the young woman lying in the woods with her throat torn out. She opened her mouth to ask him about the girl, but he talked over her. This guy was all about *him*, his pack, his business.

"The vineyard was my mate's idea. We brought in a highly regarded wine master from Livonia. Old Thiess is one of us."

Enough with the history lesson.

She had to get the conversation back on track. The murder would be treated as a separate case from the abductions, but the two cases were connected. "How well did you know the kids who went out to the park?"

"One way or another, we're all related. They're my great-nephew's pups. I usually see them at our family gatherings."

What was the relationship between the kids' disappearance and the winery?

A smart kidnapper would have dropped the boys off at some non-descript location like the outlet mall just a few miles down the road. If it were an angry vineyard employee, it would be like painting a target on the company.

"Any disgruntled former employees? Someone you fired?"

He shook his craggy head. "No. Everyone is happy here, been here forever. They're all part of the pack."

"Any unusual behavior among the members of your pack lately?"

He cocked his head and looked puzzled. "How do you mean?"

"We have to rule out all possibilities, even distasteful ones. It is possible the kidnapper or killer could be one of your pack mates."

He growled, "Absolutely not. There are no rogue

wolves in our pack."

"Sorry to upset you, sir, but under the circumstances, everyone is under suspicion. We need your maps, design plans, specs, engineers' notes, everything you have on your cellars, the surrounding areas, and the old tunnel sites."

"The mine was sealed. We followed all the rules, did *everything* according to the state's requirements. We planted thousands of trees and reforested the area, too." He closed his eyes and pinched the bridge of his nose. "I oversaw the operation myself."

Good grief. Why did everyone take these investigations so personally? On the other hand, why was he being so defensive? She needed to throw him a bone, so to speak, to get his cooperation.

"Mr. Adalwolf, this isn't about investigating you." She locked eyes with the older man. "There are still two girls out there. Don't you want to find them?"

His mouth opened, and his hand flew to his chest. "Of course, I do. What kind of animal do you take me for?"

The shocked response was either well-rehearsed or sincere. For the moment, she'd go with the latter. "This is about finding out where the two other girls might be held captive. We need to know if there are other routes in and out of these old mining shafts."

He passed a hand over his creased face again, and appeared to age before her eyes. "Tell me it's not like the Carter pack." He lowered his voice. "Please tell me it's not a jinni."

How had he heard about that case? Werewolf grapevine?

The mission of Project Aladdin was to find jinnis,

the portals where they came from a parallel dimension, and to shut them down. The assignment in Eden, Kentucky was a groundbreaking one for Eliana and Homeland Security. An applied physicist specializing in weapons, she theorized that, in the wrong hands, a jinni could become a weapon of mass destruction. She'd captured a battle between a werewolf and a jinni with low light internet protocol based surveillance cameras with high definition encoders she had placed in the woods around the abandoned mine. Specifically created by Homeland Security to assist in recording criminal activities under poor lighting conditions, the equipment live streamed real time and tamper-proof videos directly to Homeland Security. This documentation of the werewolf and jinni fight proved the existence of the supernatural creatures.

The werewolf won the battle, but the war between the wolves and jinnis still raged. Before she left Kentucky, the old alpha wolf of the Carter clan had revealed the source of the grievances between the two shape shifters, a blood feud dating back to biblical times.

The problem, however, was the jinnis weren't necessarily interested in keeping their attacks focused solely on werewolves. Contrary to popular TV images of a pretty girl in a bottle, the jinnis, or genies, were powerful shape shifters, who, like humans, could choose between good and evil. If a terrorist ever found a way to conjure and command an evil jinni, or *'Ifrit*, the world would never know what hit it. Although they'd been able to seal up that particular portal, shafts of working and non-working mines honeycombed the entire Appalachian region of the United States. Jinnis could be anywhere, even beneath her feet in the sealed up mine turned winery. She rubbed the large signet ring now loose on her cold hand.

"I'm not at liberty to discuss the Carter case, sir. All I can say at this time is right now three little boys can't recall a thing, one young woman is dead from a brutal attack, and two girls are missing."

A low growl came out through his gritted teeth. "Why us? Why our pack?"

"We don't know, but that's what we hope to find out." She wasn't about to tell Adalwolf about the energy signatures in the Summertown area caught by the satellite imagery.

A wall phone shrilled next to the winery owner. He snatched it up. "Adalwolf."

He nodded and handed the receiver to Eliana. "It's for you."

The police chief could barely speak. "Get. Over. To. The. Hospital. Now."

She'd said hospital, not morgue. That was good news. "What's going on?"

"A truck driver nearly ran over the two girls in the middle of the turnpike outside the state park."

"Are they—"

"Hypothermic. Naked. And—"

"What? Tell me."

"Visibly pregnant."

Her mouth snapped shut, and she honed in on the red exit sign. The medical examiner would have to ascertain if the dead girl had been expecting, too. In light of the urgency of the case, she doubted that important item would have been left out of the family interviews. She had to get to the hospital and talk to the survivors. "Mr. Adalwolf—" she returned the phone to him "—I must go. My team will get back to you for those blueprints. Here's my card."

The CEO pulled out a pair of reading glasses and examined the small print. "Eliana D. Solomon, Special Agent, Homeland Security, Science and Technology Directorate, Anomaly Defense Division." He raised his eyebrows. "I don't understand. Why is Homeland Security involved in this situation?"

"All the agencies work as a team now, especially in unusual cases like this. If you think of anything else, call my cell."

She raced up the narrow stairwell and mentally thanked her boss for giving her the go ahead to assemble a task force of experts for this new case. The lineup was impressive; people with years of research experience in the field and in the scholarship of jinni phenomena were anxious to assist. Here in the middle of the West Virginia Mountains, she was going to need some specialized help from someone who had personal experience with jinnis.

As soon as she'd gotten the green light, she'd known *exactly* who to ask—a tall, dark, and dangerously beguiling physician she had worked with on an extremely difficult case two years ago. Arta Shahani, an Iranian-American and Harvard trained psychiatrist, had firsthand experience in dealing with the shape shifters. The leading expert in the country on jinni possessions and a consultant to the agency on the inner workings of the minds of terrorists, the good doctor also had well-established relationships with the Baltimore and Washington Islamic community. An important consideration in a politically charged, highly sensitive arena.

Arta was, without a doubt, the best man for the job. However, he was the *last* person in the world she ever wanted to speak to again. Her stomach fluttered, her heart lurched, and her hands grew slick on the hand railing just thinking about calling him. Not that she held a grudge, mind you, but didn't she have the right to be pissed at a guy for leaving her for *dead*?

Chapter Two

Chevy Chase, MD, U.S.A., Present Day

Arta Shahani, MD, stood on the sidewalk outside a thick green hedge surrounding a brick federalist style home in Chevy Chase, Maryland. He took a deep breath, opened the white wooden privet fence, and strode up the front walkway.

What awaited him behind the solid black door? Would the entire family, minus the affected girl, greet him, wringing their hands in distress? Could he help the fifteen-year-old or would her disease overpower her? After ten years in the practice of psychiatry, he never knew what to expect, especially when called in to rule out a jinni possession.

The curtain in the narrow window to the left of the door twitched, and a dark haired man peeked out. *Ah. The father. Very well.*

"As-Salaam Alaykum, peace be upon you, Dr. Shahani. Thank you for coming to visit my poor daughter, Nur." Wrapped in a long down coat, the father inclined his head and extended his right hand. It was seventy-five degrees outside. Why on earth was the man wearing a heavy coat indoors?

"May peace, mercy and blessings of Allah be upon you, Mr. Mustafa." Arta shook the man's hand. It felt as if he'd been holding an ice pack for an hour.

"Please come in."

Arta crossed the threshold. The temperature dropped ten degrees. Mid-June in Maryland did not require this much air-conditioning. He shuddered and wished for a heavier wool suit.

"I apologize for the chill. No matter how much we run the heat, we cannot get the temperature over sixty degrees. You'll need this."

Mr. Mustafa helped him into a down jacket.

Oftentimes, in a case of suspected jinni possession, the family's religious leader or Imam would have been consulted on the case first. Referred to Arta by a mutual friend, Mr. Mustafa was convinced his daughter was histrionic at best, over-indulged at worst. Arta expected to find an upset teenager, perhaps one in need of a family therapist. He didn't anticipate walking into an igloo. Not once, in all of the suspected jinni possessions he'd investigated, had he ever encountered a chill like this one. It was like something out of a cheesy ghost hunter TV show.

"How long has the temperature been this low?"

"A month, maybe two. Technicians came out to examine the heat pump twice this week. And twice every week before." He shook his head. "They cannot find anything wrong with it. They come, it gets better. They leave, it gets worse. I think Nur slips out of her room when the women are sleeping and plays with the thermostat."

As a psychiatrist, Arta's job was to rule *out* jinni possession, to identify any medical and mental illnesses before considering a paranormal cause. Depression, anxiety, endocrine, or neurological disorders, the list went on and on for underlying issues attributed to the supernatural being. Only after a thorough family interview, mental, and medical examinations, would he rule *in* the possibility of a jinni possession.

"Tell me about Nur." Arta took no notes. The good thing about a photographic memory was he never forgot anything. The bad thing was there were some things he wanted to forget and couldn't.

"A good girl, a lovely child. Respectful, obedient." Mr. Mustafa took slow steps toward the second level. "Never gave us a moment of trouble. Did her homework, went to her Islamic classes, and loved Allah."

"What changed?" In his experience, an inciting incident always set off a chain reaction. Half the battle was finding the trigger.

The father gave a great sigh. "A boy."

Ah. A boy. Perhaps Nur *did* play with the thermostat. "And?"

Mr. Mustafa stopped and stared deep into Arta's eyes with his bloodshot, coffee brown ones. "He met her at the shopping mall. Got her name and number from her friends. Started calling and asking her out." He shook his head. "We said no. He came from the wrong kind of family."

"Can you tell me more about him?"

"He's an American."

"I'm an American. Persian extraction, born here in the United States. Is this a problem?"

The father shook his head. "She's promised to a man in our home country. When we're finished with our diplomatic assignment at the end of this year, we'll return to Turkey. Then they'll be married."

Romeo and Juliet. Nur had reason to be angry. She

probably didn't want to leave her stateside beau.

At the top of the stairs, Mr. Mustafa stood in front of a closed door. "I'm embarrassed to tell you this, but I think I should let you know my wife sought out a witch, asked for his help. The trickster told her to keep my daughter in a darkened room for thirty days and to light incense. I forbid my wife to go back to him. She still insists on burning candles scented with frankincense and keeps the room dark."

Arta nodded. "I'm sure those measures gave your wife some comfort."

The father rapped on the door. "Dr. Shahani is here to see you, Nur."

He turned the knob and shrieking commenced. Regardless of the language, the girl did not want visitors.

"The light of my life, my little Nur, is behaving badly. But she is not possessed, of this I am certain." The father paused and considered Arta with a sad expression. "The girl is simply acting like a hysterical teenager. Her mother is much too easy with her. Gives her whatever she wants. My wife wanted Imam Abdal to conduct an exorcism. I said absolutely not."

Arta knew the Imam well and respected him. One of the best-known spiritual leaders in the Baltimore and Washington Islamic community, the holy man advocated thorough medical assessments and interventions prior to any religious treatment. An exorcism was not a trivial event. The home needed to be prepared in a proper way, and medical and spiritual experts were required to be present to ensure the safety of the afflicted person, without turning it into a spectacle. An endangered soul wasn't something the

Imam wanted to have in the tabloids or evening news. Concern for the privacy of the afflicted individual was a top priority.

Despite Arta's accommodating words, he knew the Imam would not approve of Mrs. Mustafa visiting a witch, nor did he. Those charlatans preyed on the fears of the vulnerable and took their money. Nur and her family were victims who needed compassion, not deception and misinformation. Arta shuddered with a sudden chill despite the warm coat.

"My wife and her sisters take turns staying with Nur. She's never alone." He shrugged. "Still, she manages to do things, like the thermostat." He pushed the door open and nodded for Arta to go in. "I stay out here. Otherwise, she'll become more agitated."

Arta stepped inside the candlelit room. Turkish writing covered the walls, the same phrase repeated over and over. "I hate my father, I hate my life, I want to die." To put it mildly, it appeared this young woman was depressed, angry, and in desperate need of help. Mr. Mustafa called it right. She was rebelling. A lot of work waited for Arta.

Time to roll up my sleeves.

A woman sat in the near darkness in a wing-backed chair next to an empty twin bed. Wrapped from head to toe in layers of blankets, she prayed and called on Allah to help her child and to release the *'Ifrit*, the evil jinni, from her body.

Arta's eyes adjusted to flickering light as he searched the room for the girl in question. "Nur?"

The mother stopped praying and locked gazes with Arta. Eyes large and round in her gaunt face, the woman looked as if she'd stopped eating for the past two months. She pointed below the bed.

Arta went to the opposite side and got down on his knees. The temperature got even colder. His breath came out in puffs of white. *No. His imagination, nothing more.* Leaning on his forearms, he peered into the darkness under the bed and waited for his eyes to adjust to the gloom.

"Nur, I'm Dr. Shahani. Your family is worried. I'd like to speak with you. Is that okay?"

A dark lump moved.

"Nur, can you hear me?"

A muffled sound. Crying?

"What can I do to help you?"

"Kill me."

At least she responded. That was a start. Now to open the door a little wider.

"Why would you want me to hurt you, Nur?"

She kept her face turned away. "Hate him."

"Why do you say that?" He'd seen a lot of angry teenage girls in his life, a stream of them in and out of his office in upscale Chevy Chase and in jails and courtrooms. Sometimes, he wanted to shake them and tell them how lucky they were and to stop whining. Other times, his heart broke at the psychic injuries the girls revealed. The ones he met in jail in his *pro bono* work cut at his soul. So many bore deep wounds of a kind no child should ever have to endure.

"Comes at night. Makes me do things. Hurts me."

Arta tried not to jump to conclusions, but based on his medical knowledge and years of experience, he could *not* rule out the possibility of Mr. Mustafa as a perpetrator of wrongdoing with the girl. No one liked to talk about child sexual abuse, much less admit that it could occur in an individual's family. But denial and silence only added to the victim's degradation and shame. He needed to start somewhere. He steeled himself and asked the question.

"What kind of things?"

She thrust an uncovered arm toward him. Covered in red scars and lines, as well as healed and unhealed wounds, her skin resembled a crazed game of tic-tac-toe.

A cutter. A call for help. Self-loathing propelled some girls in desperation, to focus on the pain, instead of the shame.

His mind raced. Even if Arta proved Mustafa abused his daughter, what penalties would be imposed? The father was a diplomat.

A minor at fifteen, Nur would be protected from Mustafa if Arta could get her to a hospital. The diplomat blamed the boyfriend, when it looked like dear old daddy was the problem. His stomach knotted. If that was true, why did the father invite a psychiatrist into his home to treat his daughter? Was he *that* good an actor? It didn't make sense. Most abusers hid their abuse and threatened their victims to keep them silent. What did make sense was that Arta needed to get the girl out from under the bed so he could obtain help for her.

"Nur, I can take you someplace, keep you safe."

The girl's fingers uncurled and beckoned to him. He reached under the bed and held her hand. "It's going to be okay, Nur. We're going to get you well." He waited.

She gave his fingers a slight squeeze.

Good, she understood him. Now to extract her

from under the bed.

"Are you ready to come with me to a place where we'll take good care of you?"

She moved her foot, then her leg, and inched closer to him.

Progress. Relief flooded him. Once she was out from under the bed, the next step would be to work on getting the parents to agree to take her to a hospital. She slid her icy hand under the sleeve of his coat. *Good grief.* Sliced up and nearly frozen, enraged at her father for who knew what, it was a wonder the girl was still able to communicate. He grieved for the girl's suffering and pain.

Her fingers gripped his forearm. "Buzz, buzz. Answer your phone."

His phone wasn't ringing. *Was she hallucinating?* "Nur, you can let go of my arm." The last thing the girl needed was to have the impression he was violating her, too.

"I'll get out of your way so you can come out."

His phone vibrated in his pants pocket. *How had she heard the phone before he felt it?*

A sudden burst of movement, and she slammed into him, her nails digging into his flesh, and her nose touching his. Nur's puffy, red-rimmed eyes flew open, and she erupted into laughter, coarse and guttural in his ear.

"Hello, Dr. Arta. Long time, no see."

Chapter Three

Gibeon, Israel, 959 B.C.E.

King Solomon stood where Joshua once led troops to victory and offered up yet another burnt offering. So many deaths, so many sacrifices made to God. Now, despite being a man of seventeen, Solomon, the youngest of King David's offspring still felt like a boy. Without military experience, he was forced to use the captain of the guard's sword as his own, lest his kingdom topple. First his half-brother, Adonijah, then Joab, and the exiled Shimei were killed to keep his regency intact. He hated the killing. Each death tore at his heart.

He turned and faced Zadok, the only person he trusted to accompany him to the high place. "Return to Jerusalem. Tell my mother I need some time alone."

The priest made the sign to ward off evil. "What of the wild animals and bandits? Fear you not for your body, if not your soul?"

"I will keep Benaiah and ten of his men with me. They can guard me at a distance. I will fast and pray for God to come to me."

The priest's indignation burned a hole in Solomon's forehead. "God will not appear just because you summon Him."

"I am not attempting to summon our Lord like a

witch would summon the dead or a jinni. The voice of God is not only for my ears, but for my heart and soul." Weary of defending his decision, Solomon spoke through gritted teeth. "Did not a burning bush speak to Moses in the wilderness when he was *alone*? I strain my ears for the voice of the Lord, the *Bat Kol*, when I am amongst the people. If He uses his small voice, how am I to pick Him out over the din of men who shout like braying jackasses?"

Lips twisted in disapproval, Zadok's breath hissed through gritted teeth. "As you wish. I shall return to the city and tell Bathsheba of your decision." The priest shook his head. "She won't be happy."

Solomon barked a mirthless laugh. "She won't be pleased until she rules the world—through me." *All the more reason for my sacred retreat.* If *only* he knew how to achieve justice with mercy without killing everyone who opposed him.

Day after day, night after night, the voice of the Lord was silent. On the fortieth night of his fast, alone at the crest of the mountain, huddled at the base of the altar, Solomon cried out, "Lord, what did I do to displease you? Will you not grant me one word, one small sound of your voice? What should I do about my mother's plans to marry me to every ally's daughter? Each week she brings me another proposal. They number like the stars. I love women, but I am only a man. I have limits." He held his hands up, beseeching his Lord.

"Who can I trust? How can I be a good husband to so many women? How can I be a good father to an army of children? What should I do when the women bicker and fight with one another? What should I do with the building plans my father left for your Temple? Where shall I find laborers and supplies? Is there no better way to rule except by killing my enemies? So many questions, Lord, so few honest answers.

Please, I beg of you, speak to me, tell me what to do."

He fell into a fitful sleep and dreamed. A man wearing white linen appeared before him.

"God answers your prayers. I, Gabriel, bring you good tidings and the first of many gifts." The man handed him a small cedar box and vanished in a burst of stars.

A soft breeze stroked his cheek, and a small voice whispered, "Solomon."

He strained his eyes and ears, seeking the owner of the voice.

"Solomon."

He fell to his knees and pressed his forehead to the ground. Hot tears bathed the rocks beneath his cheeks. "Thank you, Lord, for hearing my prayers."

The small voice grew into a large voice and resonated in Solomon's chest like the echo of a drum. "Ask what I should give you."

This was the moment he'd prayed for, the request practiced each day, morning and night. Words tumbled out of his mouth, one after the other, like a flock of tiny birds taking flight at the first light. "I am only a little child when it comes to ruling. I don't know whether to go out or come in. Give me an understanding mind, the ability to discern between good and evil. Give me wisdom."

A sigh of wind lifted the hair on the back of his neck, and a thrill raced through his trembling limbs.

The Lord speaks. To me! How would he tell his mother, Benaiah, Zadok, and Nathan of this moment? Words could never do it justice.

Like thunder rolling over a mountaintop, the invisible one's voice shook every fiber in Solomon's being. "Because you requested this, and not long life or riches for yourself, or for the life of your enemies, but asked for discernment between wrong and right, I do according to your word."

The earth rumbled and pebbles danced on Solomon's hands.

"I hereby give you a wise and discerning mind—no one like you has been before you, and no one like you shall rise after you. I give you also what you have not asked, many gifts, riches, and honor all your life. No other king shall compare with you. If you walk in my ways, keep my commandments, I will lengthen your life."

Solomon awoke with a start. Rosy streaks of light smeared the night sky. He blinked and searched for some physical sign of the Lord's presence and promises. Nothing had changed. Yet everything was different. The sun crested the peak of the mountain, blinding him with its brightness. Songs praising the Lord exploded all around him. Every bird, tree, bush, blade of grass, each rock and grain of sand, it seemed, lent their voice, one louder than the next. *Was this clamor and chaos his gift?*

Heart hammering like a sword beating on a shield, Solomon covered his ears and shouted, "Lord, what is this uproar you send me? I don't wish to seem ungrateful, but I cannot even think with this din. Help me, please, I pray of you, to sort this noise out."

The racket subsided to normal birdsongs. Beneath the trills and chirps, he could still make out an undercurrent of chatter. "Look how the sun rises on the crest."

"Bugs, I need some bugs for my babies."

Could they not keep these thoughts to themselves? Not to be ungrateful, but how was he to separate the chaff from the grain?

A hoopoe bird swooped down, stood before Solomon, and bowed. "I offer you my services."

Tickled from his toes to the tips of his fingers, Solomon laughed until he wept. "Hoopoe bird, pray tell, what can you do for me that my army cannot?"

The bird spread his black and white striped wings and ruffled his feathers. "My vision goes for miles. I can spy on your enemies and bring you news from other countries. Not to praise myself too highly, I can do something *none* of your soldiers can do. I can fly."

The laughter died on his lips. "I beg your pardon, Hoopoe. I *am* in need of your services. Come, be with me at all times. I shall treat you with the respect you deserve."

The foot long creature flew up and perched on his shoulder. "You are wise, my King."

Despite the azure skies and bright sun, thunder roared overhead, and a ball of blue fire streaked down from the sky, landed on his outstretched hand, and extinguished itself, leaving his palm unharmed. Power coursed through Solomon from his head down to his feet. The spirit of God burned but did not consume the bush before Moses. Now it burned but did not consume Solomon. He howled with joy and turned toward the soldiers' camp at the base of the hill.

Hoopoe dug his claws into his shoulders and called, "*Oop-poo*, what is that wooden case on the ground?"

Tilted on its side, the box from his dream lay wedged against a boulder. Gabriel's gift from the Lord. *It was real.*

Solomon picked it up and tried to pry it open with his fingertips, to no avail. He shook his head. Tucking the box under his arm, he leaped down the mountain with the speed and sure footedness of a stag. The Lord answered his prayers, spoke to him, and promised him wisdom. His heart felt as if it would burst. It was a *miracle*.

"Benaiah," he shouted as he approached the cluster of men still eating their morning bread. "The Lord heard my prayers. I'm ready to go home now. Bring the horses." *Oh, dear Lord, did they talk, too?*

A black horse looked him straight in the eye, nodded, stomped the ground with his right forefoot, and neighed. *"Yes, but we can keep our counsel and your secrets. We live to serve you."*

Breathless with the excitement of each new discovery, awe swelled up in his chest. He raised his hands and lifted his face to the morning sky. "Who is like unto you, oh Lord? Let everything that *breathes* praise you—but not too loudly, please!"

Singing God's praises between each breath, Solomon relayed his miraculous story to Benaiah and his men.

The soldiers shouted "*Kadosh, kadosh, kadosh*! Holy, holy, holy, the Lord God is all mighty!" Benaiah sent half of his men ahead to prepare the way for their King and to share the news of a great miracle.

As Solomon and his bodyguard galloped up to Jerusalem, the city gates gleamed golden in the afternoon sun. Inside the walled city, people, *his* people, too many to count, thronged the route to the palace and called his name.

Solomon's soul burned with the fire of a million suns and overflowed with love for all of God's creatures. He called back to the growing crowd, "His Glory is within me. We are blessed. Praise *Him* with rams' horns sounds, praise *Him* with tambourine and dance, praise *Him* with lute and harp, clanging cymbals, strings and pipe."

By the time Solomon arrived at the palace, his voice was hoarse from singing and shouting, but he didn't care.

Joy spurred him onward. He leaped down from his blessedly silent mount, raced into his mother's private quarters, and lifted the open-mouthed Bathsheba off her feet.

"Put me down. What's wrong with you? What is a bird doing on your shoulder?"

Unable to contain his glee, he laughed and returned his mother to the stone floor.

"Hoopoe is my servant. He flies where men cannot and reports back to me."

Arms folded across her chest, her face creased in disapproval.

"Zadok and Nathan warned me your overlong fast might make you go mad. They were right."

Solomon laughed until his knees grew weak. "I hungered and thirsted for the Lord's voice." He wiped tears off his cheeks.

"He spoke to me, first in His small voice, then

booming, echoing off the hills."

She continued to gaze at him, concern carved into her face.

"Oh, Mother, you have no idea, do you? You've never felt the Lord's voice move through you, or His spirit fill you with the fire that burns, but does not consume." He grabbed her to his chest. "Feel how my heart races. It is the Lord, roaring in my breast like the greatest of lions. He is with me, Mother. God exalts me among men, fills me with His power."

She shook in his arms, and he realized she was weeping.

What was wrong with her? Couldn't she see this was good news? "Mother, please don't cry. Rejoice. Your son is now a man filled with wisdom."

She pulled away and wrapped her arms around her shaking shoulders. Silver hairs stood out alongside her high cheekbones where once only burnished brown had been. Crow's feet wrinkled next to her eyes, and gaps appeared between her teeth.

He'd only been gone forty nights. How had she aged so much in such a short time? Or was it that his vision was clear now, no longer shrouded in a cloud of memories of her youth and beauty? Tears streaked her wrinkled cheeks, and her lips trembled. "Does this mean I'm of no use to you now? Will you cast me out of your life? Send me into exile?"

Why would she think such a thing? "Mother, no, never."

"You said you would rid your life of me."

Solomon knelt before her and held her thin hands. "Dearest Mother, please forgive me. I spoke in anger, before I became wise. We are commanded to honor our father and mother."

She raised her gaze to his. "And?"

He searched her face for signs of subterfuge. Instead, he saw an old woman who feared she would be left to die in poverty, abandoned by her son. "Mother, you will always have a home with me."

"A home? But what of the throne room? Will I be allowed to counsel you?"

There was the Bathsheba of old. He had to smile. "You may give me advice, but I choose if I use it."

Her shoulders sagged. "So be it." She brushed away her tears, shook her head, and straightened her shoulders. "I'll tell the servants to prepare the feast."

As she headed for the cooking quarters, the bird whispered in his ear. "Is she always so weepy?"

"Be careful, my little friend. The lioness may be old, but she still has sharp teeth."

As Solomon rose to his feet, a servant appeared in the doorway and bowed. "Benaiah said I should give this to you." He placed the box on floor and backed out of the room.

A thrill of anticipation filled him. "Hoopoe, shall we see what's in the wooden case?"

The bird shrugged, fluttered over to the queen's dressing table, and pecked at a kohl vial.

Solomon turned the box over, searched for a gap in the wood, and tested a seam with the tip of his knife. Ornate engraving covered each side.

"It says, 'What is the greatest name of all?' That's simple. There is only one. God."

The lid flew open, revealing a dozen or more brass and iron sealing rings. He slid one onto his right index finger, held it up to the waning afternoon light, and examined the Hebrew characters in the pentacle. "What am I to do with these? Seal my scrolls?"

A blinding light filled the room. Legs trembling, Solomon wondered if God was visiting him again.

Did I displease Him?

"Lord, have you decided I'm not worthy of your gifts? What have I done?"

A swirling green mist surrounded a giant brandishing a sword.

This was *not* the invisible God. Nor was it a human. And, he doubted it was an angel. That left only two other kinds of creatures, ones he'd never encountered before, but heard stories about at his father's knee. It had to be a demon or a jinni. Either way, it looked like it wanted to kill Solomon.

Chapter Four

Aksum, 957 B.C.E.

Three years after her father's death, at the age of eighteen, Makeda climbed the stairs to begin the legal proceedings for the day. A profusion of green trees and purple flowers met her eye and lifted her heart. The gardeners had followed her instructions well, providing a calm environment to weaken the demons who fed on anger. If her days of reveling in the beauty of the land, mountains, streams, and skies, where she set aside her regal identity for a brief time and just *be* were over, at least she had this garden to remind her of her beloved countryside. Hundreds of birds in all varieties roosted in the treetops and called out to one another in a constant stream of background chatter. In addition to the comfort of having the birds close at hand, they also served as her eyes and ears when she was otherwise occupied. Vivacious and smart, the green parrots were her favorites.

She waved at an emerald male preening himself on a low branch, and patted the arm of her chair. He flew to her side, nuzzled her ear with his beak, and nipped at her gold earring.

"Pretty. For me?"

"Silly bird, you need no adornment." She rubbed his cheek and considered her next words. A few compliments and he'd do her bidding all day long. "You are too beautiful now. Who will look at me with you in the room?"

He plumped himself up. "Right you are, Queen."

"I ask a favor."

He cocked his head. "Your wish is my command."

"A troubling dispute comes before me today. The Chamberlain tells me two women, next door neighbors, are quarreling over a missing gold chain. By all accounts, each woman is honest. The piece is missing. Was it stolen or misplaced? I need someone smart and impartial to help me solve this problem. Can you fly to their houses and tell me what you see? I need you to be quick about it. Do you think you can you do it? Maybe I should ask another bird, perhaps the ibis?"

The parrot squawked. "The ibis? He can barely find his own bugs. Can't stop shouting 'haa-haa' all day long. I'm the bird for this task." With that, he spread his wings and flew out a tall window, grazing an incoming ibis.

"Haa-haa! Get out of my way."

The parrot was right. The ibis couldn't keep his beak shut. She smiled and turned to the sea of faces below her. While she'd been whispering to the parrot, the room had filled up with petitioners. A cordon of her finest warriors stood at the ready, lest bickering led to the drawing of knives and spears. She motioned to her Chamberlain to proceed. He pounded his staff of office on the stone floor and shouted for quiet. At his nod, a tightly bound cluster of four people struggled forward, knelt, and placed their heads upon the floor.

The Chamberlain, a tall man with hair sprinkled with gray, intoned in his deep voice, "Who is the aggrieved?"

Three hands shot up.

Makeda shook her head.

Wisdom. Where are you when I need you?

The Chamberlain frowned. "You can't *all* be the aggrieved. Who brings this dispute to the Queen?"

One hand.

"Rise and tell us your story."

An older man clad in a brown loincloth and a lion tooth hanging from his neck rose with difficulty. Stooped shoulders, sad eyes, head bowed, sorrow filled his body. "I gave my only daughter in marriage to that man." He pointed at the young man prostrate on the floor. "She is a good girl. A loving daughter."

Makeda interrupted the petitioner. "Is she here with you now?"

A tear trickled down his cheek. "No, my Queen. My daughter is no longer with us. Her mother and I believe her husband harmed her. Three moons have passed since we tried to visit her. That man told me she ran away. I don't believe him."

The Chamberlain poked the accused with his staff. "Rise and speak."

The young man leaped to his feet and faced his accuser. A thick twisted chain of gold banged on his broad chest, and abdominal muscles rippled beneath well-oiled skin. Hands balled into fists, he spat his words out one by one. "I gave her a good home. She couldn't cook, clean, or make love the right way. I had to teach her everything. She didn't like her lessons. Disobedient, worthless thing ran away."

The girl's white haired mother lay on the floor, shaking and sobbing. Makeda had the strong feeling the 'lessons' involved his fists. *Wisdom, please, help me. I cannot judge against a man just because I don't like him.* "Who is that woman with you?"

Makeda nodded to the Chamberlain. He prodded the young man's companion. She wore a long white dress and rose on swollen, unsteady feet. Her hair and face hooded, shadows obscured her features. Not even loose clothing could hide her belly heavy with child.

Makeda leaned forward. "Take off your head covering."

Moments stretched into minutes as the girl unwrapped the long cloth and revealed her battered face. Swollen eyes, split and bleeding lips gave mute witness to the abuse she withstood at this man's hands. A collective gasp filled the room.

"Is this your daughter?"

The old man shook his head. "This is not my child."

The younger man sneered. "She's not like your thick-headed girl. This one does what I tell her to do."

As the old woman wailed beside him on the floor, the elderly man shook his head and sobbed, "Why, Sun God, why did you take my daughter from me?"

Makeda's heart twisted at the old man's words, so like the plea of her beloved Baba. She fought back tears. *Show no weakness.*

"Do not blame the Sun God. He is not at fault." She pointed at the arrogant young man. "Seize him."

The waiting warriors jumped at her words and grabbed his arms. The expression of disdain turned into bewilderment. "I don't understand."

Without proof of murder, a death sentence was unjust. Other options were at her disposal. High on the towering platform built for her throne, Makeda stood so the prisoner nearly had to bend over backward to see his ruler and receive judgment.

"You are hereby sentenced to work in the stone quarry until you repay this man and his wife the value of his daughter and her dowry. It will not bring his child back, but it should help ease their old age as their daughter will not be here to care for them."

He grinned. "That will take a week. She was *cheap*."

The Chamberlain cuffed the side of the man's head. "Do not speak to the Queen unless she tells you to speak."

A cold fury boiled in Makeda's chest. "Each day you work at the quarry, you will receive as many lashes as the marks on this pregnant girl's body." Another thought occurred to her, as if whispered to her from on high. "I hereby send your wife back to her family, away from your 'lessons.'"

The young woman's eyes grew wild, and she shook her head.

Here she was giving the girl the gift of freedom and she was refusing it. *Why would she want to stay with that beast?*

"What is it?"

Tears trickled down the girl's swollen cheeks. "My family is dead, killed in a raid. My village is gone."

"Ah." Makeda turned toward the grieving father. "Bid your wife to rise."

The elderly woman leaned on her husband for support, and stood on trembling, stick-thin legs, her face ashen.

"Embrace your new daughter."

Sorrow, surprise, then flashes of joy flew across the old couple's faces like storm clouds fleeing before sunshine. The old woman placed her hands on the young woman's belly and laughed.

"Two heads! Double blessings from the Sun God!"

The new grandmother clapped her hand over her mouth and glanced at the Chamberlain, who shrugged and favored her with a wide grin.

"I know you cannot replace your child with this girl, but she needs a home, as do her babies. You are good people. Lean on one another for support, take comfort in the small things. Over time, perhaps you will grow to love one another, and become a real family."

The young man struggled against his captors and shouted, "You are nothing but a *woman*. You are not the king." He spat on the floor. "I do not recognize your authority." He stared up at Makeda, his face a mask of hatred.

A blanket of silence fell in the cavernous room. Even the birds ceased their conversations. All eyes were upon the Queen. Unmoving, the old couple clutched the young woman's arms as if to keep her from floating away. The waiting litigants shuffled and shot furtive glances at one another. The young man snickered, then erupted into shrieks like a hyena. He was laughing at Makeda.

How dare he jeer at the Queen of Sheba?

Her nursemaid had said she would be tested. She had prophesied well. If Makeda ignored the man's outburst, simply had him taken to the quarry, it would be seen as a sign of weakness. Soon others would fall behind him, taking his lead, perhaps even overthrowing her rule. Her father labored long and hard to raise up his nation and his people. His kingdom would not be torn down by an animal such as this one.

The Queen pointed at the smirking man with her golden scepter and said in a soft, yet strong voice, "Take him outside and *kill* him."

The man screamed all the way through the throne room. His curses echoed off the stone walls of the palace and continued in the distance, until, at last, after a final shriek, he was silent.

Makeda sat down and observed the faces of her subjects as the Queen's lessons sank into the silence.

Be kind. Smile. Show no weakness.

She inclined her head toward the elderly couple. "Go in peace. May you live long and happy lives with your new daughter and grandchildren."

The Chamberlain raised his eyebrows at the Queen as if to say, "Now what?"

The green parrot fluttered into the throne room and perched on the arm of the Queen's chair. "My Queen, I know where the necklace is and who the thief is, too," he whispered into her ear.

She nodded, and then called out, "Where are the women disputing over the gold chain?"

Two women, one heavy set and short, the other tall and skinny, pushed their way through the crowd. After they threw themselves on the floor, Makeda bid them rise.

"Who is the aggrieved?"

Shorty glared at the other woman. "Me. She stole from me. I want my treasure back."

Skinny placed a hand on her chest. "I did no such thing. I'm an honest woman, with plenty of riches in my home."

Makeda placed a finger on her cheek. "Do you have children?"

The women exchanged fearful glances.

"Yes," Shorty sputtered. "Five. I don't want her child to add to mine."

The room erupted in laughter. Even Makeda had to smile.

"I'm not saying she should give her child to you. I'm suggesting you need to search a little harder in your own home to find that necklace. Like in your little girl's water gourd."

Skinny clapped her hands, and Shorty gasped. "How do you know this?"

Makeda stroked the preening parrot. "A little bird told me. Now go home and speak to your child."

The two women rushed out of the palace, Skinny screeching at Shorty, "I told you I didn't do it!"

Thankful the last case had not required the death sentence, Makeda glanced out the window and saw the Sun God was at his highest. Unless they were at war, no one worked during this hour, even the queen.

"It is time for our meal break and rest. We will reconvene when the shadows of the trees touch the ground. In the meantime, those of you who await judgment might wish to settle your spats among yourselves."

The Chamberlain banged his staff and ordered the crowd to disperse. A cloud of dust surrounded the throng as they made their way out of the palace in search of places to eat and rest. When the last of the bickering subjects left the Queen's court, the Chamberlain approached Makeda, bent his knee, and bowed his head.

"Permission to speak?"

"Yes, please. I value your advice, dear Uncle. Tell me your thoughts."

He lifted his head and gazed directly into her eyes. "You were just and unflinching in your decisions with that renegade. You were magnificent. Your father would be so proud."

At that, a flood of tears released the tightly bound emotions she had held back all morning. "I wish to be half as good as my father. Serving my people requires strength." She sighed and wiped the tears off with a flick of her fingers. "It also requires great wisdom."

A man's voice boomed, "I bring you tales from afar, oh Queen."

"Tamrin!"

As her childhood friend crossed the length of the room, once again her father's counsel echoed in her head and heart. *"Make Tamrin your adviser. He loves you and knows he cannot marry you. You must remain a virgin. A man, babies, take too much time. You could not be a wife and a good ruler."*

Although dusty and weary looking, the broad smile Tamrin wore brought joy to her heart. She hadn't seen him in over twenty moons. A rich merchant's son, he'd joined the family business shortly after Makeda became queen. Invigorated by a young man's boldness, the caravan had grown to five hundred and twenty camels and over three hundred and seventy ships. Managing and increasing his wealth took him on long travels to faraway places.

The Chamberlain nodded and stood aside to allow Tamrin to approach the throne.

"Uncle," Makeda called, "please do not stay on my

account. I will dine with my old friend and hear news of his travels."

A short time later, after the giggling maid servants had washed the dust of the long journey from Tamrin's face, hands, and feet, Makeda bade him to join her at a gleaming brown onyx table laden with enough food for ten people. He gulped down a glass of *tej*, honey wine, and reached for a roasted chicken leg.

Makeda shook her head. The long journey had not dimmed her best friend's love for royal repasts. "Did you go to your wife and child?"

He shook his head. "I came to see you first, to tell you of the wonders of the grand city of Jerusalem. King Solomon judges cases each day, just as you do. He is a teacher, the wisest man in the world."

Makeda dropped a date pit on a gold platter and sat up straight. "Wise, you say?"

"I sat in his court room for days. He is gracious, kind to his seven-hundred happy wives, three hundred satisfied concubines, and servants beyond count. If someone errs, his corrections are gentle."

Intent on hearing Tamrin speak, Makeda slid forward on her purple seat cushion and placed her elbows on the low table, her chin in her hands.

Happy wives. Satisfied concubines. Gracious. Kind. Gentle. Wise.

"Tell me more."

"A dark-haired, handsome man, he strides among the common people, those who work on his temple. He asks the quarrymen and carpenters probing questions, not to abuse them, but to learn from them. His thirst for all manner of knowledge is like that of a camel at the end of a long desert trek."

Breathless, she nodded encouragement to her friend.

"Solomon's pronouncements come in the voice of his invisible god. A prophet among men. No dispute, no quarrel, no riddle is too hard for this king to solve."

Her heart quickened, and her face felt as warm as when she gazed up at the Sun God.

"What does he sound like? Is his voice deep? Soft? Rough?"

"His normal voice is like that of any other man. But when his god speaks, it is like the roar of a lion. Your legs shake and you fall to the ground in fear of this power." He shook his head. "I would have stayed there forever, just to be near King Solomon, to hear him teach. Oh, if only I could be here and there, that would be true happiness. I would have stayed and served him as a man servant, even worked as a slave on his temple, had it not been for my love of my queen and country— and the fact that he commands the devil jinnis to construct his Temple."

Commands the jinnis?

Tamrin's words catapulted her back to her father's deathbed confession. Baba had called her to his side and had told her to sit next to him on the bed.

"I must tell you a secret about your mother," he said. "I was out in the desert a year before your birth and saw a white snake locked in combat with a black snake. I killed the black snake. A gust of wind blew sand in my eyes. When my vision cleared, where the snake had been, a tall man stood instead. He thanked me for saving his life and said he would repay me." Her father shook his head. "He was a jinni. I told him I needed nothing." He had taken a deep shuddering breath. "The jinni brought his sister to me here at the palace the next day. She was a luminous being with green eyes, cinnamon complexion, long, straight black hair. She speared my heart with her beauty, and I desired her. He gave her to me to be my wife. Your mother was not banished from my kingdom. She went back to her people in the world of the jinnis."

If what Baba had said was true, then that meant—

A servant dropped a platter, bringing her back to the moment with a start.

"What do you mean he commands the jinnis? What manner of sorcery is this?"

A pomegranate seed lodged between his teeth, Tamrin took his time picking it out before responding. Fingers interwoven to keep them still, Makeda wanted to shake the words out of her friend.

"Not sorcery. A gift from his god. I saw the great seals on his hands. They give him the power to control the devils, keep them out of evil doing, and force them to work on the temple. One strong jinni can carry the same load in a day that it would take a dozen men to transport to the high place."

Makeda took a deep breath and blew it out through pursed lips. She was half-jinni, half-human. She was not evil. Nor was she completely jinni. Solomon's ring held no power over her—or did it?

"Tell me about the temple? Did he plan such a glorious thing?"

"His father designed it, but did not live to see his drawings become buildings. King Solomon carries on his father's vision. His needs are many for this marvel."

Makeda seized the opportunity to avoid distressing thoughts about this king and his jinni-commanding seals. "We can trade with the king for many of our exports, frankincense, ebony wood that resists termites, cinnamon, reeds for writing. What does he offer us in return? Olive oil? Wine? Slaves?"

Tamrin motioned to a hovering servant for his glass to be refilled, took a deep gulp, and shook his head. "He gave me much gold this trip. It is almost as if the streets and houses of Jerusalem are covered in gold and silver. What we need is protection."

Breathless with the audacity of the proposal, she fell back on her cushion. "What do *we* need defenses from? The mountains are treacherous to outsiders. Our warriors are well trained with weapons, horses, and chariots. We can defend ourselves."

"Not our land. Our trade routes."

"So in exchange for our tribute, he will continue to protect our merchants? Do you think this is a fair trade?" Tamrin was her one true friend who never let her win a game as a child just because she was a princess. She loved him like a brother, trusted him with her secrets and life. Now she needed his honest advice before she placed her country at the mercy of the King of Israel. What would be next if she acceded to this command? Would he wish to annex her nation? That would *never* happen.

"Without Israel's protection, our goods can't make it to the Red Sea, much less to the shore of the Great Sea. We passed a caravan on our way to Jerusalem less fortunate than us. Every single man butchered, or left to die of thirst. Camels and goods stolen with no recourse, no king or queen to turn to for justice. Our lives and livelihoods in exchange for things we can spare? Yes, this is a fair trade."

Smile. Be kind. Show no weakness.

She nodded. "We will show this king we are not some weak nation, easy to be conquered, our bones picked by his buzzard troops. When we send our tribute, we shall do it with abundance *and* strength."

Tamrin grinned. "Of course." He glanced out the window. "The tree shadows are almost at the ground. You need to get back to your court proceedings, and I need to go home." He began to rise and stopped. "With your leave, of course."

She waved him away. "Give your wife my greetings. Take some dates for your boy. I know he loves them."

Tamrin bowed low, stuffed a handful of the sweets in his pocket, and exited the queen's dining chamber.

Makeda leaned back and closed her eyes. Part of her was tantalized by the stories Tamrin shared about King Solomon. She imagined drops of honeyed wisdom falling from his lips. If only she could gather his knowledge and bring it home to Sheba. She sighed. If Jerusalem were closer, she could go there herself, not just rely on Tamrin's eyes and ears. Six moons to cross halfway. Such a long journey. Who would rule her nation in her stead? Who had the respect of her people? And what about the evil jinnis? Would the devils recognize her as half-jinniyah and share her secret with the handsome king? Would he command her with his seals? What would he order her to do? Would he force her to come to his bed? That would never happen. She could never be with a man. She needed to be a virgin queen. She promised her father to protect and serve only her nation, never a man, not even one as great as King Solomon.

Above all else, you must seek wisdom. That is your destiny.

Did she need to travel to Jerusalem to learn wisdom? Was this the true meaning of Metatron's prophesy?

"Oop-poo!" The call of a bird startled Makeda out of her reverie. On the inside edge of the window perched a hoopoe bird with a gold and silver filigreed tube tied to his leg.

She approached the striped creature. "Well, hello, my little friend. What is that?"

He cocked his orange head and gazed at her with dark, intelligent eyes.

"A summons. Your royal highness is commanded to appear in the court of King Solomon."

Chapter Five

Chevy Chase, MD, U.S.A., Present Day

Throat tight, heart attempting to jack hammer out of his chest, Arta whispered, "I thought I rid the earth of your *'Ifrit* stink two years ago in a jail cell in Arizona. What are you doing here?"

The girl's face shifted and contorted as if a million insect larvae burrowed beneath her skin. The evil jinni struggled with Nur for control of her tongue and won.

"What kind of a hello is that for an old friend?" She coughed in his face, and acrid fumes singed Arta's nostrils. "I gave you a terrorist, you gave me an eviction notice."

Eyes stinging, he jerked his head away from the sulfurous stench. "You forced that young man to become a bomber. He had no evil inclinations until you whispered into his ear."

"*La, la.* No, no, my friend, he always dreamed of becoming a martyr to the cause. I just helped him get there sooner."

Feet kicking the underside of the bed, Nur choked, trapped in a power struggle for her own body. Arta had to get the *'Ifrit* out before the girl asphyxiated. He hated having to speak to the jinni, it only encouraged him. Now the creature had a real audience, someone who recognized him and his power. The evil one was in no rush to leave. He was having a good time.

"Release this girl. She's a mere child, no player in your game." While Arta worked at putting force into his voice, his mind whirled with questions and memories. How had the *'Ifrit* survived? At the time of the incident in the desert, he was sure the jinni was gone.

In the name of all that was holy, what happened?

Eyes narrowed, voice guttural, the *'Ifrit* laughed. "I might consider leaving this worthless body. For a price. The plus side for me is her father is a diplomat. Much political fodder here, don't you think?" Coarse laughter followed. "And, the delicious possibility of 'child sexual abuse' with obtuse American doctors meddling in 'repressive cultures.' What fun. I can stir up a diplomatic nightmare, if not an outright war between Turkey and the United States. Ah, but I digress. You wanted me to go."

"Leave this child. Let Allah heal her scars, let the holy one, blessed be He, protect her from further attacks from you and your kin."

A sly expression came over Nur's face. "Did you bring a wolf with you to eat me?"

"Only witches and frauds keep wolves to eat jinnis." Not that he would object to having an entire pack of them with him right at the moment. Arta was losing ground, needed to think of something quickly to gain the upper hand. No amount of blowing or olive oil bathing would rid Nur of this *'Ifrit*. He needed something stronger. He might not be a holy man, but he knew how to call on a Higher Power.

"In the name of Allah, the Beneficent, the Merciful, Praise be to Allah, Lord of the Worlds, The Beneficent, the Merciful. Owner of the Day of

Judgment, Thee alone we worship; Thee alone we ask for help. Show us the straight path—"

"Boring." Yawning, the *'Ifrit* rolled Nur's eyes. "Just give me what I want."

Sweat trickled down Arta's brow, despite the freezing temperature in the room. "I don't negotiate with terrorists or *'Ifrits*."

"C'mon, Arta. Do what you did back there in the desert when you left your Jewish girlfriend for dead."

The psychiatrist's neck hairs stood on end.

With one swift movement, the girl reached over, grabbed Arta by the throat, and choked him with superhuman strength.

Bright stars swam before his eyes, and the narrow world under the bed telescoped to darkness. He prayed for a miracle. Just as he thought he would pass out or die, Arta felt the girl's hand fall away from his neck. The laughing *'Ifrit* swam back into his view, but his vision was as clear in the shadowy hollow as if it were daylight. Beneath the over-sized down coat, his made-to-order Hong Kong suit and shirt stretched and shredded into a million threads. His hands were now feline paws and his feet exploded out of his shoes. Curved claws tore through his fingertips and toes, and Arta roared in pain.

Not again, not now.

The *'Ifrit* chortled with glee. "I knew you'd do it."

The girl bucked in a seizure and shrieked in pain.

Arta tried to shout, "In the name of Allah, the most gracious, the most merciful Allah! There is no God but He—the Living, the self-subsisting, the eternal—" but all that came out of his mouth was a roar of a lion that rattled the walls and sent Nur's mother screaming and slamming the door as she ran out of the room.

The 'Ifrit provoked him into an uncontrollable rage and into shape shifting against his will. Now the evil jinni would pay for his crimes against Allah and His creations.

He placed his paw on the girl's forehead. She writhed and foamed at the mouth, and he continued to recite the Verse of the Throne—except now it came out in gusts of lion's roars instead of words.

"No slumber can seize Him nor sleep. His are all things in the heavens and on earth. Who is there can intercede In His presence except as He permits? He knows what appears to His creatures as before or after or behind them—"

Nur's eyes closed. Her head rolled to the side and her mouth fell open.

Was she dead?

Arta touched her neck with a gentle paw. A weak, but steady pulse. Life still flowed in her, thanks to Allah. His senses now amplified to that of a predator, he sniffed the girl's breath. She needed to bathe, wash her hair, and brush her teeth, but the signature jinni stench of struck matches, was absent. She was safe. The *'Ifrit* was gone. But Arta's problem remained.

Although a Persian lion was smaller than an African one, the space under the bed afforded little opportunity for him to move. Pushing at the carpet with his front paws, he attempted to extract himself, only to back into the wall next to the bed. No going forward. Nur was in front of him and needed medical attention. He only had one choice. Crouching low on his belly, he flicked his tail and smacked the too-close wall. Arta gathered his strength and leaped to his feet. The bed flew into the air and crashed into the wall—just as Mr. Mustafa tore open the bedroom door.

His mouth in a huge "o," the man froze in place.

Despite being in tatters, the down jacket was still recognizable from the cloud of feathers floating in the air. Arta roared in a lower decibel in an attempt to apologize for terrifying Mrs. Mustafa. Then he nuzzled Nur and pushed her toward her trembling father.

"Is she—" Tears welled up in the father's dark eyes. "My daughter, what did you do to her?"

Annoyed, Arta shook his thick mane. He needed to get through to Mustafa. He worked in political minefields. Should be prepared for tense situations.

The man calls himself a diplomat?

Mustafa took three swift steps to his daughter's prone body and lifted her into his arms. He stroked her forehead and felt her wrist for a pulse. "She's alive. And that terrible stink is gone." His gaze travelled over the room and back to Arta's face. "The window is locked. There was a doctor here, my wife, and Nur. Then there was a roaring sound. My wife bolted out of the room. Now only the lion and my daughter remain."

Arta nodded and sat down, flicking his tail. *Okay. Now they were getting somewhere.*

"You are the doctor?"

Another nod. *Mustapha was smart—he put it all together. Good.*

"This is unbelievable. Insane. Outrageous."

Couldn't have said it better himself. If he didn't roar, that is.

"How did you do that? How do you become a man?"

Arta put a paw over his face. If he knew the answer

to that question, he wouldn't be sitting there playing twenty questions when they needed to get the girl to an ER.

Nur moaned. "*Baba*? Is that you?"

"Yes, my child." Mustafa held her face tight to his chest and closed his eyes. "You are safe now—you have been saved from the evil jinni by—"

"The grace of Allah." Arta said in real words, not roars. He was a man again, and a shivering, naked one at that. He grabbed a white sheet out of the pile of bedclothes and wrapped up as best he could.

The girl turned her face toward Arta. "Praise be to Allah that you didn't give up. I fought the *'Ifrit* as best I could, but I am a weak daughter. I tried and tried, but he overpowered me. Thank you for saving my life, Imam."

He opened his mouth to tell her he was not a spiritual leader, then changed his mind.

"Do not thank me. Thank Allah for his blessings and mercy. It is from Him that all goodness flows." He turned to the father. "Take her to the George Washington University Hospital Emergency Room. Tell them she has the flu and had seizures. They'll check her out, make sure she doesn't have any residual damage. Say nothing about a jinni possession."

Mustafa nodded and stared at Arta. "I don't understand what happened here, but I do know Allah has blessed you with special powers. Thank you. As-Salaam Alaykum, peace be upon you, Dr. Shahani."

"May peace, mercy and blessings of God be upon you, Mr. Mustafa."

"Your work takes you to dark places. I suspect you will need the protective light of Allah more than I."

Arta's phone buzzed at his feet. He picked it up, read the text, and felt the air go out of the room. Homeland Security needed him in Summertown, West Virginia with the last person in the world who would want to see him. The agent he'd been forced to abandon when the terrorist interrogation went bad. The only woman who made him want to recite poetry and the only one he'd ever truly loved at first sight—*Eliana Solomon.*

****

Summertown, West Virginia was only a few hours from Maryland by car, and mere seconds away by phone and text messages, but Arta seemed to take forever to respond to Eliana's call.

"Eliana, this is Arta. Are you okay?"

Her mouth dry, heart racing at the sound of his rich baritone, Eliana lost focus on the case for a split-second. She wanted to ask him what happened in the desert.

Why did you leave me for dead? Why didn't you come visit me in the hospital? Why didn't you call me?

She shook her head, straightened her spine, and forced herself to be professional.

"Hi Arta." She paused for effect. "I'm alive."

Did that sound bitchy? Too bad.

"We need your help here in West Virginia."

Eliana launched into a nothing-but-the-facts description of the case, right up to the phone call from the police chief. "The two girls are in the hospital now. Getting rehydrated. Talking. Healthy." She paused. "With some anomalies." *An understatement.* "Like the boys, these two girls can't recall anything about the time between entering the state park on foot and waking up in the middle of the highway. One thing their parents state with complete certainty is on the day they entered the state park, they had no babies on board."

"Now?"

Here comes the bomb.

"They're visibly pregnant."

A sharp intake of his breath told her she had his attention.

"How could that be?"

"Army Military Intelligence called Homeland in when the Imagery Intelligence Technician identified the jinni energy signature on satellite video images. I smelled sulfur on the dead girl, which screams jinni. Paw prints surrounded her body—large canine ones, which implicates werewolves. To top everything off, the surviving girls' blood tests indicate hormonal levels consistent with over three months human gestation."

Impatience gave his voice an edge. "You're talking in circles. Which isn't like you. Can you please cut to the chase? It's been a long day."

She wanted to say, *You've had a long day? What about that day in the desert?* She choked the words back.

"I'm trying to give you the *full* picture, Arta."

"Sorry."

"Ultrasounds confirmed the presence of healthy, kicking, four-legged fetuses. With tails."

"Well, if they're werewolves, wouldn't tails be normal?"

"Yup, after they are a year old. Plus, werewolves have a longer gestation period. The only mammal close to this timeframe is an opossum. Unlike these pregnancies, werewolves are in human form from conception to birth. Plus, the moms almost always give birth to multiples, not singles."

He made a humming sound. She swore she heard him stroking his chin.

"So, if the girls fooled around, they weren't mating with one of their kind."

Interesting way to phrase it. Was he trying to tell her something about their relationship?

"Not to put too fine a point on it, I'm just gonna put it out there right now. I think they're were-jinnis." *Boom. Take that Dr. Shahani.* A long silence. She glanced at the phone to make sure she had a connection. "Did I lose you?"

At last, she heard him swallow.

"That's not possible. Since the time of the great Prophet King Solomon, we've known wolves and jinnis don't get along. He commanded the jinnis with his seal. The werewolves were his supernatural enforcers. Legends say powerful ones can *eat* disobedient jinnis."

"In biblical times, maybe, but these days, jinnis are attacking werewolves, particularly their young women. It happened in Kentucky. And, I'm telling you, it's happening again here in West Virginia. Same *modus operandi*, grab a girl, get her pregnant. Jinni's are made from different matter from humans and live thousands of years. Their reproductive life is not the same as ours. The combination of the species seems to have triggered an extremely accelerated gestation."

"This is an abomination. The implications are—"

"Apocalyptic?" She gave a dry laugh. "Welcome to my world. Let the games begin, my friend."

"I'm not sure I'm the man for this case. I'll find you another psychiatrist, one more objective, with less history."

Her heart caught in her throat.

Less history? What did he mean?

The only case they'd ever worked together involved a Pakistani man two years ago. Found in a tunnel between Arizona and Mexico, surrounded by bricks of C-4, the man appeared to be dazed and confused. U.S. Customs and Border agents attempted to interrogate him, and he began alternating in speech from Latin, Arabic, Greek, to Aramaic. Eliana received the call to investigate the case. She asked for a reputable psychiatrist who dealt with suspected jinni possession. She got more than she expected with Arta Shahani, MD, who turned out to be a hot Persian man with a devastating smile. She shook her head to clear the memories of his dark brown eyes, rugged jaw, and broad shoulders.

"Sorry, Dr. Shahani. Your country needs you. No one else is cleared for these matters. You need to put away your feelings about—"

About what? Her? Just because she got hot and bothered thinking about him, didn't mean she appealed to him. "About were-jinnis."

"It wasn't the were-jinnis I was referring to." He blew out a long breath. "I'm talking about us. Something happened between us, didn't it? "

Her cheeks burned, and her heart thundered in her chest. She couldn't give into an emotion that defied words. Yearning swooped through her limbs and left her breathless. In a moment of weakness, she confessed, "It would be a lie if I said I didn't find you attractive. The timing was—"

"Terrible. Rumi said, 'Through love Ghouls turn

into angels.' Did I treat you like a ghoul, Eliana? "

"Don't be silly, Arta. You're no monster. It was a horrible case, gone sideways."

Where was he going with this? Why was he asking her about ghouls, evil jinnis that live in graveyards and other deserted places?

"Are you sure you want to work with me again? I feel so bad about—"

"We're professionals, Arta. Whatever happened in Arizona, should stay there."

He was the only person with the credentials she needed. It was essential to have him on the case. Pissed off or not, if she stayed in close range with this man, she couldn't guarantee to keep her promises to her dead mother to save her virginity until she married.

"It wasn't Las Vegas. You need to understand—"

"We need you here in Summertown. We want you to spend some time with the boys, examine them, elicit memories, something, anything." She needed to get back on track. Her voice brusque, she rattled off instructions. "Pack warm clothes and good walking shoes. The area is riddled with mines and caves, a jinni's dream landscape for portals."

He sighed. "I'll be there as soon as I wrap something up here. Tomorrow morning, lunchtime at the latest."

This time tomorrow, he'd be here at her side. A shiver of anticipation ran down her spine. A school girl's giddiness over a star football player bubbled up before her brain engaged.

Give it a rest. Focus on the case.

They had more important things to deal with than her sex hormones, ticking biological clock, and blessed virginity.

"I know we're supposed to be objective, sift through all the clues, wait for all the evidence before we come to a conclusion. But, these pregnancies, these were-jinni babies, are scary. Whatever ammo you own against these supernatural creatures, bring it with you, Arta. My gut is telling me this is going to be bad. If evil jinnis succeed with one of the most established werewolf packs in the United States, they can take over all the werewolf packs in the world."

Her mind raced with questions. Why did they need hybrid creatures? What was their real agenda? What could a were-jinni do that a regular jinni couldn't do? Were the legends true? Could were-jinnis really be supernatural weapons of mass destruction—worse than an evil jinni? The fate of the homeland and the world depended on her finding answers. And soon.

Chapter Six

Jerusalem, 957 B.C.E.

Row upon row of jinnis, men, wolves, lions, and birds stood at attention as King Solomon strode before them. He stopped before the gathering, arranged a signet ring on each of his fingers, placed his fists on his hips, and demanded, "Where is my Hoopoe? Why is he absent?"

The giant jinni remained motionless and silent, held in check by the power of the great seals. The wolves and lions, shape-shifters who could become men, shook their heads, howled and roared. Not one of them had seen or heard the bird.

"How can it be that not one of you has seen him?"

The men, unfettered by the king's seal, muttered in annoyance that a mere bird would command the ruler's attention and force them to stand idle while the sun beat their overheated brows. The king turned to the closest worker, a bricklayer coated in red dust and splattered with mud.

"I hear every word you say. Tell me where he is. I won't punish you. He, on the other hand, has to answer to me."

The man shook his head. "I'm sorry, my King. He's difficult to miss, what with that big wingspan of his and those stripes. I'd be the first to tell you."

A woman's voice interrupted the king's obsession with the missing bird.

"Solomon, a word with you please?" Bathsheba held a stick in one hand and her squalling five-year-old grandson, Rehoboam, by the ear with the other.

He sensed what was coming. The dark-haired child was in trouble on a daily basis.

"Now what?"

Bathsheba released the boy, who ran to clutch his father's legs.

"This child has to learn to respect his elders. He wanted some sweets, but I told him to wait, it would spoil his meal. So he ran to the cook and demanded dates. Cook told him to wait, too. He shouted, 'I am the royal prince, you must give me what I want.' Then he hit her with this stick."

Solomon leaned down and peeled the little beast off his legs. A wet mass of snot lay in the center of the king's purple tunic. "Rehoboam, what am I to do with you? You cannot behave this way toward your subjects. Your actions are unbecoming to a member of the Royal House of Israel."

The child stomped his foot and howled, "I want, I want."

"You can want, but you may not hurt people. Apologize to the cook. As penance, you must wash pots and pans the rest of today."

The child threw his shoulders back, put his fists on his hips, and glared up at his father with fiery eyes. "I don't do women's work."

"Well today you do. Keep this up, and you'll get a thrashing, followed by a day of pounding laundry on the rocks." Solomon grasped his defiant son by the wrist and handed him back to Bathsheba. "Mother, please tell me I didn't act this way when I was little."

Her silver braid whipped back and forth. "I blame his mother, Naamah the Ammonitess. She allows him too many liberties. Mark my words, Solomon, this young one's selfishness will be his undoing. He should not be your successor."

"Despite my many wives and concubines, the Lord has not blessed me with another living son." Solomon patted the unpleasant child on the head. "He's the only one."

"Then we'd better try to undo Naamah's bad work while there's still time." She dragged the shrieking boy away. "Stop wailing, you're not a baby anymore. Try behaving like a king instead of an evil jinni. Don't make me use this stick on you." Her scolding trailed off in the distance.

Solomon closed his eyes and shook his head. *God, give me strength.* If only he could manage his wives and children as easily as he commanded the jinnis. Sadly, his magic seals had no effect on his women and offspring.

"Oop-poo!"

"There you are, my friend." He waved the jinnis, men, wolves, lions, and birds away, releasing them to return to their duties. "You worried me with your long absence."

"I bring good news."

Solomon motioned for the bird to hop on his shoulder. "Yes?"

"Tamrin, the merchant, told us the truth about his virgin queen. I traveled to the territory where he said his people lived. A beautiful woman rules over them.

Tall, with a cinnamon complexion, huge green eyes, and hips and breasts to rival those of the largest Asherah in your kingdom."

The king's face felt as warm as if he sat in front of a blazing fire. "You make me hungry with your words, bird."

Hoopoe inclined his head and ruffled his top feathers. "You taught me well with your seven-hundred wives and three-hundred concubines."

"Is she as wealthy as Tamrin claimed?" He stroked the bird's soft neck.

"Yes, even more than he said. She has a magnificent throne, made of ivory, gold and jewels, a marvel to behold."

A kingdom that rivaled his in wealth. "Did you deliver my scroll to her?"

"Yes, but I must tell you more. The people worship the sun as a god, not our God, the All Knowing and Supreme Ruler."

A problem, but nothing insurmountable. "They need a judicious teacher. What was her response to the summons?"

"I thought she'd throw the scroll at me after she read it. She summoned her counselors and conferred with them at length."

Solomon stroked his beard. "The Queen surrounds herself with advisers. That is the sign of a good ruler, the mark of wisdom."

"First she thought to send you an abundance of wealth in her stead. But our friend, Tamrin, told her that would only kindle your wrath. She argued with him and an old gray haired man. She called him Uncle. At last she sent them all away, picked up a reed, and wrote upon a scroll." Hoopoe held out his leg. Where once the gold and silver tube had been, a solid gold one encrusted with red and green stones dangled in its place.

He laughed. "She sent me a much more valuable one than I sent to her. A subtle, but direct way of showing me how rich she is." Solomon unbound the gem heavy message written in Aramaic. "With my deepest respects, I make preparations to meet you, King Solomon. Barring thieves and murderers, I shall be in Jerusalem in twenty-four moons. Makeda, Queen of Sheba."

He held the paper to his nose and inhaled sandalwood, frankincense, myrrh and some unknown, mysterious aroma. Was that perfume, he wondered? Or was that *her* fragrance? His pulse quickened and his loins stirred at the thought of burying himself deep in the scent of this woman, a virgin queen who smelled like rain on parched desert sands. Was she the one who could give him a son to be proud of? Twenty-four moons. How would he wait? The only thing that could distract him that long would be the construction of the temple. Impatient as his rebellious son, Solomon prayed God would protect the Queen of Sheba and hasten her to his side.

****

Makeda stood before her high throne and surveyed the residents of Aksum and beyond. Warriors, merchants, farmers, landowners, and messengers, everyone she needed to spread the word and give notice to their workers stood before her, awaiting her announcement. Anxiety weighed heavy in the room. Even the birds' tongues were still. Grateful for her long white dress which hid her trembling legs, Makeda had to be strong for her country, for her subjects, for herself. Her kingdom had to be protected at all costs. No sacrifice was too large for Sheba.

"Listen my people," she called in a voice she hoped sounded strong and confident. "The Sun God has heard my prayers for wisdom. Each time a dispute comes before me, I pray to him to give me the understanding and to show me the bright light that directs my heart to justice for my subjects. We are wealthy as a nation, yet I ache with the need for the priceless gift of wisdom."

She took a deep breath and focused on her uncle's face. She had practiced this speech with her father's brother and Tamrin for days, writing and rewriting each word with care after each rehearsal. He gave her a warm smile and nodded for her to go on.

"My people, what I prayed for has arrived, at last. I have been invited to visit the king of Israel, the one who keeps our trade routes safe from bandits, the wisest of men, King Solomon."

A woman wailed, "Oh, Queen Makeda, do not leave us. You are wise *now*, we need you *here*."

The woman's heartfelt plea touched Makeda. She recalled her words to Baba as he lay on his deathbed. She had begged him not to leave her, too. She thought of her father and his voice came to her, almost as if he stood at her side and whispered in her ear.

I am with you Makeda. Be strong my daughter, you are doing the right thing.

A well of strength, hitherto untapped, flooded her veins. "Do not mourn. I do not seek death, but rebirth. I do not go on bended knee, but standing straight and tall.

I do not go as a servant, but as King Solomon's peer. My duty is to serve our great nation as best I can. I will return with deeper understanding, for *you*."

"We will all come with you, oh Queen," shouted a merchant. "We serve you."

"I cannot allow farmers to leave their animals and fields. No families will be uprooted to follow me on this quest. That road leads to the downfall of our nation. My feet will stay on the path of the bright and shining light of wisdom. It will lead me there and back to you."

"The road to wisdom is surrounded by bandits who hide in the darkness of evil," a warrior shouted. "We will come with you, to serve and protect you." The legion of men standing behind him cheered and thumped their spears on the ground.

She was prepared for this. The fierceness of these men was matched by their unflinching loyalty to her. They adored her, but she did not wish to impose hardships on their families. Young men who sought adventure would be welcome on this trip. Married men would worry about the families they left behind.

"Of course, I will take warriors." Women cast anxious glances at men. "We also need men to stay here and protect our kingdom. Those with wives and children shall remain here." A collective sigh of relief rose in the room, giving support to her decision.

"I am working with my advisers to prepare for this journey. No hardships should be imposed on our nation because of this. If you receive an invitation to travel with me, you have the right to decline." Not one of those called to serve would refuse. The list had been reviewed with care to ensure the selection of the right people for this delegation.

Tamrin, planted on purpose in the back of the room, called out with his pre-arranged question. "Who will rule in your absence?"

"My Uncle will serve in my stead while I am gone." A murmur of approval rolled through the crowd, transforming the mood in the room from mournful to joyful.

"It would give me pleasure if you would gather along the road and see me off when I leave. For now, please return to your homes and your work."

The dispersing crowd's chatter and laughter enhanced with bird song and parrot squawks, lifted Makeda's spirits. *Thank the Sun God that was done.* She waited for the room to empty before she climbed down the stairs to stand alongside her uncle and Tamrin.

She inclined her head. "Your thoughts?"

A tear trickled down her uncle's face. Makeda reached up and wiped it away with her thumb.

"Your father would be proud."

"Baba spoke to me today."

Uncle's eyebrows shot up in surprise.

"I feared I would burst into tears, and he whispered to me to be strong." She put her hand over her heart. "He is here with me now and always."

Tamrin nodded. "He always knew how to calm you. And *terrify* me."

Makeda burst out laughing. "That he did, my friend. Now, to our preparations."

The next month Makeda relied on her childhood friend's extensive experience with trade routes and caravans to equip her momentous journey. At last, the traveling city of warriors, merchants, cooks, animal tenders, servers, waiting girls, and Makeda set out with seven-hundred and ninety-seven laden camels, innumerable pack mules and asses. Bags of frankincense, myrrh, cassia, cinnamon, medicinal herbs, and other lightweight commodities needed were guarded by warriors. Timbers of ebony, the world's hardest wood, impervious to termites and other insects, were loaded onto oxen-drawn carts in numbers sufficient to build a palace.

One hundred and twenty talents of gold, gathered from the tribes in the neighboring country of Sasu, were loaded on innumerable carts pulled by paired oxen. Makeda's father had begun the tradition of trading with these people by sending merchants to exchange slaughtered oxen, chunks of salt, and iron for gold nuggets. Over the years, her father's traders had brought back huge stores of the precious metal, enough to keep the kingdom in a strong trading position with the rest of the world. Once again, Makeda was grateful to her father for his foresight and wisdom.

Makeda rode at the head of the caravan, well aware of the complaints from the caged beasts they brought as tribute to impress the wealthy King Solomon. Despite her previous conversations with each animal, the black-maned lions roared their disapproval, the baboons screeched, the parrots shrieked and squawked, the cattle lowed, and the sheep and goats bleated. They hated the cages and the fact that they could not protect her as she rode in front, an easy target for bandits. At some point along the trip, she would have to speak with them again. Right now, however, she had to focus on smiling and waving to the cheering crowds that lined the highway as she rode out of Aksum on her favorite horse. At least the mare wasn't complaining. Yet.

Makeda turned as they passed the city gates and took one last look at the only home she'd ever known. The Sun God rose behind the mountains she had climbed as a child, caressed the meadows where she had played hide and seek with the rats, and stroked the petals of the abundant purple flowers she used to perfume her clothing.

A sharp stab of longing shot through her, making her falter. It wasn't too late to turn around, to cry out, and say, "I cannot do this." Fears assailed her with each heartbeat. Would she ever see her palace again? Would the great King Solomon welcome her with dignity and respect, or would he treat her as a concubine, a subject to be ruled? Would she truly return to her people reborn with wisdom as she had told that woman, or would she die in her thirst for knowledge and good judgment?

She closed her eyes and took a deep breath, praying for her inner resolve to turn from water to iron. Makeda blinked, looked up into the clouds and gasped. High overhead, an enormous eagle the color of a young antelope rode the wind, heading in the direction of Jerusalem. The color of the bird, identical to that of the angel she met in the cave years before, told her their caravan was protected by none other than the great and powerful angel, Metatron.

Chapter Seven

Summertown, Present Day

Throwing off her blazer, Eliana commandeered a computer in the command center room and scoured databases available only to those with the highest security clearance for information about Summertown. She needed to know more about the relationship between this geographic location and the jinni energy signature seen on satellite images just two days before the children disappeared. If she'd received the message sooner, she might have been able to arrive in Summertown in time to track the jinni, prevent the kidnappings, and killings. A moving target in a honeycomb of old mine shafts and tunnels complicated rescue efforts. Just as she was about to call her boss and fill him in on the latest events, the mayor strode in with Lowell Adalwolf at his side.

"Ladies and gentlemen," Mayor Schaeffer announced. "Effective immediately, we are putting a gag order on this series of events. Speak to no one outside this room about the details of these cases. Keep your speculations to yourselves. The hiker who found the body is aware of the need for silence and agreed not to speak to the media. There was no *murder*."

Eliana snapped her mouth shut. Talk about overstepping boundaries. The mayor wasn't a judge. He couldn't issue a gag order. They paid for that hiker's silence. She shot out of her chair.

"Homeland Security's investigation is in progress. I hope you're not telling *us* how to do our jobs."

The mayor glared at her.

"No one wants a satisfactory conclusion more than I do—except perhaps, Mr. Adalwolf."

Lowell Adalwolf nodded. "As of midnight last night, the ME ruled my grand-niece's death a random attack by a wild animal. As many of you know, there are over eight thousand black bears roaming all across West Virginia. Her death is a warning to all that we can never be too careful in our state forests."

The Medical Examiner declared it a bear attack? This wasn't a TV show. No reputable lab could process the DNA that fast. The paw prints weren't ursine. They were canine. This was a cover up. She made eye contact with the only other female in the room, the red-haired police chief who was convinced the girl was killed by a rogue were-wolf. The chief rolled her eyes as if to say *what a load of bear shit*.

The mayor declared the meeting over and departed, leaving a sullen silence in his wake. Adalwolf prowled through the crowded room and dropped a thick sheaf of papers in front of Ellie.

"Here are all the documents you requested," he growled. "I doubt you'll need them now we know what killed my niece."

It took all of her training to keep from snarling back at him.

"Thank you, Mr. Adalwolf. We *do* need them. Did you visit your other grand-nieces, sir? They're in pretty bad shape. Practically catatonic. I hope you haven't forgotten *them*."

He looked as if she'd just hit him with a rolled up newspaper. Adalwolf placed a hand on his chest. "I am *deeply* offended by that remark. I haven't forgotten my nieces, or the seriousness of the crimes against them."

"Good. I'm glad you feel that way. A black bear didn't get them pregnant." She tapped the blueprints. "Everyone in this room wants to find out who abducted the kids and where they're hiding—before they can grab any *other* girls. And, by the way, I examined the paw prints. They weren't bear."

He glared at her. "They're my family. I'll do whatever it takes to find out who did this to them. We don't need bad press right now. The county fair is one month away, mid-July. That, plus our summer destination weddings and wine festival, brings in tens of thousands of people and millions in revenues." He lowered his voice. "Four weeks. We must find who did this and capture him. I'm telling you, no one in my pack would do this. The ME caved in to the mayor, gave him what he wanted. Those paw prints were a ploy to throw us off. Werewolves are being framed. It's a *human*."

"A human? The girls are pregnant with four-footed fetuses. How could the father be human?"

"With so many intermarriages over the centuries, anything is possible. It could be someone who isn't purebred werewolf."

"Guess I need to learn more about Summertown genealogy."

"Find him," he growled. "Otherwise, this lovely little town will suffer a financial blow so hard, it may never recover."

Adalwolf turned on his heel and stalked out of the room.

Hmm. Maybe the report overstated the cordial relations between the werewolves and the humans in this little burg.

She tugged at the long sleeves of her button down shirt and unrolled the mining plans. Lines and scribbles meant nothing to her. She needed an expert to decipher the blueprints and decide where it would be best to send in a robotic FINDER—short for Finding Individuals for Disaster and Emergency Response—a suitcase size smart device that emitted microwaves and could detect heartbeats and breathing. If a perp—human or werewolf—was hiding in those tunnels, the FINDER would track him down. A jinni? Well, that was a different story. Made from smokeless fire, a jinni body's properties differed from humans'.

Where was her team? Twenty-four hours after her call and still no help? That wasn't right. *The engineer should be here now.* She grabbed her phone to track down her expert, and dropped it on the desk when it began to roar like a lion. She swore she'd changed the ringtone to the default setting. She snatched up the snarling cell and found a text from Arta. His plane was on the tarmac. Early. Too early. He wasn't due for another hour. She wasn't prepared for him. Then again, would she *ever* be ready?

She texted him her ETA at the airport, an hour. A small lie. It was forty minutes if she drove like a little old lady who couldn't see over the steering wheel. She needed time to collect her thoughts and calm down. She gulped down the rest of her tepid coffee, threw her jacket on, grabbed the blueprints and case file, and strode out to the parking lot.

Deep breaths, Eliana. Do not think about two years ago. Do not think about the last time you were with Arta, just before the room exploded and shards of glass drove themselves into your scalp, forearms, and chest. Don't think about the hospitalization and the pain. Above all, do not think about the roars of a lion you heard just before you blacked out.

****

Arta Shahani stood at the curb of the one runway Summertown Airport, took a deep breath of clean air, and admired the pristine mountains. An eagle floated overhead, enjoying the updraft. He wished he could ride the wind with the bird, and watch the green vistas and mountains roll under him again. One of the hazards of living in the Washington D.C. area was he sometimes forgot the more remote, less populated portions of the country. No matter, once he was with Eliana, it didn't matter where he was. *"With thee, my love, hell itself were heaven..."*

He tapped his foot and jingled the change in his pocket and then stopped, suddenly self-aware of his mannerisms. Arta felt a flush of embarrassment dashed with a tinge of boyish anticipation. *Eliana.* All he had to do was *think* her name and crazy things came over him. His pulse raced, muscles tensed, blood rushed to all the wrong parts of his body. He knew the term for it, flight, fight, or f—

The sharp blast of a car horn interrupted his musings.

The object of his fascination sat in a black government sedan in front of him.

Eliana.

For a frozen moment, he stopped breathing. His stomach plummeted, and his pulse kicked into erratic beats. He couldn't stop staring at her. Her green eyes sparkled with humor, and a mischievous grin spread from one flushed cheek to the other. Just as lovely as the first time he met her and took her hand. A jolt of joy headed for his pants. That would never do. He placed his briefcase over his groin and waved.

"You're looking well," he called to her through the open window. "I like what you've done with your hair."

"Are you flirting with me, Dr. Shahani?"

"Is it working?"

"Keep trying." Eliana leaped out of the car and popped the trunk. "Did you empty your closet, bring your complete wardrobe? You always struck me as a clothes horse." She laughed. "Trust me, you won't need much in the way of formal wear here."

Her laughter reminded him of the tinkling of crystal. Their assignment in Arizona hadn't given them any time for dining out. A leisurely meal, time spent alone. Time to man up and explain what happened two years ago. *With thee hell would be a mansion of delight.* Their last case together had been hell, but the time without her had been worse.

He dragged his larger bag over to the back of the car. "I wish it was just clothes. I stopped by to see my friend, the Imam. Told him I had a confirmed *'Ifrit* possession in another state, and a local Imam to help us. It was the only way I kept him from coming with me. He filled my bag with an anti-jinni arsenal, special weapons—conventional and unconventional—given to him by his predecessor."

"Smart of you to give him that cover story, tell him

we had a local religious leader on the case. No way to predict community response to his presence. With everyone on edge, the town's a tinderbox."

She bent to slam the trunk of the car, affording him a view of one of the wonders of the world, her lovely round ass. Unlike other women who starved themselves to be stylish, tall, curvy, and *luscious* Eliana paid no attention to the media telling her she should be tall and skinny.

"Hey, you coming? Or you going to stay asleep on your feet all day? We've got work to do. I'll get you up to speed on the way to the hospital."

He pulled open the passenger side door. "Yes, of course. Your beauty dazed me."

"Flirt. What's next? Poetry?"

He raised his eyebrows. "Will that help?"

"Maybe, if it's not too schmaltzy."

He shook his head. "Then I am at a loss. I specialize in Rumi's love poems."

She started the engine. "Save them for another day."

"Has something happened since we last spoke?"

"You could say so." She briefed him on Mayor Schaeffer's edicts. "This little burg has as many hidden and not so hidden agendas as our nation's capitol. Don't expect a lot of help from the locals. They want this all to go away as soon as possible."

"No one likes it when you interfere with business. The timing does make me wonder. One month before a major festival, children disappear and reappear, a girl is found mauled by an animal, and two young women are pregnant—from a supernatural rapist. If that news gets out, the mayor is right, aside from extremists who might want to picket and protest the town, no one will be coming to West Virginia, much less Summertown."

A werewolf howl filled the car, and Arta jumped. "What is that?"

"My phone. The ring tones are a mess." Eliana yanked her mobile out of her pocket and glanced at the caller ID. "My boss, Bert Blackfeather. Gulf War veteran. Won the purple heart and a few other awards he refuses to discuss." She pressed speaker. "Solomon here. You're on speaker, and Dr. Shahani is in the car with me."

"Fine. I needed to talk to both of you anyway. The forensic engineer you wanted is tied up with a ten-story parking lot collapse in Chicago. Got any second stringers in mind?"

"Crap. Not off-hand." She frowned and turned to Arta. "Do you?"

The only engineers he knew taught at universities and seldom practiced their profession. He began to shake his head, then stopped. "There is one guy. He worked on the structural investigation of the twin towers after 9-11. He's at Columbia University in New York City."

Eliana gave him a thumbs up. "Sounds promising. What do you think, Bert?"

"What's his name?"

"Hong Feng. American Chinese. Second generation. We spent a lot of time in detention together in high school. It's a wonder we graduated."

Blackfeather guffawed. "Take one rebellious Chinese-American guy, one unruly Persian-American guy, and one disobedient Ethiopian-Moroccan-American and put them all in West Virginia. Sounds like the opening line of a bad joke."

"You forgot one Native American boss to order them around. Thanks for your vote of support. You gonna run a background check on him?"

"Is there a choice? I just hope I can convince him to drop everything and run off to the Appalachians to help."

Arta chuckled. "If he balks, tell him I'll post those photos on the Internet.'"

Bert was still laughing when she pressed the off button.

"You own incriminating pictures of Feng?"

He shook his head. "Embarrassing not incriminating. Before and after shots of the worst haircuts ever seen, given to him by his mother his senior year. A bowl cut, I swear. At his request, I took clippers and shaved his head. His parents were on the phone with my mother for days."

"Ohmigod. I can only imagine. My father would have killed me." Eliana laughed until tears streamed down her face. "That photo. Is it on you?"

"Sorry. For the purposes of national security, I am required to keep it in a safety deposit box." He reached over and brushed back a strand of long black hair that had fallen out of Eliana's tight ponytail. "You never told me you were Ethiopian *and* Moroccan. That explains a few things."

"Like?"

"Your fascination with jinnis, your quick wit, your facial structure, your beautiful skin." *My burning desire to speak in love poems every time I'm with you.*

Color crept up her neck, and she locked gazes with him. "I owe my complexion to my parents. My father's

Moroccan; my mother was Ethiopian. I was born in the United States. First generation."

Mesmerized by her green eyes, he spoke as if from miles away. "Your cultures also include a double dip on supernatural entities with *zar*, the Ethiopian equivalent of jinnis."

"The *zar* meetings, the singing and dancing, those are a form of support groups in countries where women are suppressed. Besides, my mother said male *zar* spirits only visited lonely spinsters or widows, women who wanted male company. The *zar* never bothered women who were happily married." She sighed. "My mother was happy, married, and beautiful. That is, until acute myeloid leukemia took her away from us."

"You must miss her."

"I do." She bit her lower lip and stared ahead.

He yearned to reach over and stroke her cheek, run his fingers down her neck, and pull her close. Did her lush red lips taste like wine? Honey? Cinnamon? He could practically feel her lips on his. He wanted to run his hands over every inch of her, visit her secret gardens of pleasure. When this case was over, he was going to do something more than just file the paperwork and say good-bye.

She placed her right hand on the center console. "She gave me this on her deathbed." Hebrew letters covered the face of a large signet ring. "Made me swear to wear it at all times. Claimed it came from King Solomon. Told me it would protect me from evil jinnis."

Arta traced a fingertip over the intricate script surrounding a pentacle. "Does it work?"

She gave a weak laugh. "I doubt it. The case I

worked on in Kentucky three years ago, the alpha werewolf wore one nearly identical to mine. He said *his* was the real signet ring handed down through the generations. The last Emperor of Ethiopia, Haile Selassie, claimed *his* was the original. Hard for there to be more than one *true* Solomon's Seal, don't you think?"

He tapped the ring. "Did you authenticate it?"

Eliana locked gazes with him. "What? And ruin the mystique? No. This way, my memories of my mother and her stories about our Ethiopian lineage are still intact."

Arta tore his eyes away from hers and stared at the ring. "Eliana Solomon seems a bit short for a woman with such long family history. What's your full name?"

"Eliana Dameka Solomon."

For a moment, while she sat with her gaze fixed on the road, her profile reminded Arta of ancient Middle Eastern coins in a museum case in the Smithsonian.

"What does your middle name mean?"

"Little woman." She laughed. "Not a good fit for me. It's a family name. My mother's name was Dameka, and her mother's, all the way down the line back to Ethiopia, I'm the odd woman out with a different first name. My father's request. 'Too many little women', he said. Enough about me. What about you?"

"My family fled Iran with the deposal of the Shah, when the Americans were taken hostage. My father, Ardeshir Shahani, was the Shah's private physician, trained in the United States. The prince allowed my father, and only my father to treat him when he was ill. Said he cared for him like no other doctor. The

Ayatollah overthrew the government, and my parents feared for our safety. It wasn't good to be a favorite of the Shah during and after the revolution. They packed their car full of all their belongings and drove from Tehran to Turkey in the middle of the night. Before the revolution, my mother, Azedeh Shahani, was a university professor of poetry and literature."

"Ah. Now I understand your love of poetry. You can't help it, can you?"

"My mother specialized in Rumi's work. Were you aware he was also a musician and a Sufi mystic? His message was always about love and forgiveness."

"We could all use that, couldn't we? How did your family get from Turkey to the United States?"

"My mother delivered my sister, Tahmineh, in Ankara. They emigrated as soon as it was safe for her to travel. I was born in Maryland. A massive heart attack killed my father when I was a child. I attended the University of Maryland Medical School on a scholarship, and you are well acquainted with the rest of my resume." When this case was over, Arta was going to take a chance and tell her the truth about his father's special healing powers—and *what* he really was.

"We're the first generation born in this country, both from a family of immigrants. Our parents placed all their hopes for a better future on us, didn't they? What about Feng? What's his claim to fame?"

Arta patted his pants pocket, searching for his phone to pull up his friend's university home page with Feng's research activities. *Where was the damn thing?* Was it in his briefcase? Arta reached down to pick up the bag just as the car screeched to a halt. His head smacked the padded dashboard. He yelped and bounced back, grateful he'd fastened his seatbelt. "What happened? Are you okay?"

Eliana whipped the car over to the side of the road and jumped out the door. She ran to the tree line and shaded her eyes with her hand. "Did you see that?" She yelled.

Arta extricated himself from the seatbelt and the vehicle and rubbed his brow. His forehead was developing a lump already. "Lots of very green trees— that's it, nothing more."

She wheeled on him. "There was a pack of black dogs running through the woods."

He turned, and followed her pointing finger, straining his ears and eyes to sense movement. "Sorry, no—wait—"

Closing his eyes, he inhaled deeply, and his stomach rolled with nausea.

"Jinni stink. He's here."

Chapter Eight

Jerusalem, 955 B.C.E.

Solomon paced the length of his throne room and stopped in front of Benaiah, captain of his soldiers, bodyguard, and confidante. He pitched his voice for his friend's ears only.

"Your men were positive it was the queen and her servants, not a merchant's caravan?"

Benaiah grinned. "Who else brings wagons laden with ebony and cages filled with wild animals? The men have been waiting almost as long as you, my friend. Your anxiety is theirs. Your wishes, theirs. Your hopes, theirs. They live to serve you, just as that silly bird does." He nodded at the hoopoe bird, preening on a decorative brass perch Solomon had commissioned for the striped creature.

"Excellent idea. Why didn't I think of that?" Solomon whistled and the bird flew to his side. "Hoopoe, find the queen's caravan. Tell me where she is."

Benaiah's eyes followed the bird as he rose into the sky. "You know, rumors say she's a jinniyah."

Solomon nearly spat with disgust. Ever since the announcement of the queen's upcoming visit, his people had been eager to share stories from their distant relatives, none of whom lived in Sheba, but all of whom allegedly saw the woman with their own eyes. God only knew what stories they told about him in far off lands. Perhaps to the people of Sheba, he was a two-headed monster who ate children for breakfast.

He shook his head. "How can you listen to such tales? I took you for a wiser man. God tells me I must judge someone for myself, not violate His commandment of telling falsehoods about our neighbors."

Benaiah shot back, "She's not our neighbor. She's a foreign queen. What if she plots to steal your kingdom? Even with the route under our guard, her escorts are armed to make the journey. For all we know, she's planning an invasion. I'm the commander of your guard. I must consider the woman a threat."

"My friend, I love you as a brother." He thumped Benaiah's shoulder. "You have been fighting so long, you forget for everything there is a season, and a time for every matter under heaven—even peaceful state visits. She is no more a jinniyah than I am a jinni."

Like a dog with a bone, Benaiah would not let the matter go. "They say her legs are hairy and her feet those of a goat." He hooked his thumbs into his sword belt and pursed his lips. "Didn't Hoopoe report on her to you?"

"He said *nothing* about hooves." Solomon's stroked his beard. "Look, if she's a jinniyah, I should be able to command her with my seal, just as I do the big one over there." He pointed at the jinni standing at attention by his throne. "In fact, I think I will surprise the queen with a special gift for her arrival." He motioned for the giant to come to his side. "I want you to do something special for our guest. Something that will make her feel at ease." He beckoned for the jinni to come even closer and whispered in his ear. The scowling creature disappeared in a burst of green light, leaving Solomon dazzled for a moment.

Blinking, Benaiah glanced around the courtroom. "What did you tell him to do?"

"All in good time, my friend. Now what test shall I give the queen?"

The captain crossed his arms over his broad chest. "I want to see her feet."

Solomon shook his head. Benaiah was a good man, but his mind travelled on one track—firebrands, arrows, swords, and death. Protect the king at all costs—even if it made the sovereign weep with frustration.

"You won't let this rest, will you? We *can't* ask the Queen of Sheba to lift her skirt in public so we can stare at her toes."

"What if she needed to raise it to go over a stream? Send our men out to tell her there was a rockslide. They can direct her to the creek just outside our walls. Together, you and I can witness her lifting her skirt to keep it out of the water. That will give us proof of what she is or is not."

His patience snapped. "Are you mad? That's not a stream, it's dirt and filth, waste matter from our city. What kind of welcome is that? We'll do no such a thing."

Benaiah's face darkened, and he opened his mouth to protest.

"Not another word. Cease this foolishness. Go sharpen your sword instead of your tongue. Leave me in peace."

The soldier's mouth snapped shut. Spine stiff,

Benaiah turned on his heel and marched out of the room.

Solomon sighed. He hated to be so curt with the man. Yes, he was trying to protect his king, however, Benaiah's fears made him sense danger in every shadow. He needed a respite from the soldier's suspicions. He needed time away from being the head of state, away from the eyes that followed his every move, away from his guards, hangers-on, and elders giving him unwanted counsel. Only the wolves and lions knew when to keep their thoughts to themselves, it seemed. He longed to sit up in the hills and just *be*.

"Ooo-poo!"

"The Queen of Sheba and her people are at the gate. Her train goes for miles. Wagons laden with gold and ebony, carts full of boxes. Spices, so many spices, the smells made me dizzy. Camels, lions, leopards, cheetahs—"

Laughing, Solomon held his hand up. "Your report lifts my spirits. Rest yourself and your wagging tongue. Stay at your perch. I need you to stop your chatter so I can pay close attention to our guest."

Would she be as beautiful as Hoopoe said? Or had the long desert trip blinded the bird? So many stories. How could anyone, man or woman live up to them? As much as his other wives and concubines were beautiful and amusing, he thirsted for conversation of a deeper kind than household gossip. Would the Queen of Sheba be wise or foolish? Would her voice be melodious and soothing, or harsh and irritating? Would her skin feel like silk or wool? So many questions, soon to be answered.

A wide-eyed servant raced into the court room and

begged permission to speak. His words tumbled out between gasps. "She's through the gates and coming up the hill—and so are her soldiers, farmers, and animals. Where shall we put them all?"

Solomon nodded to a maid to give the man a drink. "We set aside an entire house for the queen and her handmaids. The others will set up camp with our soldiers." Mindful of Benaiah's concerns, Solomon's warriors would observe the foreigners and ensure their visit was peaceful. At last, it was time for him to leave the palace and greet his royal visitor. Solomon sent a servant to find Benaiah and Zadok. He nodded at the musicians who followed him with trumpets, cymbals, psalteries, harps, and voices raised in song.

Solomon tried to calm his drumming heart. The sun hung overhead, blinding him as he emerged from the cool interior of the palace. He shaded his eyes with his hand and a servant rushed forward with woven palm fronds. Behind the gauzy curtains of a bejeweled litter carried by six strapping men, he discerned a slender figure. The slaves grunted as they placed the elaborate carriage on the brick surface. Three hand-maids clustered about the enclosure and worked to extract their mistress. Two sandals decorated with gold and silver emerged between the hovering women. Contrary to Benaiah's hand-wringing, her legs ended not in goat's hooves, but in ten normal, but tiny, toes.

The nation of Sheba had sent a child.

He turned, caught Benaiah's eye, and raised an eyebrow. The man shrugged. Solomon bit the inside of his cheek to keep from laughing. What was he to do with a woman who hadn't even had her first cycle with the moon? He wanted serious discourse, conversations about trade, treaties, and treasuries. Disappointment speared his heart and he closed his eyes to block out the scene before him. So much for his dreams of this meeting between nations. In his thoughts and desires, he'd built up the long anticipated day into an exalted event, one worthy of recording for all generations to come. He'd even told the scribes to attend and to record each thing they saw and every word they heard.

Where was Solomon's wisdom now? Gone. Flown away with the chattering Hoopoe, leaving a foolish monarch in its place. He blinked, shook his head, and sighed. No matter. He had to greet his guest with courtesy and respect as behooved a visiting dignitary.

Assisted to her feet, the girl stood and turned toward Solomon.

She was much older than he first thought. Chin up, back erect, she stared at him with unwavering obsidian eyes. *Hoopoe must have been mistaken about her eye color*. The boldness of her gaze took him off guard, halting the annoyance of a begrudged welcome, and replacing it with admiration. He wished he could have been that calm under pressure when he was younger. Or was she play-acting like he did before he became wise?

Wrapped in billowing linen and silk, a gold breastplate covering her chest, the dark-complexioned young woman held her head erect under the weight of an ornate wig. A beauty with long lashes and almond shaped eyes, the Queen reminded him of Pharaoh's daughter, one of his growing numbers of wives. A blasphemous arrangement according to Zadok, the marriage to the Princess of the Nile was a political triumph. With Egypt as an ally, not even the Philistines dared to attack Israel for fear of incurring the wrath of the Pharaoh's armies. The generous father even threw in the city of Gezer as a dowry for his daughter. What more could a king want?

Love.

That's what he truly wanted. Each of his wives was beautiful, yet not one had captured his heart like his father's had been by his mother. On the other hand, look how their passion had torn up their lives. Was yearning for a love match *wise*?

When the royal stood before Solomon, her chaperone, a tall woman covered from head to toe in white linen, her face concealed in shadows, intoned in the language of merchants and travelers, "Behold, the Queen of Sheba appears before you with great treasures. Our nation sends you one-hundred and twenty talents of gold, abundant spices, precious stones, and animals from throughout our land. If you accept her gifts, please take the Queen's hand and bid her to join you in feasting."

He grasped the tips of the young woman's fingers, and began to intone the well rehearsed words, "Splendid are the offerings of your nation. Your gifts are accepted with awe and gratitude. We are honored by your presence." He leaned in to kiss her hand. A fresh burn, still in the early stage of healing, caught his attention. He turned her wrist and examined her palm.

Solomon clutched the young woman's hand, yanked her close, and growled into her wide-eyed face, "Where is the Queen? What did you do to her?"

Trembling beneath his grip, she spoke not a word. A single tear trickled down her cheek.

"Your eyes are not green and your hands are burned from cooking and callused from hard labor. Did you murder your mistress? Who helped you?" He motioned to Benaiah. "Seize this woman, take her to be interrogated."

Guards grabbed hold of the girl's arms, her wig toppled to the side, and her gold breastplate twisted on its chains.

The chaperone's voice rang out over the buzzing crowd, "Stop."

****

Makeda's legs shook beneath her long dress, and her heart leaped like a young antelope at the height of a run. Tamrin had not done the king justice. Yes, he had a regal profile, that much was true, but her friend hadn't spoken of Solomon's expressive eyes, as brown as her father's and just as terrifying when enraged and glaring at her as he was right now.

What had she been thinking?

"Who dares to interfere with the will of the King of Israel?"

Hands trembling, she threw her head covering back. "Makeda, Queen of Sheba."

Her gaze caught in his, and she lost track of time and place. She fell into the dark pools of his eyes, and the rest of the world disappeared. All sounds ceased, except the rush of the blood in her ears and the rasp of her breath. She reached out for help from her animal friends, yet for once in her life, all were silent.

How could that be? Not even the prattling Hoopoe bird spoke.

"You," he whispered. "Why did you seek to make a fool of me?"

At his voice, ripples danced across her skin, as if a cool breeze caressed her. She squeezed her shaking knees together in a failed attempt to quell the growing warmth between her legs. Was he controlling her thoughts with his rings? Mouth dry as sand, she chose her words with care.

"I had no intention of making you look foolish. I needed to see if you were truly as wise as people said. This was my riddle for you. 'When is a queen not a queen?' I ordered my hand maid to switch places with me before we entered the city."

His response, a roar, reminded her of that fateful day in the cave. He sounded like Metatron, huge blasts of laughter exploding all around, echoed now by the crowd.

"This is the best test anyone has ever given me." He wiped a tear from his eye and turned to his captain. "Release the handmaid. She shall be rewarded. Not once did she seek to save herself. Only a true leader can inspire loyalty to the death."

He grasped Makeda's hand and stopped.

"Your palms. They are callused, almost as much as your handmaid's. Do your people not serve you?"

At his touch, her spirit went out of her. Weakness washed over her, and she longed to cling to this man. Controlling her wayward body was more challenging than rendering death sentences. *Lust is for animals*. At length she spoke with what she hoped was a queen's reserve.

"My handmaid just put her life at risk for me. What more service could a ruler demand? Would your people do the same for you? Or am I not speaking to the *real* King Solomon?" She pulled her hand out of his and pointed at a guard. "Perhaps that man is the true ruler of Israel?"

The soldier placed his hand on the hilt of his sword. "You dare insult our king?"

Solomon raised his hand. "Benaiah, keep your peace." Eyes locked with hers, the king spoke loud enough for all to witness. "I meant no insult. The Pharaoh's daughter came to me with hands as soft as a newborn's. Yours tell me you do not sit around all day, waiting to be waited upon."

"My responsibilities take me away from many simple pleasures, but hunting is one I will not and cannot forgo. My father led the men, now it is my duty, one I enjoy."

Solomon's eyes grew wide. "A queen who hunts? God never ceases to amaze me. Perhaps we can ride to the hunt while you visit with us? Now, *that* will be a story for the scribes." Taking her hand again, he smiled and turned to his musicians. "Let there be music and merriment and feasting."

High-pitched howls and ululations erupted from the women in the courtyard and bounced off the stone walls, echoing her joy and forbidden desire. She wanted to kiss his full red lips and lie all night with his head between her breasts. *Oh, dear Sun God!* Why did this fierce reaction come from his touch? No mere human body could experience this explosion of sensations. Controlled by the seals on his hand, her jinniyah half must be betraying her human half. Part of her wished to squash the response, the other part wanted to drag him into bed.

No. Impossible. She promised her father she would remain a virgin, married to her kingdom, not a man. Her nation needed her. Sun God help her, she would need the strength of a lioness to resist this man's powers.

He smiled and pulled her into the shadows of the courtyard.

Had he read her thoughts? Was he taking her to bed? Was this the meaning of Metatron's prophesy? Was this wise man her destiny?

"Our children and our children's children will marvel at the story of our meeting and rejoice in God's plans for our nations." He paused in front of a doorway blocked by armed men. "A surprise awaits you."

Had the man not heard of her promise to her nation? No children would be coming forth from her womb.

He nodded at the soldiers, then led her into the throne room.

Her gaze snagged on Hoopoe. He bowed his head to her, and she gave a laugh of relief mixed with disappointment. "Your bird is too clever by far."

The king smiled. "Keep looking."

"Your throne is covered with gold eagles, lions, wolves, sheep, doves, hawks, animals of every kind. It is a magnificent seat for a king."

"Yes. But that's not your gift."

She stepped deeper into the shadowed room and came to a halt.

A carved ivory throne overlaid with gold leaf and encrusted with jewels sat next to King Solomon's.

A chill glided down her spine. *Impossible.*

She strode over to the seat and ran her fingers over every jewel, flower, and leaf pattern. "This is a wondrous piece of work. My friend Tamrin must have drawn you a picture of my throne. I must congratulate him on—"

There on the right arm of the throne, in her own hand was the design she'd scratched into the wood, written over and over while she grieved and prayed for guidance as the new ruler of Sheba. Only she had ever seen that word.

Baba.

Anger restrained by years of training, Makeda wheeled on her host. "What is the meaning of this? Who conspired with you to steal my throne? How did it get here ahead of my arrival?"

"You are so far away, I thought you'd like a reminder of home. To answer your other questions…" Solomon beckoned to someone hiding in the shadows. "When I asked him, this one told me he would bring it to me before I rose from my station, for he was strong and trustworthy."

A mountainous creature stepped forward. Her skin prickled as if on fire and sweat trickled down her back. Fear made her voice harsh. "Who is this?"

Solomon motioned for the creature to approach.

The closer it came to her, the more her skin burned with the stings of a thousand insects. She glanced down at her hands, certain she was covered in blisters. Nothing, not even a welt, appeared. The urge to flee called for her feet to run, but her father's lessons, pride, and anger rooted Makeda to the brick floor. The Queen of Sheba did not run away.

"This is not a who, but a what. A jinni. And a powerful one, at that. He tried to kill me when we first met." Solomon waved his bejeweled fingers. "If I did not bind him with my seals, he would destroy us and everything we have built. Instead, he does my bidding and holds his tongue, except when I prompt him to speak."

The brute's brazen stare burned with rage and bore into her soul. His eyes widened for a fleeting moment. Then his lips quirked.

The jinni knew.

Chapter Nine

Summertown, Present Day

Eliana stood at the edge of the asphalt and peered into the green mists cloaking the forest. Only half past three in the afternoon, but shadows beyond the tarmac were thickened by the trees. Jinni stink clung to the plants like noxious fumes at the gates of Hell, violating the forest with its presence. Skin tingling with pins and needles, the urge to run after the jinni almost irresistible, she took two steps toward the wooded area and paused. Her mother would tell her to run, not walk, *away* from the jinni-infested site. How many times had her mother clutched her hand as they walked past decaying houses in their old Baltimore neighborhood? Her mother would hold up her ever-present signet ring given to her by her mother, Eliana's grandmother, and say, "Jinni stink. This is no place for people like us."

People like us.

What had her mother meant by that? Ethiopians? Moroccans? Jews? With a Moroccan rabbi for a father, they lived in a Jewish neighborhood and walked to their warm synagogue filled with the comforting sounds of the small congregation. Women sat behind a screen in a balcony, watched their babies, and chatted with one another. The men wrapped in prayer shawls rocked, prayed, and shouted "Amen" in unison at the proper times. Little boys ran up and down the aisles in defiance of all rules of decorum in any other setting.

At the end, families converged on the sidewalk calling, "Good *Shabbos*, good Sabbath" to one another as they hurried home to dinner, timetables of Jewish life set by *Adonai* and the commandment to honor the Sabbath and keep it holy. Eliana and her mother would rush home to set the table, prepare the wine, *Kiddush* cup, and the candles for their prayers before dinner. They needed to beat the setting sun.

While they hurried through the lengthening shadows, her mother taught her about the jinnis. Made from smokeless fire, created by God along with angels and man, these invisible beings came in all varieties— Islamic, Jewish, and Christian. In some places, families of jinnis lived with human families, the humans unaware of the invisible beings at their side. On occasion, this closeness in living arrangements led to accidents. Sometimes humans hurt jinnis without knowing. Jinnis lived for thousands of years and never forgot a slight, intended or unintended.

Their long lifespan allowed them to bide their time to exact revenge, generations later. The more powerful the jinni, the more devastating the blow. To avenge a perceived wrong, the evil ones, the *'Ifrit,* destroyed everything in their path—human or non-human. God forbid a terrorist gain control of one like the one she was tracking right now. The jinni was close, time was of the essence, but she wasn't about to go in unprepared.

"Arta?"

Eyes closed, breathing with his mouth open, the psychiatrist stood rooted to the spot where he first called out the signature sulfur smell. Arta turned toward her. His eyes, normally brown, appeared to have a golden cast to them. He blinked, and the illusion disappeared.

"What do you want me to do?"

She gave him a once over and stopped at his spit-polished loafers. "First, change your shoes. You'll break your neck slipping and sliding in those."

He glanced down at his feet.

"Second, grab whatever you can carry that the Imam gave you and follow me." The tingling sensation was ebbing. If she didn't get moving, she was going to lose the jinni. "I'm going after him."

"Wait. I'm no park ranger. You leave me, I'll never find you."

"If I don't go now, I'm going to lose him." She didn't have time for an argument. The tingling was almost gone. She jogged to the car, placed her too-loose signet ring into the center console, pulled out an ashtray filled with change, and poured the coins into her pocket. "Follow the money."

"Eliana—"

"Later, Shahani." She ran into the forest, sniffed the air, and prayed for the pins and needles to reappear. She glanced over her shoulder. Arta bent over the open trunk of the car. She hoped he brought those hiking boots and a pile of holy weapons of *'Ifrit* destruction. She dropped some quarters and moved as fast as she dared, her senses on high alert, her mind wandering back to her childhood, to the time Eliana and her mother encountered an evil jinni.

On their way home from synagogue, a new member of the congregation's burial society stopped her father. He needed to know the correct way to pray when practicing *shomrim*, guarding a body from desecration and *dybbuks*, during the time between death and burial. Her father sent them on home when it became obvious the conversation was going to be a long one. Despite living only a few blocks from the synagogue, the shadows falling across the decaying houses made it seem as if they were miles away from home.

"*Ima*, Mommy, what's a dybbuk?"

"The spirit of a dead person. Sometimes they try to crawl into the recently deceased person, take over a body. That's why we have *shomrim*."

"Is a dybbuk like a jinni?"

She clutched her daughter's hand harder and pulled her coat tighter. "Nothing like a jinni. Walk faster."

Eliana struggled to keep up with her mother's long legs. "Ima, I can't walk faster." Her skin began to tingle. "Ow. You're making my hands and arms sting."

Her mother stopped under a street lamp and put her hand over Eliana's mouth. "Hush. We're not alone."

The lamplight dimmed, and shadows closed in. A whirling dervish of paper, leaves, and plastic bags coiled around Eliana and her mother. The prickling grew worse, until her arms felt as if they ablaze with flames, and her entire body burned. She wanted to ask who else was there. Was it a *dybbuk* angry about her question? With her mother's fingers pressing her lips closed, she could not say a word.

Her mother pulled Eliana closer pressing her into her breasts. She began to pray in Hebrew, Amharic, and some other languages Eliana didn't understand. At last, shaking and weeping, her mother raised the hand with the large ring and shouted, "It is the Sabbath. How dare you desecrate this day? In the name of all that is holy, God, Allah, Blessed Be the One, leave us."

The tingling stopped. The street lamp grew brighter. The wind disappeared and dropped the debris at their feet.

"My arms, Ima. They hurt so bad."

Tears glistening on her cheeks, her mother leaned down, slid back the sleeves of her puffy coat, and stared at her reddened inner arms. She kissed Eliana and hugged her tight. "*That* was a jinni. They know who we are. They *want* people like us. Never, ever forget that feeling. It tells you when a jinni is near. Run away as fast as you can."

One year after the attack, her mother died of acute myeloid leukemia. The specialists asked how long her mother worked with ionizing radiation. The answer: not at all, not once, never. Despite her scientific training and applied physics doctorate, a tiny corner of Ellie's mind believed if her mother hadn't had the confrontation with the jinni—or whatever that energy field was—that evening, she'd still be alive today. Her mother would be furious with her daughter for making it her mission to run *toward* the jinni-induced sensation, instead of away from it, as she did now.

Her skin stung as if she'd run through a nettle bush. She picked up the pace, jogging deeper into the darkening woodland. Branches whipped at her face, and roots grabbed at her ankles. Warm blood trickled down the side of her face. She wiped it out of her eye, and felt the back of her hands explode with a million barbs. Breathing hard, she stopped and turned in a circle, her body a prickling compass attempting to settle in the right direction. She inhaled, and focused on the sounds of the wild—or rather the *absence* of sound. Not a single bird chirped. No bugs hummed in her ear. No squirrels chattered at her from above. Silence shrouded the forest.

Just as she exhaled, a twig snapped to her right. She wheeled in that direction and froze in place. Less than fifty feet away, a huge gray wolf stared at her with glowing orange eyes.

Gazes locked, Eliana placed her hand on her left hip, searched for her cell phone, and stopped. No signal penetrated these woods. Not daring to blink, she placed her hand on her right hip, and her fingers curled around the reassuring grip of her Sig Sauer.

Lips curled, huge yellow teeth dripping with saliva, the creature's growl made her heart stutter. She took a deep breath and spoke in a firm voice. "Are you one of the Adalwolf pack?"

The gray raised an eyebrow, cocked his head, and softened his growls.

Hand still on her hip, she took a cautious step toward him. "My name is Eliana Solomon."

He sat down.

"If you can understand me, please nod."

He shook his head, ears flopping.

Close enough.

"I'm trying to find someone, he's—" Her skin burned with the stings of a million wasps that weren't insects, and the stench of sulfur filled her nose. The jinni was close by, practically on top of her. *Where was he? Did she dare take her eyes off the wolf?*

As if in response to her thoughts, the wolf lay down, put his head on his paws, and stared over her shoulder.

She glanced to her right and screamed.

****

Arta ran toward the scream. What happened? How far away was she? The scream, so out of character for this woman with more courage than most men, made his heart falter.

"Eliana?"

Arta's voice came out in a growl. The jinni stink grew stronger. Nose up, he lunged through the woods, pushing past the snapping branches, swiping bushes, and leaping over fallen logs. As shadows lengthened in the forest, his vision grew sharper, more intense, as did his sense of smell. He flexed his fingers and the sharp edge of a claw grazed his palm.

Oh shit. Not now. Not again.

His mind went to the first time he met Eliana.

His rendezvous with her had been at the agency's private plane at the Baltimore-Washington International Airport. He had checked the photograph in his phone three times to make sure she was the right woman. The headshot from her Homeland Security ID did her no justice. She was taller than he expected. Blue blazer, long-sleeve button down white shirt, black slacks. All business. But when she removed her sunglasses, the green of the irises of her eyes, surrounded by a rim of black, mesmerized him. Contrary to his expectation of a wild-eyed fanatical jinni hunter, this woman appeared to be calm, collected, and cool.

He dropped her hand. "What can you tell me about this case?"

Eliana pointed toward the waiting Lear jet. "We'll chat onboard."

Throughout the long flight, she shared her voluminous notes and thoughts with Arta. The testimony of the Border Patrol Officers and the comments of the priest called in to translate the man's ravings read like something out of a Grade D horror movie, stereotypical and absurd. Despite her solemnity, or perhaps because of it, he chuckled.

Eliana gave him a stern look. "Dr. Shahani, what's so funny?"

"Call me Arta, please." He shook his head. "I'm afraid this may be a ruse on this man's part. He's originally from Pakistan and moved to India. The belief in jinni possession in both countries is quite prevalent, especially in the rural areas. How did he come to be in Mexico?"

"Vacation, supposedly. God only knows what the Mexican government thought when they approved his VISA. The man lived in Bombay, worked as a customer service agent for a US Credit Card company."

Arta touched the tips of his fingers together in a steeple and tapped his chin. "Lots of Internet access and time to search for instructions on how to build a bomb."

"Yes, I'm sure between Americans calling to complain about their credit card bills, he played on the computer."

Quick, smart, and exuding a devastatingly female scent of flowers and spice, Eliana Solomon embodied the word, 'distracting'. She took a deep breath and pushed a strand of hair away from her eyes.

"The Indian government has promised to assist us in the investigation, but—"

"You're not depending on their help."

She nodded, leaned back in the leather seat, and

crossed her long legs. The plane banked to the right, and he glanced out the window. Brown and red, interspersed with patches of green for lawns and the blue of swimming pools met his eyes. Descent, at last, thank God. Close proximity to this woman gave him reckless thoughts about gardens, perfumed silks, moonlight, and love poems. He needed to focus on the investigation. The little jet touched down on the tarmac and bounced once, twice, jolting him out of his thoughts.

Arta unbuckled his seat belt. "Let's go meet this young man and find out if he's hallucinating, possessed, or a fake."

A short time later Arta took control of the situation at the local police station where the gibbering Pakistani sat in solitary confinement.

"I'm a physician. I have an obligation to assess this man in private."

Eliana and the Sheriff protested, citing national security, the Patriot Act, and danger to the doctor's life. "Okay, I get it. He's a danger to himself and others. Do you have a room with a one-way mirror so you can watch the interview?"

Shackles clanked as the man shuffled into the room wearing a one-piece orange jumpsuit. Arta took off his jacket, loosened his tie, and rolled up his sleeves, as if preparing to play a hand of poker, instead of probing the mind of a terrorist. Video running, he began with easy questions, "What is your name? How old are you?"

The young man across the table bared his teeth and responded with a potpourri of multiple languages.

"You're not making much sense, my friend. Pick

one language, please. Tell me your name in English, French, Farsi, Turkish, or Arabic."

A low guttural sound, more a growl than words, emerged from the man's curled lips, then worked themselves into Arabic. "You say you are an *'Ifrit*, an evil jinni." Arta nodded. "Can you tell me more?"

The Pakistani babbled about how he was going to destroy the world. The man became more agitated with each word. Although manacled to a metal chair bolted to the floor, he shook and rattled the chains and the chair with each word. Something hissed, popped, and crackled. Arta yawned to clear his ears of the air pressure changes from the plane ride. More hisses and crackles. *The sound system must have a malfunction.* Arta glanced at the one-way mirror and shrugged.

Turning back to the Pakistani, Arta realized the *suspect* made the bizarre sounds. The man's voice alternated between a booming bass, hisses, and clicks. To his horror, the bolts holding the chair to the floor rattled, loosened by the man's exertions.

Arta rose to his feet, shouting at the prisoner. The next thing he knew, his shouts turned to roars, and glass exploded. The power went out and darkness enveloped the station. People yelled to get the generator up and running. Despite the blackout, Arta was able to distinguish everything in the room. Shrieking, the suspect jumped at him. In the melee, Arta found himself standing on the suspect's chest, his hands, now gigantic paws, pressing on the terrorist's throat. The man's head fell to the side and Arta thought he killed him. Just before the generator kicked in, Arta fled into the desert. Three days later, a cleanup crew removing trash on tribal lands found him by a dried out riverbed, dehydrated, disoriented, and naked. The workers told him he was lucky he wasn't eaten by a pack of feral dogs.

With the recording equipment destroyed in the explosion, and the ensuing chaos in the blackout, the investigators were forced to piece events together. After an extensive autopsy, which revealed radio transmitters implanted in the terrorist's false teeth, they decided the devices were responsible for the bizarre sounds, shattered windows, and resulting chaos. The medical examiner determined the cause of death was asphyxiation—on his tongue. Eliana was peppered with shards of flying glass, one of which lodged in her chest, and was rushed to the hospital with massive bleeding.

For his part, Shahani thought he'd suffered from hallucinations caused by inhalation of toxic fumes. He'd told himself the same story so often, he'd begun to believe it. Until he went to see Nur. What did you call someone who shape shifted into a Persian lion and drove out jinnis? *Crazy.* He wasn't crazy, and he was a shape shifter. The first time he shifted was in Arizona. The second time in Chevy Chase. In each instance, he confronted the same *'Ifrit.* Could he control his shape shifting? Could he will himself to become the powerful cat when needed?

Shouts and high pitched yelping came from close ahead of him in the shadowy woods. A few more feet, and he'd be at her side. He wanted to call her name, but all that came out was a hoarse roar. He leaped over yet another fallen tree and landed on all fours. When he glanced up, Eliana was ten feet in front of him, on her back, fighting for her life with not one, but two growling, snapping wolves, one of which was dark brown and twice the size of the other. He leaped at the beasts and a gun exploded.

Chapter Ten

Jerusalem, 954 B.C.E.

King Solomon paced the cool courtyard at dawn, unable to sleep one moment more, in spite of the soft comforts of his bed and one of his seven-hundred wives. Yet, *she* was not the one he wanted. The woman he longed for with every breath he took was the only female he could think of day and night. She haunted his dreams and every waking moment. *The Queen of Sheba.* Just thinking about her caused his loins to stir. She insisted he call her Makeda, which he did at every opportunity.

Makeda. Makeda. Makeda. Makeda.

Each thump of his heart repeated her name, echoing in his ears like a drumbeat. Shouts of frustration would be roaring to the skies if he were alone, but the soldiers standing guard nearby might think demons drove him mad, like King Saul. He suffered from a disease worse than demon possession. He was sick with *love.*

God delivered a love match to him, a woman equal to him in every way. For a year now, Makeda remained a royal guest in Jerusalem. From the moment she lifted the white linen from her head and locked gazes with him, her intelligent green eyes penetrated to his soul, capturing and keeping his heart hostage. Love brought strong men to their knees, made them do foolish things, undid years of training and wisdom. Solomon yearned for a love match like David and Bathsheba's. Not *once* did he ever suspect his wish would come true. God's plan? Or a divine joke? Who else but the Lord would deliver his love match to him in the form of a queen who was required to remain a virgin?

Every other female swooned at his feet, overwhelmed by his wisdom and God-given powers, regardless of country, culture, or chastity. Not this one. She demurred, smiled, joked, and drove him mad with desire. His hands itched to explore every inch of her statuesque body, from her long graceful neck to her bejeweled fingers and toes.

Her toes.

Mid-step, he stumbled a bit on the dew slicked rocky surface. A soldier lurched forward to help, but Solomon waved the man away.

He'd never seen her toes.

Dressed in her finery, her feet were always tucked beneath her throne. Not even a glimpse of her toes peeked out when reclining on pillows to dine. Makeda managed to make his countrywomen appear clumsy by seating herself without flailing arms and legs.

Damn Benaiah for planting a seedling of suspicion. The woman was modest. *That was all.* Her country expected her to cover her legs and ankles. When they went hunting, Makeda wore a sand-colored outfit that fit like a second skin and boots made from the hide of an antelope. Hair pulled away from her regal face, spear at the ready, no extraneous cloth impeded her lightning fast pursuit of the prey. Her prowess shamed the mightiest man in his guard. Benaiah remarked to

Solomon about her hunting abilities, albeit in a begrudging tone of voice, saying if he had one warrior like her among his men, they'd never go hungry.

Even the self-righteous Zadok remarked on her intelligence. She'd attended every festival over the past year, including the high holy days, and participated in every ritual. On the Day of Atonement, at the tossing of the scapegoat from the cliffs, Makeda asked for her sins to be taken with the animal. She fasted and prayed for her name to be inscribed in the book of life. His beloved rejoiced at the sounds of the rams' horns sounding from the great walls of Jerusalem at the end of the day. And, at the harvest festival of Sukkot, Makeda formally rejected the sun god. His God was her one and only God, and the new God of the people of Sheba. Overwhelmed by her piety, Solomon fell more deeply in love with the Queen of the South. He wanted her more than ever. She was his true love. And she *was* breaking his heart.

He closed his eyes, raised his arms, and prayed, his lips moving in silence. "Lord, I beg of you. Take this love sickness away from me. Make me the man I was before she arrived. Restore me to the stalwart, wise man you created that night on Gibeon."

"May I approach?"

As if summoned by his prayer, Makeda stood before him, a lion at her side. His breath came in short, shallow puffs, and his heart thrummed in his ears.

"Solomon, are you unwell?"

He shook his head to clear away the fog seizing his brain and made his thoughts take flight. "Never better, now that you are here. I see your constant companion is still at your side."

The lion inclined his head and lay down before his king.

She rubbed his ear. "He is a noble fellow, brave and handsome."

"The Kingdom of Mannai sent me seven of their finest lion-men. They guard me where men cannot. Shirzad is yours now. He is the best, one of my favorites." Solomon smiled. "Neither man, nor beast, nor shape-shifter can resist the charms of the magnificent Makeda."

She smiled and flushed from her long, lovely neck to the roots of her gold and jewel bedecked hair.

"I'm here to share my travel plans with you. It is time for me to go. I cannot stay any longer."

His stomach plummeted. *His prayer had been answered.* Go? She couldn't go. Not now, not ever. "No, please don't leave me."

Makeda's green eyes widened, and her eyebrows rose. He closed the gap between them and grasped her arms. "Marry me. I will make you queen of my nation, my primary wife. You will be the mother of my children, heirs to not one, but two great dynasties. You can keep your kingdom."

"You know I cannot do that. I must remain a virgin or lose my people, my throne. *Everything.*"

He pulled her closer, risking the disapproving expressions of the soldiers who looked on and committed every word to memory for Benaiah. He didn't care. He fell into the green pools of her eyes. Sandalwood, frankincense, and myrhh enveloped him in a heady mixture, sending shuddering waves of heat to his groin. He wanted to press his lips to hers, skim his hands across her silky skin, plunder her hidden treasure trove with his tongue, and be with her every night of his life.

"Did your father intend for his dynasty to die with you? How can you have an empire if you don't have offspring? Did he not wish for you to have the pleasure of a family? The joy of children's laughter? The love of a man who wishes to fulfill your every desire?" Eyes blurry, voice husky, he whispered, "Do you not care for me?"

Tears filled her eyes and spilled down her cheeks. Shoulders shaking, she shook her head. "I'm not made of stone. I feel much for your people, for you. I've wanted to be with you from the moment we met. Would you break the laws of *your* fathers? Would you abandon *your* nation? Please, don't make me break my promise to my father and my country."

In a flash, Solomon saw she was as wretched as he. The heavy chains of royalty weighed each of them down, shackling her to a lonely destiny, him to a heartbroken lifetime. He pulled her tight, kissed her forehead and cheeks. He choked out the words he wished he would never have to say. "Go therefore and be well. And may God protect you on your travels and guide you safely home."

Before his resolve weakened, Solomon turned and headed toward his private chamber to grieve. Never again would he love a woman so hard, so deep, so strong. Never again would he write love poems for his beloved, her dove eyes, and her pomegranate lips. Never, ever again.

****

Solomon receded into the shadowy recesses of the palace. The soldiers closed ranks around the king and followed him, leaving her alone in the courtyard with the lion and her broken heart. She wanted to run after him, to stop him, demand that he bed her right now. Why must he be so...so...wise? Her resistance to his charms had dissolved over the past months as she observed him with his people. With each dispute, each verdict, she viewed him with new eyes. The judgment she loved the most was also the one that turned her bowels to water with terror.

One day two harlots had appeared before him carrying two babies, one dead, one living. One prostitute claimed the other rolled over on her own son, smothered him, and then stole her baby. The other woman claimed the dead child was not hers. Instead, she said she went to sleep with a live baby on her breast and awoke with a dead one. The other woman stole *her* baby and replaced him with the dead one.

Solomon mulled aloud. "One says, 'This is my son that lives, and your son is the dead. The other says, No, your son is the dead, mine is the living one.'" He motioned to Benaiah. "Bring me a sword."

His captain offered his own.

"Now." Solomon gestured at the living baby. "Split him in two. Each woman shall own half a child."

One woman shrugged. "Fine. Divide it."

"No!" The other woman cried out. "Give her the child. Let him live."

Solomon pointed to the second woman, the one willing to give the baby up rather than see him die. "Do not slay the infant. That is the real mother. Return the child to her."

He turned to the liar. "You will rue the day you came before me and bore false witness. You will pay this woman the equivalent of two weeks of work."

The woman opened her mouth to protest.

He held his hand up. "You may no longer ply your trade within the walls of Jerusalem. If I hear from any of my soldiers that you are inside city limits, I will not be kind to you again."

Throughout the judging, beneath her impassive mask, Makeda's heart was in her throat. Her wet palms still gripped the arms of her throne when she felt her breath whoosh out. When the court paused for meal time, she turned to him. "How did you discern the correct choice?"

"A real mother would lay her life down for her child, not take it away."

That day he had won her head and her heart. But to what avail? Other kings would have forced her to be his concubine. Without her virginity, she would be freed from her promise, both a blessing and a curse. Despite his obvious desire, he did not force himself on her.

He was right. Who would be her successor to the throne upon her death? Who could she groom and educate to take her place? Where would she find such a person? If she didn't, her kingdom would be in turmoil. She need only recall that dreadful man she ordered to be killed on the spot. There would be other rebellious youths like him, muscular men who equated strength with privilege. Unearned rights, stomping on little people. Is that the legacy she'd leave to her nation?

Makeda shook her head. She'd made a promise, a sacred oath that could be broken only with death or dishonor. She sighed and the lion stood. He gazed at her with large golden eyes. She reached over and stoked his head. "I'm sad to leave you, too, Shirzad, my friend."

The sting of a thousand insects prickled her skin and jinni stink wafted to her nose.

Makeda whirled. "You again. Leave this place. I do not wish to see you."

The huge jinni who lurked in the shadows each time she visited the king, smirked and slid across the rocks, drawing closer to her, dragging along an unbearable stench.

Frantic, Makeda searched for an exit. The brute blocked the only way out of the enclosed space. She tried to scream, but nothing came out, not even a whimper. What did he do to her? How did he silence her?

She turned to run into the palace, but could not move.

What happened to her legs? They shook like branches in a storm.

The burn of the stings jinni stench became unbearable. The creature reached out to grab Makeda.

The lion roared and leaped at the jinni.

The evil one vanished in a puff of green smoke.

Released from whatever spell the jinni used, screams erupted from Makeda. The great cat roared along with her. Soldiers poured out of the palace, swords at the ready.

Shirzad sat in front of Makeda and shook his head at the men.

Fingers wrapped in his black mane, she choked out, "Find the king, I must speak with him *now*."

Trembling, thoughts raced through her head. What if the king allowed him to speak? The jinni would reveal her secret in a heartbeat. What if the jinni followed her? Even if she left Israel, he could appear anywhere along the route and attack her, take her against her will. No. She couldn't allow that to happen. Ever.

After her father told the truth about her mother being a jinniyah, Makeda sought out every wise man and woman she could find to tell her everything about the jinnis. No one had a sure method to destroy them. However, one ancient crone told her how to capture them. There was no other choice. That jinni was a danger to her and her kingdom.

"Makeda, what is it? What's wrong?" Disheveled, red-eyed, hair sticking out at odd angles, Solomon strode across the courtyard. For the king, the lion stepped aside.

"I changed my mind. I cannot live without you. I will marry you."

Solomon's face lit up as if a thousand suns rose in the sky. He grabbed her hands and kissed the palms. "You are my beloved, and my beloved is mine."

"Under *one* condition."

Face glowing, he pulled her close. "Do you hear my heart? It clamors with joy. I will give you anything, whatever is mine is yours. My kingdom is your kingdom. Your wish my command."

"That evil jinni must go."

The king tilted his head. "I don't understand. He's my strongest worker."

"That brute hides in the shadows, follows me, and attempted to attack me after you left my side." She shuddered. "If not for Shirzad, God only knows what he would have done."

Solomon stroked his beard. "My love, my seal controls him. He could not harm you."

"He turned me to stone, sealed my mouth with some sort of binding curse. I tell you he is evil."

The king considered her words. "That he is. If not for the seal, I would be dead by his sword."

She grasped his hand with both of hers. "He knows your feelings for me. The demon seeks to rip your heart out by harming me. His malevolence toward you has no bounds."

"A menace to me endangers the kingdom. What shall we do?"

"There is only one way to deal with him." She lowered her voice for his ears only. "Then and only then, can I be yours in every way."

The following day, Solomon, Makeda, Hoopoe, and Shirzad set out for a trip on the Dead Sea, accompanied by the minimum number of bodyguards. The Queen of Sheba instructed her followers this was a private matter, and they were not to accompany her. A few exchanged anxious glances, but Tehetena, the handmaiden who pretended to be queen when Makeda met Solomon, hugged her mistress and gave her a knowing smile.

Let her think it was a lovers' tryst. Better that than the truth.

Benaiah grumbled, but agreed with Solomon that the Shebans might fear for their queen in her absence and grow restless. He stayed behind to keep an eye on the visitors' encampment.

Wishing to avoid the eyes of the curious or the conniving, Makeda insisted on a late departure. The captain set sail as the sun headed toward the horizon, turning the sky purple. A light breeze sprang up, sending the small vessel skimming across the water.

Just as the sun kissed the water, Makeda turned to Solomon. "It is time."

Solomon ordered the captain and the men to cover their eyes and raised his hands. "My strongest jinni, I call you to my side. I have need of you."

Green mist swirled and coalesced before them on the deck. The giant inclined his head to the king—and smirked at Makeda.

She drew a sharp breath. If his tongue was loosened, he would reveal her secret. She had to act fast. "Now."

A puzzled expression crossed the jinni's face. Then he spotted the iron amphora sitting on the deck. His features twisted with rage.

"With this seal, I, King Solomon, command you to get in that jug and remain until the stopper is removed."

His voice returned to him, the jinni shrieked, "Nooooooo—" He twirled like a tent in a sandstorm. His feet lengthened and became threadlike, entering the mouth of the bottle first, then his legs, hips, and chest. Palms pushing upward on the lip of the bottle, the jinni howled as he was drawn in, inch by inch, until his head was sucked in with a popping sound. Solomon pushed the lead stopper into the opening and bound it with iron chains. Together, Makeda and Solomon lifted the weighted urn and tossed it overboard.

Heart racing, Makeda leaned over the side of the boat and peered into the depths. The bottle twirled downward, headed to an eternal rest.

Her arm around Solomon's waist, she pointed at the water. "We did it, my love. We are free of that evil jinni."

"Now we can be one." He nuzzled her ear. "We

must announce the royal wedding."

"I am my beloved's and my beloved is mine." Love swelled her breast with joy, tinged with guilt. According to her father's decree, she chose dishonor. Was it? Wouldn't it be a greater disgrace if her father's work for his nation died with her? With the Wisdom of Solomon, she made the right decision. Marriage and children with this great king would ensure her father's line endured. Makeda sighed. The beast was gone, the threat of discovery destroyed. She glanced back at the water one last time.

A bubble exploded on the glassy surface and a deep voice roared, "I curse you and your family for all generations to come. Your children and your children's children will suffer the revenge of my people."

Chapter Eleven

Summertown, Present Day

A cross between the screams of a human and the high-pitched, yelping howl of a wolf filled the woods as the dark-brown werewolf's ear erupted with bright red blood. Were those her screams? The only thing that mattered was the King Kong of werewolves had, to her breathless relief, turned tail and taken off. No silver bullets required. The tingling was subsiding. She had to pursue him. It. Whatever. Now. She rolled over to her side and came face to face with—

"Arta?"

Shadows danced and blurred his features. His nose thinned, his eyes grew rounder and darker. He shook his head and his hair, long, luxuriant, almost a black mane, returned to his business man's cut.

She blinked. *What the hell was going on?*

He reached out and touched her cheek, his brow furrowed, eyes glinting with flecks of gold. "I got here as fast as I could. Are you okay?"

"I'm good." She searched his face. Had he just shifted? No. He couldn't be—Or could he? "You— you're—"

"Fine." Arta rolled over and leaped to his feet.

Eliana holstered her Sig Sauer and rose to her knees. He extended his hand, pulled her upright, and yanked her closer than expected. Her breath caught in her throat and came out in a husky whisper. "Thanks."

"You scared me half to death." He held her hand a second longer than needed and searched her face. He brushed at her hair. Bits of dead leaves fluttered free. "You are fearless in the midst of the sea of fear."

A shaky laugh escaped her. "More poetry?" Her hand trembled at his touch. Better to move away, before his words unraveled her and she did something foolish. She stepped back and gave him the once over. "Your clothes. They're torn."

"Thorn bushes. Thought I'd never get free of them." He pointed behind her. "You know him?"

Six feet away, a gray-haired man lay bleeding, unconscious, and naked.

She nodded. "Lowell Adalwolf, the alpha wolf of the pack."

Arta moved to the older man's side and began to examine him. "Pupils equal, reactive to light. Pulse is weak, thready." He rolled the man over and winced. Arta removed his blazer and handed it to Eliana. "Careful. There's an antique Koran in my inner pocket." He pulled off his button-down oxford shirt and cotton tee, and fashioned a makeshift bandage. "Nasty gash. He needs stitches and IV fluids." He wrapped the arms of the shirt around Adalwolf's torso. Deep scratches seeped crimson around the edges of the cotton. "We need to get him to a hospital."

Eliana peered into the dark woods. The burning sensation from her jinni radar was gone. A blue jay's angry squawk broke the silence of the forest, underscoring the creature's absence. She returned her attention to the injured man and the shirtless Arta. Dark hair tapered to a vee down well-defined pectoral muscles giving new meaning to six-pack abs.

Good grief. *Was the man a body builder in his spare time?* If she knew poetry, she'd be quoting it soon. 'Swoon-worthy' was the word that kept running through her mind, but somehow even that did the man no justice.

"Grab his feet." Arta placed his hands under Adalwolf's shoulders.

She tore her eyes off his sculpted body and snapped to attention.

"Hold on." Tucking her blazer into the makeshift bandage, the jacket gave Adalwolf a modicum of modesty. At least some of the older man's dignity would still be intact if he came to in the car. Perhaps.

Adalwolf's limp body required rest breaks, each one an opportunity for catching her breath—and unobstructed views of Arta. Covered in a sheen of sweat, stripped to the waist, his glistening skin golden, the normally sedate psychiatrist resembled an ancient Persian warrior carrying a fallen comrade off the field of battle. On the third stop, Eliana dragged her eyes away from the unexpected beefcake before her, fanned her neck, and wiped her brow.

Adalwolf groaned and opened his eyes. "What happened?"

Arta crouched beside the man. "Thanks to Eliana, you're alive."

"Arta bandaged a terrible gash."

The old alpha wolf sat up, stared at his blazer-covered groin, and frowned. "The other werewolf?"

"One of yours?" Eliana asked.

Adalwolf's frown deepened. "Not one of my pack

mates. Too big. Too smelly."

"Jinni stink," Arta said.

Eliana shot a glance at Arta. "We're not sure—"

"Stop." The alpha wolf shook his head. "That's been your party line ever since you arrived in Summertown. I've seen a lot of werewolves in my very long lifetime. Thousands. This *thing* was nothing like any I've ever seen before. Rabid werewolves are sick. They don't get bigger. They become anorexic, shrink into themselves, crawl into a cave, and die. This is the biggest, craziest one I've seen in my life. It was as if he was taken over by something else—"

Arta's eyes fixed on Adalwolf. "Possessed?"

"Exactly."

Arta and Eliana locked gazes. This was worse than they thought. *Much worse.*

"We'll discuss this later," Eliana said. "You need stitches."

Adalwolf chuffed. "You sure? Why don't you take a peek first."

Arta lifted the bandage and shook his head. "Unbelievable. The wound is healing already."

"Werewolves heal fast. Our immune systems resist almost anything, except rabies. Vaccinations are mandatory in my pack." He shook his head. "I was out for a run. Just wanted some time to myself. Then I ran into you." He nodded at Eliana. "I didn't recognize you at first because I was in wolf mode. That was the ugliest werewolf I've ever seen. So much for time to myself." He got to his feet. "Drop me off at my house. I don't need stitches, but I do need rest."

"He bit you. We need to swab you for DNA and we need a statement. Your body is a walking evidence locker."

****

Arta gave the older man the front passenger seat to accommodate Adalwolf's long legs and to give himself time to think. Something had changed since his last shape-shifting incident. In Chevy Chase, as in Arizona, he'd been taken off guard and unable to control the change. Today as he raced through the woods, the change notified him of its impending arrival, like an aura before a migraine. He ran into the fray, praying for the strength to accept God's will and the ability to do right by the one who gave him this gift. The pace of the change slowed. Only his hands and face morphed, sparing his clothes from the shredding they took in Chevy Chase. He prayed for the integrity to use his lion powers when needed and prayed Eliana would not see him in lion form—not yet. Somehow, he'd been able to control the change, slow it down, make it specific to the two most needed areas and reverse it faster than the two previous times. By the time he arrived at her side, the reversal to his human form was almost complete. Almost, but not quite. Her expression had telegraphed that she'd seen *something*. He was grateful she'd let it drop—for the moment.

He glanced at Eliana in the rearview mirror and they locked gazes. She quirked an eyebrow, as if to say, "Well?"

She'd seen. With all her experience with shape-shifters, she must know. What should he do? Would she be understanding or repelled if he told her about Arizona and Chevy Chase? Even with all his research, it was still hard for him to believe. How would he explain it to her? Despite his self talk about hallucinations, he'd conducted blood tests to be sure he wasn't harboring some exotic illness and found no abnormalities.

After the incident with Nur, he went home to Silver Spring to visit his mother, a widow since his childhood. Perhaps she could shed light on his strange transformation. The same photograph he'd seen every day of his youth had greeted him as he walked in the door. This time, however, it took his breath away. His father stood next to the Shah of Iran at the twenty-five hundred year celebration of the Persian Empire in the ancient city of Persepolis. A stone wall with raised carvings of Persian soldiers soared up to the blue sky behind them. All these years, he glanced at that photo as he came into the house. On this particular day, it was not his own features mirrored in his father's smiling expression that caught his eye. Instead, his gaze snagged on the men above the Shah's head. Persian men who faced one another and protected a regiment of stone soldiers.

Men with the bodies of lions.

He roared in shock and disbelief. His mother ran out of the kitchen into the foyer and froze when she saw her son glance between her and the photograph.

"What is it?" She asked in Farsi. "What's wrong?"

"Why didn't you tell me? When were you going to let me know about—"

"Come." His mother motioned for him to follow her. "Let's drink some tea."

Stunned at his mother's casual manner, he stomped after the still svelte brunette his high school buddies had nick-named Mrs. Robinson because of her strong resemblance to Anne Bancroft. "Mother—"

She put her finger to her lips, turned, and clattered mugs on the counter. "The gazebo is lovely now." Steaming cups in hand, she led her bewildered son outside.

Golden rays of the setting sun streamed through cracks in the thicket of wisteria giving the space a sacred aura.

His mother pointed to a cushioned white wicker seat. "It's not safe to talk about this in the house. There are listeners, watchers. Everywhere."

His breath caught in his throat. "How long have you felt this way?"

Eyes cast down, she whispered, "Since the day you were born, my darling son."

Her words drove shards of guilt into his heart. Kicking himself mentally for not visiting her more often, he leaned in and spoke in a soft voice. "Mother, are you saying the American government is spying on you?"

She laughed and nearly spit out a mouthful of tea. She caught her breath and said, "If *only* it were the CIA."

"You're worrying me."

"I'm not crazy, but you should be worried. More about that later." Her eyes darkened, and her lips thinned. "What happened to you?"

Arta blew out a long breath and told his mother about the two incidents. She said nothing as he spoke, simply sipped and nodded to encourage him. When he finished, he said, "Your turn."

"You must never speak of this inside my home. People much more dangerous than the NSA or the CIA monitor this house. These assassins work for the

138

Ayahtollah." She gripped her cup so hard her knuckles turned white. "Your father didn't die of a heart attack. He was stabbed with a poison-tipped dagger during a cocktail party."

Arta's head spun.

Assassins? Poison-tipped daggers?

Stuff of Persian legends, not modern times. The gazebo, once so airy and light, closed in on Arta, choking him. He stood and began to pace like a caged lion. "Why was I never told about this?"

"Your father said you were protected, because I was a human. You were never supposed to turn into…into…him." She caught his hand in hers. "The *'Ifrit* must have triggered your change. Nothing else makes sense."

He stared into his mother's eyes. "Tell me everything."

In a matter-of-fact voice, she shared the story of the shape shifting lions that protected the royalty of Persia for centuries, all the way back to Shirzad, a fabled lion-man companion to the great King and Prophet, Solomon. First in their half-man, half-lion forms, later in their human forms as bodyguards and trusted confidants, the shifters always guarded the throne. As physicians, they excelled in casting out demons and jinnis. His father was one of the last of the long line of shifters to care for a Persian prince. Worried about the changing political landscape in Iran, the doctor selected a human mate to protect his family and future generations.

To the best of his mother's knowledge, during and after the revolution, all the other lion shifters were hunted down and murdered. Even now, decades later, the fanatics listened in on her constantly. Not only was she a "dangerous" feminist, working for women's rights in Iran, she was the wife and potentially the mother of a shape-shifting lion.

"Neither your father nor I ever predicted you would be able to shape shift. And I certainly never expected to be forced to tell you the truth about your Persian lion family tree and your father's death." She reached across the table and clutched his hand. "I swear, I thought you were protected from this threat. Between your non-lion related name, your choice of psychiatry, a scorned profession among the revolutionaries, and your work for Homeland Security, I was positive you were under the radar. Safe. If the assassins ever get wind of your abilities, they'll be after you, too. Now you must be on guard every minute, day and night, just as I have been for the last thirty years."

He shook his head and forced his thoughts to the present, and his relationship with Ellie. If he struggled to understand himself, how could he expect her to accept this other part of him? How would he explain it to her? Poetry leapt into his mind when he tried to talk to her. He was a scientist, a psychiatrist. He ought to be better at this sort of thing. She was a professional. Eliana would finish the assignment, wrap things up, file her report, and say good-bye. Forever.

"Dr. Shahani," Adalwolf interrupted his thoughts. "In your opinion, is it possible for someone to have multiple personalities?"

Grateful for the distraction, Arta replied with care. "You mean like the book, *Sybil*?"

"Yes, exactly. What if what we all witnessed in the woods was a mentally ill werewolf? One not able to distinguish between right and wrong."

"Multiple personality disorder doesn't mean a person doesn't know right from wrong. Are you going for an insanity defense ahead of a trial?"

Adalwolf harrumphed. "Aren't insane people entitled to use it?"

Arta let out a long breath. "Defendants' attorneys have the right to mount a defense to the best of their abilities. Whoever the defendant may be."

"Even a giant, snarling, drooling, vicious werewolf?"

"Every monster is allowed his day in court. Trust me, there are plenty of them. My job is to assess them for the legal system."

Arta fell silent, thinking back on all the child abusers, rapists, and murderers who used the insanity defense. None of them, however, was possessed. A tough sell in any country, he wondered how it would play in an American court? How would he, an American trained psychiatrist with expertise in jinni possession, provide credible testimony to a jury of the possessed person's peers? He hoped he was never involved in such a trial. A shape-shifting lion might be accused of possession, too. Then what? He knew the answer. And didn't like it a bit. There was a reason the Romans called their entertainment zones the circus.

Eliana called Chief Novak and told her to meet them at the ER in ten minutes.

"I told you to take me home," Adalwolf barked at Eliana.

"Mr. Adalwolf, we must document your injuries, even if they are healing. We also need to swab you for DNA samples, remember?"

"I didn't give you consent," he snarled. "This is false imprisonment. Kidnapping. I know my rights."

Before Eliana recited the USA Patriot Act, Arta jumped in. "Mr. Adalwolf, you defended Agent Solomon against someone, something, who may be responsible for the attacks on your family members. You are covered in the attacker's DNA. The ME had DNA samples from the deceased young woman. Fetal samples are not feasible at this point. The girls are traumatized enough; they need to consider their options, give consent. And, there is a risk to the unborn" he struggled for the right word—"child."

The back of Adalwolf's neck turned bright red. "I'm a prominent man in town. It's one thing for people to know I'm a werewolf. It's another thing for them to see me naked."

It was a good thing Eliana had put her blazer over the man's groin. He could only imagine Adalwolf's embarrassment if he'd regained consciousness before then.

"If I give you my trousers, will you go to the ER?"

He growled assent.

Arta struggled to remove his pants without pulling off his underwear, no small trick. He caught Eliana staring at him in the rearview mirror, amusement crinkling her eyes. He shook his head and shrugged. So she would see him in his boxer shorts. No biggie, right? How different was that from swim trunks? In the aftermath of nearly losing her, the confined space of the car, and her eyes darting between the road and his backseat striptease, the moment became intimate. Captain Happy Pants liked it and rose to the occasion. Eliana's eyebrows hit her hairline. She turned a deep crimson, stared straight ahead, and the car lurched forward plunging toward the hospital, civilization, and clothes.

Arta choked off a laugh, pretended to cough, and failed. She glared at him in the rearview mirror. In a loud explosion of coughing, he handed Adalwolf the pants over the seat. "Wear them in good health."

Eliana pulled into the Summertown Medical Center ER entrance with a screech and parked behind a police cruiser. Chief Novak leaped out of the unit and approached the car. "Are you okay?"

Eliana nodded. "I'm fine. We need to get him inside."

Novak spotted Adalwolf in his odd assortment of rags and clothes. "What the hell?"

Arta waved through the rear window. "Hello, Chief. If you could pull my suitcase out of the trunk and find me a shirt and a pair of slacks, I'd appreciate it."

The red haired woman's eyes practically bulged out of her head.

"This is one story I *want* to hear."

Eliana ushered Adalwolf out of her car. The man looked as if he was going wading in his borrowed trousers. At least he didn't balk at the fit.

Arta couldn't imagine what the pack leader was going through. First Adalwolf denied any werewolf involvement, now with incontrovertible proof snapping in his face, the alpha wolf was already in high gear, trying to come up with a defense for the attacker. Not guilty by reason of insanity.

You'd think he'd want to hunt the abomination down and kill it, not defend it.

Meantime, they had to find a match for the DNA

on Adalwolf's body, no small task, even in a small town. Would they be able to get the townspeople on board? How would they convince the male residents to line up for a cheek swab?

He tucked his shirt into his pants and strode into the ER waiting room. A cluster of nurses whispered and shook their heads. No one spared him a glance.

Eliana came out of a hallway, her face a mask of anger.

"What's wrong?"

"One of the pregnant girls miscarried."

"Is she okay?"

Her jaw clenched. "No."

He grabbed her hand and squeezed it. "Tell me."

"She bled to death. A nurse found her on the bathroom floor."

A commotion erupted at the entrance to the ER, growing noisier every second. A woman with hair the color of burnished steel strode to the front of the throng.

"I'm looking for Special Agent Eliana Solomon." She glared at the nurses and swung her laser beam of a gaze around the room. "I know she's here. I want her front and center. Now."

Arta grasped Eliana's hand. "Who's asking for her?"

Eliana nodded. "That would be me."

The woman, blue eyes blazing, looked him up and down, then focused on Eliana. "I'm Winifred Schaeffer, wife of that horse's ass, Mayor Schaeffer. My husband complained the most about you and how you gave him a hard time over this investigation, so I knew you were the one I wanted to talk to. He's so wrapped up in making the town money, he's forgotten the real reason he was elected. He's supposed to be representing the *people*." She took a deep breath.

"Now the Adalwolf family has lost another girl. I'm here with every mother, sister, aunt, cousin, and grandmother in town. We aren't going to put up with this macho crap one more minute. This predator can't attack any more girls. What do you need us to do?"

A look of astonishment wreathed Ellie's beautiful face. She stepped forward, out of his protective grasp. He longed to pull her back, his hand suddenly cool with the absence of her warmth.

"Chief Novak needs DNA samples from every male over the age of thirteen in this town. We need to rule suspects in or out." She glanced back at Arta. He smiled and nodded, mentally urging her to go on. "If you really want to help us, then we need you to be our census workers, going house to house to find, enumerate, and convince men to go to the Community Center to be swabbed. Crime scene technicians will be there to maintain the chain of custody, collect, catalog, and store the samples. Can you help us?"

Mrs. Schaeffer turned to the buzzing crowd behind her. "Ladies, it's time to round up the troops, get their butts in here. No arguments. This is war. We will fight this monster with everything we've got. And we are going to win."

Eliana fished in her pants pocket. "Mrs. Schaeffer, I'm going to put you in charge of the volunteers. Here's my card. I suggest you divvy up the town and assign your ladies to work in teams of two. I'm thrilled with your help. You'll probably be more successful than uniformed officers. Call me with names and contact information as you complete sectors. We'll organize the collections."

The mayor's wife took the card, nodded, and turned to the crowd. "Come on ladies, let's go back to my house for coffee and strategy planning. Start picking partners now, dress in sensible walking shoes…" Her voice trailed off as she led the Amazonian army out of the ER.

Arta stepped next to Ellie.

"You know," he said, "I'm a little afraid for the men of the town."

She nodded. "Mrs. Schaeffer is a force to be reckoned with, isn't she? Organized, resourceful, and pissed off. Her husband should watch his back. Winifred could be the next mayor."

Ellie's phone played the violin solo from *The Fiddler on the Roof*. "My father."

"Hello, my little woman," his voice boomed out of the phone.

Arta suspected the entire ER could hear him.

"*Abba*, I'm not deaf."

He lowered his voice a decibel, still audible to people within ten feet. "I had a bad dream. You were in terrible trouble."

"I'm fine."

"You can't fool your father. I bet you almost died."

She said nothing, just rolled her eyes at Arta.

"Where are you? I need to see you, I have to tell you something."

"This isn't a good time. I'm on a case."

"A dangerous one, right? I have to tell you something that could save your life. It's about your ring."

Chapter Twelve

Jerusalem, 954 B.C.E.

Makeda stood on a short stool in front of a tall polished bronze shield, eyed her watery image, and wished she had the obsidian mirror from her palace back home. *Home.* A pang shot through her. She'd been in Jerusalem so long, she wondered if the people she left behind would even remember her. She closed her eyes and thought of the highlands, rainy season, and the lush meadows surrounding the Great Lake and the Blue Nile, so different from the dry countryside of Israel. Her birds. How she missed hearing their banter as she listened to cases in the courtroom. Hoopoe was talkative, but not nearly as entertaining as the ibis and the emerald parrot when they bickered. Tears pricked her eyes.

Am I doing the right thing?

Her father's voice whispered, "You must stay a virgin. You cannot be a wife and mother and a queen. You must stay focused on serving your kingdom." But the voice of Solomon responded in her head. "She will be ruler of two nations; she will bring glory to Sheba and Israel." Metatron, the right hand of God, led her here. She had to trust in God and follow His guidance, as Solomon did. She blinked and wiped her cheek, lest the servants see her weeping. It wouldn't do to appear sad tonight of all nights.

The royal seamstress stepped back and gazed at her work. "Are you happy with your wedding raiment, Queen Makeda?"

"It is like none other. How did you fasten the pearls and gems to the material along the neckline?"

"My son is a goldsmith. He creates the strands of gold and jewels, and I sew them to the cloth. I chose the emeralds because they go well with your eyes. I designed a different one for each of King Solomon's wives."

Makeda stepped down, nodded for her handmaiden to give the woman a bag of gold, and waved the servants away. As the sun set on her life as a virgin, she needed to be alone. Her reflection stared back at her. The brass revealed her true feelings: uncertain and shaky.

"Each of King Solomon's wives."

The thought of being wife number seven-hundred and one fell heavy on Makeda's heart. How could he call her his love match amid his harem of seven hundred wives and three hundred concubines? She understood well most of the marriages secured allies, often at Bathsheba's urging.

Yet not all of the women were selected by his mother. Some he chose on his own. Like her. Unable to contain his joy after disposing of the jinni and winning Makeda's consent, Solomon had told everyone about the upcoming wedding. He insisted on having the ceremony before the next moon. He burned with desire to be with Makeda—and she with him. But marriage was not an easy road, no matter how much one's loins smoldered. How long would it take before the glowing embers became ashes? Which woman would he turn to after an argument with Makeda? Whose breasts would console him if she fell short of his wishes on their wedding night? She had her suspicions.

Over the past week, two of the other queens had made a point of visiting her in her separate quarters, not to welcome her into the harem, but to advise her to go home. Oh, each tried to disguise her hostility, to no avail. Their hidden barbs had pricked her heart. Some worse than others.

The Pharaoh's daughter brought gifts of olive oil and wine, along with stories of how difficult it was for her to stay here in a desert country, so far away from her beloved fertile Nile. Her pet, sitting on her lap the entire time in its jeweled collar was more direct.

"Leave us," the spotted creature hissed for Makeda's ears only. "Go home."

She appreciated the Egyptian cat's candor, if not his tone of delivery.

Naamah the Ammonitess, mother of Rehoboam, arrived with a snot-nosed child clutched in her hand and introduced him as "the next king."

"The Elders convened a special gathering," Naamah said, handing her son a large handful of dates from the bowl on the table between them. "They don't want another queen. What they say is the law. If I were you, I'd be planning my trip home." She waved around the room. "With all this, your slaves should start packing now."

Despite wanting to douse the other woman with water, Makeda sipped it to keep from speaking.

Gulping wine, Naamah sneered. "Even if Solomon knew you, even if he gets you with child, even if you have a boy, Rehoboam was born first. Your child will never be heir to the throne of Israel."

Makeda took another, larger swallow. She understood the mother was looking out for her child. However, the vinegar-tongued woman did not need to know whether she and Solomon had been together. If Makeda had an heir, he or she would have another kingdom to rule. Sheba was enough for any king or queen.

The thought stopped her breath for a moment.

In her kingdom, no one slid verbal spears into her side, unless they wanted to die on a real one. Who needed this constant intrigue and backbiting? She could lead a peaceful life alongside all manner of beasts—except Solomon's other wives, it seemed. The girl in her wanted to run home to the high plains and play. Perhaps it *was* time to leave, return home, and be rid of this flock of female birds of prey.

Makeda shook her head. There would be no backing out. She had made a promise. The marriage had been announced by messengers to all the surrounding kingdoms. Tomorrow when the sun stood at its highest, the rams' horns would sound. Preceded by her guard, accompanied by her handmaidens, and followed by her entourage, the Queen of Sheba would walk from her quarters to the high place where the priests celebrated festivals and rituals while awaiting the completion of the temple.

King Solomon would be waiting for her, wearing the crown his mother gave him for his wedding day. Zadok, the high priest, would call for God's blessings on the union, as above, so below. Was she truly ready for the joining together of two important kingdoms?

Was she prepared to join with Israel's king? In the dusky light, the mirror shimmered with movement. Her beloved stood behind her. Legs trembling beneath the purple cloth, Makeda held her breath and waited for him to speak.

"I could not wait any longer. I had to come to your chambers." He placed gentle hands on her arms and turned her around to face him. He kissed her forehead, nibbling down the side of her neck, nuzzling her ear, sending feathery delight down her spine. "I want you now."

Her heart raced like her mare's, and the room began to twirl. She closed her eyes to stop the whirling.

He pulled her closer and pressed his hardness into her warm recesses. He moaned into her ear. "See what you do to me? I cannot think, I cannot speak, I cannot do anything but dream of lying with you, running my hands across your breasts, suckling at your nipples, and lapping between your legs."

Back arched, she could barely breathe. He loved her. That was all that mattered.

I am dark and beautiful, daughters of Jerusalem. Solomon comes to me, not you.

Girl no more, the woman in her took charge, pulled his face close to hers, and spoke her deepest urges.

"My countrymen and women tended to their desires. Yet, I was never allowed to do the same. My father made me guard my virginity. He thought a woman could not rule if she was distracted by a husband and children. If I chose that path, it would be at the cost of my heart. My love, my soul mate, I have found the wisdom I sought in your arms. Your love is better than wine. You have come to my chambers.

Tonight we will rejoice in each other's arms."

"You are the most beautiful woman I have ever seen. Your neck is bejeweled, but you don't need adornment, your eyes are like emeralds. You speak, and my heart skips like a gazelle. Let us lie together and celebrate our love."

Makeda took his hand and led him to her bed. She lit a single candle and removed her finery with care. Naked, she stood before him and held her hands out.

"My heart is your captive. I only ask you give me what I desire—you and you alone. No robe, no crown, no seals. Just you."

Eyes shining, never taking his gaze from her face, Solomon removed his crown, placed his seals in a leather pouch, pulled his tunic over his head, and stood before her. "I shall give you whatsoever you ask, my beloved."

She gasped. *Great king, indeed.* "You are like a buck, or a young stag, standing on the mountain, ready for the doe."

He closed the gap between them. The heady scent of myrrh and incense washed over her. "Will you run from me, my doe, or allow me to kiss your apple flavored lips above and below?"

"Your locks are luxuriant, black as the raven. Your legs marble pillars. Your loins are of smoothest ivory, I wish to caress them. Your mouth is sweet. All of you is desirable. You are my love, my mate. I am no doe. I will not run. I shall shout from the highest place to the Jerusalem girls, I am going nowhere. I am *home*."

His kisses burned a path between her breasts, down her belly, to her dew-drenched recess. He knelt before her and pulled her closer, his tongue probing her secret place. She moaned, and nearly fell. He lifted her, swung her onto the bed, and placed his left hand under her head. His right hand stroked her breasts and sent burning ripples of desire through her core. Each touch, each kiss branded her. Begging for entrance, his hand pressed against her wet center, and she moaned. Drunk with love, she opened her body and soul for her darling, and he set his seal upon her heart.

****

Solomon awoke at dawn, rolled over, and gazed upon Makeda as she slept. Her lovely black curls flowed across the pillow like rivulets on a parched plain after a rainstorm. Her arms, which held him tight as they rode the stallion of desire into the night, were thrown over her head in surrender. Her breasts, sweet suckling twins, called to him. Beneath the blanket, even more delight awaited him.

"My love." He traced her nipples with his tongue.

She smiled and opened her eyes.

"You fill me with yearning." He pressed against her moist center, entreating her with his hardness. Only she could satisfy what he craved. Last night, to his delight, her appetite had been equal to his. She urged him on with her cries of pleasure and pulled him deeper into her womb. If he planted a seed each time, she would carry a dozen babies inside her. Only exhaustion and sleep ceased their lovemaking. Rested, he was ready to begin anew. She pulled his lips to hers and rose to welcome him inside her again.

Bathsheba called from outside. "Solomon, you need to prepare for this wedding. Now."

Solomon groaned, closed his eyes, and rolled onto his back, his desire a fading memory. "My mother's spies are everywhere."

Her face covered with her arm, Makeda shook so hard he thought she was crying. He gently pulled her arm away to console her—and stared at her.

"You dare to laugh at your king?"

"If you're so wise, shouldn't you know your mother would find out where you were on the eve of your wedding night? Every palace produces eyes, ears, and mouths that whisper to different loyalties."

The absurdity of thinking he could keep secrets from anyone, much less his mother, struck down his momentary flash of indignation. He guffawed and shook with laughter, too. "At least Hoopoe didn't eavesdrop on our lovemaking."

Makeda pointed at the window. "Are you sure?"

The bird sat on the ledge, spreading his striped wings in the sun. *"Oo-poo!"*

Solomon tossed a pillow at the bird, and he fluttered away. "He'd better keep his beak shut, or he'll be served at our wedding feast."

Laughing, Makeda mock-begged, "Please, don't."

"I could never eat that bird, he's all bones."

Makeda swatted him. "Go to your mother."

He stood and pulled his tunic over his head. "I'll tell her I was sampling the Sheban spices."

A shoe narrowly missed his head. He strode back to the bed, sat beside her, pressed her luscious breasts to his chest, and kissed her swollen lips. "My beloved, by giving me your sandal, you made last night's vows of love binding. Even without the priest's blessings, we are legally married. Today's festival will be for the people—and my mother."

Solomon nodded at Makeda's giggling

handmaidens as he rushed by. They would enjoy the day with their mistress, talking about him, no doubt. He hoped she told them every last detail, including how much she loved him. He wanted to shout his thanks to God and announce, "She is my beloved, and my beloved is mine." A few goblets of wine and he'd be merry enough to climb the walls of Jerusalem and sing his latest poem, his song of songs, regardless of how much the wretched priests and miserable prophets disapproved. *All* love came from God.

Bathsheba stood in the shade of the wall of Makeda's quarters, her arms crossed, never a good sign.

"What's wrong, Mother?"

"You dare to ask me what's wrong?" Hands on her hips now, a frown furrowed her brow. "Dawn came and went. You're lying about in bed when you should be preparing for a state affair. Visitors arrive from every kingdom, including your future wife's. You need to greet them. This is a royal event. Everything must be done correctly, or the Kingdom of Israel will look like a bunch of Philistines."

She took a breath, and Solomon seized the moment.

"Am I supposed to be cooking, cleaning, or preparing the table?"

"Don't be ridiculous."

"Are the servants not doing as they are told?"

Lips pursed, she spat out, "That's not the point."

"Why do you reproach me? I was with Makeda, in her chambers. What was so important that you had to interrupt me? Did one of the other wives send you?"

Her face reddened.

"Was it Naamah?"

She averted her eyes.

"The Ammonitess spits out jealousy laced venom with every word." Despite his annoyance, wisdom forced him to pursue truth. "Why would you listen to her?"

"She begged me to think about Rehoboam and the future of Israel. What if Makeda conceives a boy? Joab killed Absolom, your father's other son, to prevent a war. We don't need more challenges for the throne of Israel. It could divide and destroy the nation."

"Naamah has passed her bitterness on to her son." He shook his head. "His temper is uncontrollable. He tries my patience with his selfish actions, as does his mother."

"But, Solomon—"

"Tell Naamah I gave Makeda *all* she desired."

"All?" Bathsheba's eyes widened. "You cannot mean—"

"Last night God spoke to me with His small voice. He blessed Makeda."

His mother's shoulders sagged. "There will be war."

"It's Rehoboam we should be worried about, Mother, not Makeda's unborn child." He took her hands. "Didn't we agree it was time for you to stop meddling in my affairs?"

She lowered her eyes and nodded.

"Go, now, prepare yourself for the wedding. We shall be joyous and celebrate a momentous day in our nation's history. Two nations, one family." He paused. "Who came from Sheba? Is it her uncle?"

Bathsheba shook her head. "The merchant, Tamrin, said he needs to speak with Makeda."

Solomon waved his hand. "She's busy getting ready for the biggest day in her life. He can visit with her at the wedding. That will be soon enough."

He watched his mother dash toward the palace, her handmaidens scurrying to keep up with the older woman. No doubt she was racing to tell Naamah the news. A rival for the throne? Not likely. As long as he found favor in the eyes of the Lord, Solomon would never allow Rehoboam to reign over Israel.

Benaiah caught up with Solomon as he strode up the hill. "I heard you spent the night with the beautiful Makeda."

Solomon shook his head and kept walking. Every rock and tree gave tongue to his sexual activities, it seemed. "Are there no Philistines for you to slay?"

"Not today. It's your wedding day."

"I wager that would be the time to strike an enemy, when people are merry with wine."

The captain laughed. "Your enemies are kept too busy talking about your latest bride to wage war. Even *they* want to know if you saw her feet."

"Her feet?" Solomon shook his head. "Not that again."

"There is still time to call off the marriage."

The king bit his lip and stared at his friend.

"My friend, you command the jinnis. They build the temple and work hard. There's nothing wrong with having a jinniyah pleasure you." Benaiah paused. "Marriage? Children? That's not acceptable. Any offspring would be neither jinni nor human. They'd be half-breeds. I ask you as a friend, and as one who lives to protect you and the House of David. Are her feet like a goat's?"

Not wishing to start a fight hours before his wedding, Solomon bit back harsh words. "All of her is desirable." With those breasts and loins, only a man dead from the waist down would examine Makeda's feet. He was not made of wood. Even now, his flesh warmed at the thought of his lover. "I explored all of the Queen of Sheba, and she is without blemish."

Chapter Thirteen

Summertown, Present Day

Eliana counted to ten. This wasn't the first time her father had tried to convince her of the magical powers of the ring, nor would it be the last, she was sure. If her mother hadn't given it to Eliana as she lay dying, she wouldn't keep the damn thing. A semi-precious stone glinted at each of the six points of the star engraved on the face of the brass and iron signet. Etched between the gems was the tetragammaton, Yod, He, Waw, and He, or YHWH, the four letters in Hebrew that stood for God's divine name. Despite her father's role as head rabbi of a tiny Sephardic congregation in Baltimore, she did not share his unshakable faith in the legends of the ring—or her mother's strict religious customs.

Her mother was an observant Jew, a woman of valor, who kept the Sabbath and scrutinized her household to keep it in accordance with the laws of Moses. If devotion to rituals was any measure of her goodness and faith in God, then she should have been spared from dying a painful death at a young age. An aggressive form of leukemia took her away from them one year after her diagnosis. Angry with God, Eliana fell out of love with religion and refused to go to synagogue ever again. She attended the William Harvey University Center for Talented Youth and fell in love with physics.

"*Abba*, I'm in the middle of an investigation. I'll call you when this is over."

"Your *life* might be over if you don't pay attention to me." He took a deep breath. "Your mother, may she rest in peace, was of Solomonic descent. Her father was a holy man, a *Kesim*. He kept the Jewish customs alive through storytelling and oral history. During Operation Moses, your grandfather put your mother on the plane in Ethiopia and sent one of the last Torahs written in the ancient language of *Ge'ez* along with her to Israel."

An artery began to throb in her right temple, harbinger of a migraine to come. She pressed on it and wished for the meds that sat in the trunk of her car in the parking garage two blocks away from the hospital.

Arta touched her arm and whispered, "Are you okay?"

She shook her head and mouthed the word "migraine." He patted his pockets, pulled out a green bottle, placed it in her hand, and held up a finger. His steps receded behind her.

"*Abba.* Please. I know the story."

Irritation flashed in his voice. "Why do you act like it's a fairy tale?"

"More like the Arabian Nights. If my mother was a direct descendant of the Queen of Sheba and King Solomon, then why didn't she live in the palace with Emperor Haile Selassie instead of a mud hut in the highlands of Gondar?"

"Menelik, the son of Makeda and Solomon, had many wives, concubines, and children. The concubines' children could not lay any claims to the throne. He gave the ring to his favorite child, a little girl he named

Dameka."

"My great-great-great-grandmother a zillion times over was a concubine. Not even a real wife."

"Did you forgot everything you learned in Sunday school?"

She could almost see him pulling at his long gray beard, a sign of exasperation with a slow pupil, a stubborn daughter, or both, in her case.

"*Abba,* you of all people should know information gets jumbled in oral history. It's like playing 'Gossip.' By the time the story got to Ima's parents, it evolved into a new, colorful story, one that made the family seem more important than just being dirt poor farmers."

"Don't be disrespectful. Your grandparents, the Beta Israel of Ethiopia, were a biblical people who lived their lives according to the Tanakh, the teachings of Moses, the prophets, and the writings. That's more than *some* people can say."

She chose not to take the bait. Today of all days, she lacked desire to debate her non-observance of religious customs, like not driving on the Sabbath.

"I'm suggesting family legends may contain a bit of truth within them, but usually that nugget is buried beneath layers of creative story telling."

"That doesn't negate the power of the ring. I'm sure that's why you were able to find the evil jinni in Kentucky. Don't you see? It's a homing beacon for jinnis."

"Homeland Security Operations Center's satellite technology spotted the abnormal energy pattern and transmitted them to the Science and Technology Directorate and the Anomaly Defense Division, just like we track any other irregularities. The werewolves destroyed that entity, not me. With what they say is *their* real Seal of Solomon."

"Why are you being so stubborn? Can't you just accept your special connection to the world of jinnis through this ring? Four great religions agree Solomon commanded the jinnis—yes, I know some called them demons—with his seals. *Plural.* He owned more than one, my darling hard-headed daughter. Four religions can't all be wrong."

She closed her eyes and gripped the phone harder, the throbbing in her head the percussion of a ball peen hammer. How could she tell him she wasn't wearing the ring when she chased the jinni into the forest? In the cold, the loose band kept slipping off, so she removed it and left it in the center console when she grabbed the fistfuls of coins to leave a trail for Arta. The ring bore no relationship to the tingling she felt. It was almost as if she became supercharged with electricity when she was near the entity, the stinging growing stronger as she approached it and receding when the creature disappeared. None of her education or training in applied physics prepared her for a sentient being that could harness that kind of energy—whatever it was.

Eliana blinked and Arta stood in front of her holding a bottle of cold water to go with the headache pills. "Thank you," she mouthed. She spotted the date on the calendar on the wall behind his head, and her heart dropped. Today was one month away from the anniversary of her mother's death. The grief she and her father shared over the loss of his wife, her mother, never truly dissipated. Subversive sorrow burrowed deep beneath day to day activities, until the scent of a perfume, the flavor of a favorite food, a piece of music, or a date on a calendar set it free. Her mother would never be forgotten.

"*Abba*," she said gently, "I promise I'll be home for Ima's service. We'll watch home videos, eat *injera* bread, make spicy stew, and drink lots of Ethiopian coffee in her honor." Her eyes filled with tears. "I miss her, too. The best thing about this ring is it connects me to Ima and her blessed memories. I won't forget her, I swear." *I won't forget the promise I made to her.*

"Eliana—please—you're my only child, all I have left of your mother—" He choked up.

"I'll be careful. I promise I will wear the ring at all times."

"Thank you." He sniffed. "Now, get back to work. Your boss is waiting for you."

She looked at Arta and shook her head. "The man you heard talking to me is not my boss. His name is Dr. Shahani. He's working with me on this case."

"Shahani? The guy you worked with in Arizona? The guy who took off and left you bleeding to death? I can't believe he's been assigned to work with you again."

"I asked for his help."

Dead silence.

"*Abba?* I need to go now."

"You tell him if you get hurt again," her father spat out the words, "I'm coming after him."

****

A short while later they sat in a coffee shop in a booth that had just been vacated by five nurses on break. Arta stirred his tea while Eliana sipped her coffee and pressed the side of her head with her fingertips.

"I'm sorry you heard that. My father means well."

Arta nodded. "Understood. He loves you and wants you to come home safely." He took off his jacket and placed it on a chair at the end of the table. "Tell me about your mother."

Years of weariness fell away as she spoke of her mother. A smile played over her face, and the small crow's feet around her eyes disappeared.

"She was always *Ima* to me, the Hebrew word for mother. Musical, like her. She sang night and day, songs about Ethiopia, her childhood, the highlands, and her flight to Israel. Each morning she called to me in a low voice, like a flute. 'Wake up, my heart.' Each day, she walked me to school, stopped at the sidewalk, crouched down to my level, and said, 'You're a big, strong girl. Stand tall. Ask lots of questions.' Then she would kiss my forehead and say, 'May God bless you and keep you safe now and always.' Every night she read to me from Psalms. Each night, I fell asleep to the songs Ima said were written by our ancestor, King Solomon."

"Your childhood memories are so beautiful. She sounds like an Ethiopian June Cleaver." His mother, by contrast, had become a passionate activist the moment she hit American soil. Anger at the loss of women's rights under the Ayatollah Khomeini spurred her to establish an American foundation to raise money for the Women's Organization of Iran. She used her education, prose, and poetry as weapons, turning the words of Rumi and other mystics back onto the religious fanatics, pointing out their logical inconsistencies and blatant misogyny. Labeled a dangerous activist, even now his mother was banned from visiting elderly relatives who remained behind. His childhood was filled with the sounds of his mother working the telephones, calling newspapers, and raising funds to support her Persian sisters.

She held his gaze with those amazing green eyes. "I had a lovely childhood—until that night."

"What happened?"

"The only time my mother raised her voice in anger was at something I couldn't see." She stared at a spot over his head. "It was the first time I met a jinni."

The hair on the back of Arta's neck stood up.

Down boy. Control the lion. No need for shape-shifting now.

"We were leaving synagogue and a member of the funeral committee detained my father. It was fall, getting dark early. My mother said we'd have to hurry to get home in time to light the Sabbath candles." Her hands trembled, and she set the coffee cup down. "We walked past boarded up houses. So spooky, and Halloween was coming, too. She held my hand like a vise, practically dragged me down the street. A wind blew up and enveloped us. I felt like I was being bitten by a million fire ants."

She stopped. Tried to lift her cup, but her hand shook so hard, the coffee spilled. Eliana set the mug on the placemat.

Arta reached across the wooden table and grabbed both of her hands into his.

"Ima screamed in English, Hebrew, and languages I didn't understand. Ordered someone, something to go away, and called on God." Tears rolled down her cheeks. "The wind stopped and the tingling subsided. My mother told me to never forget that stinging and to run away from it. She said, 'They know who we are. They *want* people like us.' A year later, she was dead from acute myeloid leukemia. The disease came on so fast, so hard, the oncologists asked my father if she'd worked with uranium or radium." She closed her eyes and shook her head. "No *human* activity did that. She shielded me from an '*Ifrit*. And died because she protected me."

"Your survivor guilt is completely normal."

Anguish twisted her beautiful features. "Why was I spared? She was the kindest, most loving person in the world. After she died, I decided my life's work, my mission, was to track this creature and destroy him. Whatever it is, this *thing* has the power to kill humans. He stole my mother and my childhood. Now he's destroying the Adalwolf family. I feel so helpless."

She wiped away a single teardrop and gazed into the distance.

Arta stood and slid into the booth next to her. He put his arm around her shoulder and lowered his voice. "'Come, come, whoever you are, wonderer, worshipper, lover of leaving, it doesn't matter, ours is not a caravan of despair. Come, even if you have broken your vow a thousand times. Come, yet again, come, come.'"

Her voice hitched. "That's so beautiful. Is that your poet—Rumi?"

"Yes. It means you should be kind to yourself. Don't despair. You can stop running away from forgiveness. It's waiting for you."

"My mother wanted me to run the other way." She palmed a tear off her cheek. "But I can't. I must avenge her death. Maybe then I can forgive myself."

166

He nodded. "The Imam gave me some things to help you. And I need to tell you something important. Can we go someplace private?"

"Sorry. I'm not normally this emotional. It's this case. I keep thinking about those three girls and the babies. With only one girl alive now, I worry he's gearing up to attack others. The focus on werewolves, and the were-jinni babies, this isn't random. He's planning something."

"It's been bothering me, too." Arta slid out of the booth and offered his hand. "Your mother's story, none of this adds up. In all my research and the conversations with jinni experts, no one ever mentioned a jinni using radiation to attack a human. Even the *'Ifrit* we're dealing with now is using physical violence. Wait. The girl's throat had to have been covered in saliva. Did the police examine the body in the woods for radioactivity?"

Eliana stared up at him. "I don't remember seeing *any* radiation monitors. There's a handheld RID, a radiation isotope identifier, in the trunk of my car. Homeland equipped me for any and all hazards. Let's grab the RID and find the survivor and the girl who just died. If the alarm goes off, then we can let Chief Novak know we found a way to track this *'Ifrit* down. We'll need to let my boss know, too. He can get us more equipment. Something tells me the town is too small and too short on cash to equip their first responders with radiation monitors."

She slid out of the booth and stood in front of him.

"What did you want to tell me?"

"It can wait. This is more important. You're on to something." The case needed to be solved and with this possible lead, other things went on the back burner.

Would there ever be a good time to tell her what really happened in Arizona?

"No. It was you. You got me talking about my mother. You put the pieces together. You're a genius." She threw her arms around him, pulled him close, and planted kisses on his cheeks. One on the left, then right, then left.

Stunned by her affectionate assault, his brain took a leave of absence. His body was happy to respond on his behalf. He spoke for her ears only. "The next time you do that, we need to be somewhere private."

Flushing from her neck to the roots of her curly hair, she stepped away from him—much to Arta's disappointment. He cleared his throat and placed his folded jacket in a strategic location.

Her eyes sparkled with mischief. "When this case is over, you and I are going to have a long, intimate conversation. In the meantime, we've got work to do."

After a quick walk to the garage and a search for her car using the remote control panic button, Eliana pulled a beige metal unit the size and shape of a small shoe box with a black handle out of the trunk of her car and pressed the power button.

"Everything's a computer these days. I have to log in to use it. Takes a few minutes to get ready."

Arta peeked over her shoulder. "That thing resembles a clothes iron. How does it work?"

She glanced back at him and grinned. "Appearances can be deceiving. This is a small but powerful portable radioisotope identification system, or RID. It's sensitive to a wide range of radioactive materials. We can get real time visual results on this dial screen." She pointed at the gray area of the dial. "The default setting is 'Dial' and 'Finder.' When the needle's in this zone, the unit is detecting normal background radiation. Green means unusual activity. Red means get the hell out. I turned the audio on. The faster the clicking sounds, the greater the radiation."

"Are you picking anything up in here?"

She surveyed the garage. "These concrete walls serve as a shield. Good as any place to get a background radiation level."

She waved the unit over the closest internal wall and shrugged. "Gray zone. A couple of clicks. No big deal. Put your hands out, palms up."

"Why?"

"Checking you out. Humor me."

He complied and enjoyed the view of the top of her head and the side of her neck as she bent to her work. He suppressed an urge to bend down and nibble on her lovely, shell shaped ear.

"You're clear." She glanced up, caught him staring at her, and smiled. "Pretty eyes. Sometimes they're hazel, other times they're golden brown, almost like a cat."

Almost like a cat?

He wasn't quite ready to tell her that was because he was a shape-shifting Persian lion. He shrugged. "Trick of the light."

"Maybe." She pointed toward the exit. "The RID is still stabilizing, so I'll leave it on while we go back to the hospital." She started to walk and stopped short. "Hold on. I promised my father I'd wear the ring." She opened the driver door, reached in, and plucked out the seal.

"There." She slid the ring on her left hand. "You're my witness."

They walked down the stairs and the RID clicked once, twice. They hit the street and the clicking sound grew louder and more frequent.

"Hold on." She glanced down. "False alarm. The color is still gray. Must be cosmic radiation."

Arta scanned the intersection. Five in the evening and what passed for rush hour traffic in Summertown filled the street. A black pick-up stopped at the red light and blared country western music. The light changed to green and the truck driver honked his horn, once, twice, then leaned on it because some poor gray haired woman didn't hit the gas fast enough to suit him. The starter ground and the guy shouted, "Come on, lady."

Arta shook his head. *So much for country hospitality.*

Eliana pressed a button on a light pole and glanced down at the instrument. A bird chirped to indicate it was safe to cross. "Still gray. Let's go."

They hit the middle of the street. The cacophony of street noises paused for a moment and the distinct clicking sound of the RID grew louder.

"We're in the green zone."

"Should we stop?"

"Hell, no. We're on to something." She began to jog and Arta followed suit. Just as they were about to enter the hospital driveway to the ER, the unit went off like an enraged army of giant crickets.

CLICK, CLICK, CLICK, CLICK, CLICK, CLICK.

Eliana screeched to a halt, gasped, and pointed to the screen.

Buried in the red zone, the needle looked as if it was trying to jump off the dial.

His heart raced almost in time to the clicks. Cotton-mouthed, he could barely croak out the words. "What's going on?"

"Gamma rays. Cesium isotope. We need to evacuate the hospital and lock this place down. If the radiation isn't coming from our victims, we may be looking at a dirty bomb."

Chapter Fourteen

Jerusalem, 954 B.C.E.

Makeda's handmaidens giggled as she regaled them with every delicious detail of her night with her beloved. He deserved his reputation as a kind and gentle lover, especially since it was her first time with a man. As they prepared for the wedding and dressed Makeda in her raiment, all she could think of was how much she would enjoy spending more time with her new husband. After only one night, she knew he would give her all she desired every time they were together. Makeda closed her eyes and thrilled at the memory of his touch. She could hardly wait for the ceremony and festival to be over. She wanted him here and now.

"Look at yourself, my queen."

Makeda blinked and returned to the moment.

Her hairdresser held up a polished brass hand mirror for her to admire the jewels embedded in her hair, framing her face and twinkling in her braid.

She stared at her reflection. "Lovely."

"You are beautiful. You glow with a light from within. You found your heart."

"Queen Makeda?" One of the cook's children, a stick of a girl, stood in the doorway, her knobby knees shaking, and her eyes round and fearful as she twirled her hair around and around.

Her handmaidens shouted at the child to leave, she didn't belong here.

The little one began to cry. "He said it was important. He said he had to see you."

Makeda held her hand up and silence fell.

"Who? King Solomon?"

Eyes big as goose eggs, the girl shook her head and raised her hand high.

"A tall black man with a robe of many colors. He said I reminded him of you when you were a little girl."

"Tamrin." Makeda jumped to her feet. "Where is he?"

Solemn, the girl spoke in hushed tones. "Amay told me to bring you to him."

Makeda laughed. Cook was protecting her honor. "Tell your mother to bring him here. I'm surrounded by chaperones. No man shall touch me other than King Solomon." She nodded to the closest handmaiden. "Give the child a reward. She earned it."

The little one snatched the gold coin and ran away.

A short time later, the scowling Cook stood in the doorway.

"My daughter said you told her to bring him here." She peered into the queen's chambers and nodded. "Come."

Head bent to fit through the doorway, Tamrin stepped into the room, stopped, and stared at Makeda. The brightness of his smile dimmed, and he frowned as he glanced around the room.

"I was on my way to Jerusalem with tribute for the Temple and to bring you news from Sheba when tales of your wedding reached me." His handsome face twisted with grief, and tears welled in his large brown eyes. "I thought they were vicious stories told by your enemies to ruin your good name. Now I see it's true."

Heart in her throat, Makeda spoke to her closest handmaiden with a shaky voice.

"I would speak with Tamrin alone."

"My lady—"

"This man is my childhood friend and my trusted advisor. He will not harm me. Go."

Anxious whispers swept across the overcrowded room. They obeyed, but dawdled overlong, leaving the queen's chambers slower than she wished. "GO."

The women tumbled out the door, tripping over each other in their haste.

She pointed to a cushion and invited Tamrin to sit. He refused. The muscles in his jaw worked as if he were chewing on a horse's bridle. *He'd never been one to hold back. Why was he now?*

"Your eyes speak what your mouth won't. Go ahead. Tell me of your displeasure."

Fire filled his glare. "I doubt you want the truth."

Tempted to strike the stubborn mule of a man standing before her, she spoke through gritted teeth. "I. Said. Speak."

His words exploded from his lips, filling the room with his anger.

"What of your promises to your father and your kingdom to remain a virgin queen?" He twisted the hem of his garment with both hands. "You betrayed them both. How could you do this? You were supposed to come home, not stay here the rest of your life. Have you forgotten Sheba?"

A quiver of heated arrows flew from her lips. "How dare you. I was born to serve Sheba. All I do is to serve Sheba and my father's blessed memories. You urged me to come here to meet the wise King Solomon, remember? Then he ordered me to come to his court. To show myself. What choice did he give me? Our kingdom's survival hung on my obedience."

He shook his head. "You have changed. You would have never spoken to me like this before. So bitter, resentful. You, of all people, should know what you owe your kingdom."

"What about me? What do I owe myself? Don't I ever get to be happy? Can't I be in love and still be a queen?"

He fell to his knees, bowed his head, and wept.

"I have always loved you and could never marry you. You were the night sky, the moon and the stars, beautiful, smart, and beyond my reach."

Her vision blurred. She knelt before him and took his hands in hers. "Please don't hate me. I never expected to succumb to Solomon, to give my heart to any man. He is all you said he was and more. I consider you my brother. Don't abandon me."

His eyes narrowed. "There can only be one reason for this wedding. You are with child."

She dropped his hands. "What if I were?"

"Then you would not be able to be Queen of Sheba at the moment when we need you most." His glare burned into her soul even as his jaw locked into a hard line.

Her heart flew into her throat. "What is wrong?"

"Wogesha says the blackwater demons visit your uncle because you did not return to Sheba. He fears for your uncle's life."

She put her face in her hands. *First her father, now*

her uncle. Was there no end to these demons and their torture?

"Your grief will not force the demons to depart. Only your return to Sheba and taking back your throne can do that." Bitterness crept into Tamrin's voice. "But you are no longer a virgin and are about to marry a foreign king. You cannot be *our* queen. You may as well send a host of evil jinnis to destroy your kingdom."

Rage possessed her. She leaped to her feet and walked away from the man, lest she strike him. "You know *nothing* of evil jinnis, you stupid, jealous *boy*. This past year, each day an evil jinni filled with lust followed me. He wanted my sacred maiden-head, my virginity. Do you know who saved me? A shape-shifting lion. Yes, a man who can become a lion roared at him and drove him away. My beloved forced the jinni into an iron bottle with his seals."

Tamrin's mouth opened and closed like a fish.

"We weighted the jar with rocks and threw him into the Dead Sea. He is gone. Never to be released again. Would you prefer me to be taken by *that* creature?"

Shamed, her childhood friend cast his eyes down and shook his head.

"I watched King Solomon govern for over a year. He has shown me the way to be a good ruler and be happy. His invisible god has blessed him and is my God now, too. When I return to Sheba, I will still be queen and the nation will bow down to Adonai, who makes all things possible. He even made a queen wise enough to understand her virginity was never about being pure, but about waiting for her destiny."

Tamrin's shoulders shook, and his voice traveled to her on a sad sigh. "Will the wedding festival still take place?"

Captured by the power of the Lord, who surely spoke through her, she failed to recall that she was to appear at the ceremony to seal the union between the nations, even as she and Solomon sealed their love match the night before. Her wedding day joy plunged to despair. Two—no three hearts would be broken today. Sheba called. And she must go.

****

The rams' horns sounded, again and again. But instead of joy, they announced Solomon's sorrow to the world. He told his mother to feed the visitors and the guests, give them wine until they staggered home or passed out. It mattered naught to him. The person who understood him as a man and as a ruler, who made his heart leap with joy each morning he arose, the only woman he ever loved was leaving. Tears blurred his vision, and he wanted to howl with the pain that tore at his heart like a vulture.

He wanted her. She wanted him.

She could not stay. He could not go.

Only God knew what was to become of them.

Makeda, surrounded by a whirl of packing servants, wore the white garb she arrived in one year ago. Her purple dress, bedecked with emeralds and gold, lay across the bed, like a shriveled corpse of their nuptials.

He clasped her hand with his. "I cannot live without you. I will come with you."

She shook her head. "For a wise man, you are sounding foolish, my heart. You are needed here. If you leave, who will rule in your stead? Rehoboam? He is but a child and a spoiled one, at that. Israel needs you. The Temple remains incomplete. God will not be pleased if you don't obey Him."

His throat closed and choked his voice. "If only you could stay with me. Tamrin wants you for himself. What if he is lying about your uncle?"

"I ordered my women to spy on his caravan. All the travelers were talking about my uncle's illness. It is true." She removed her necklace, a gold medallion embossed with a pomegranate. "Keep this to remember me always."

He clasped it in his hand. "I will never take it off. I have something for you."

"My love, you gave me all I desired."

"After I left you, I returned to my chambers and napped. I dreamed of a brilliant sun which shone on Israel for years. And then it flew away to Sheba and stayed there in all its brightness, forever. I wanted the sun to come back to Israel, but it would not return to us. You are my light, my sun."

She sighed. "Solomon, I must go."

"You cannot go without my gifts. Everything that you wish for of splendid apparel, and riches are yours. Camels and six thousand wagons laden with beautiful things will go with you, along with a dozen of my finest horses, female and male so you will possess the best breeding stock. My soldiers will guard your route and oversee your journey to your border. Your throne will be returned to your land by another jinni."

"It is enough. Your love is enough." Tears filled her eyes. "God sends us on a journey we cannot understand. Only He sees the plan."

Solomon took off one of his rings and pressed it into Makeda's palm. "Take this to remember me. If the seed I planted in your womb is a boy, send him to me when he is a man. This ring shall be a sign he is the child born of our love."

She stared at the ring. "I will wear it always, and give it to our son when the time is right."

Unable to bear watching his beloved leave, he pressed his lips upon her forehead and said, "May God protect you and our child. Go in peace and know I will love you forever."

Solomon knocked into servants as he strode out of the room. He needed to be alone. The hills called him to return to the place where God first spoke to him and gifted him. He needed to go to Gibeon.

Benaiah caught up to Solomon as he rode toward the gates of Jerusalem. "Where are you going? You can't leave the city without a royal guard."

Solomon snarled at his captain. "I'm sure you and your men are happy now Makeda is leaving. Forgive me if I don't join you in rejoicing." He kicked the horse's flanks, ignoring the animal's startled protest. He was too hurt, too angry, to pay attention to anyone else's aches. His anguish was greater. The love match he prayed for had come and now she was leaving.

God laughs at our plans.

Benaiah shouted at men to mount their horses and follow the king.

Solomon's thoughts were a tumbled well of despair. Let the Philistines attack him, his heart had already been ripped out of his chest. Little was left of him now but an empty urn. He rode hard and furious, the wind tearing at his face, his eyes leaking. Sobs racked his body. Never again would he find such a woman, such a love. Beautiful, smart, gifted, noble, everything any man could wish for in one angelic form.

Makeda, Makeda, Makeda. Makeda.

The horse's hooves pounded her name into his heart and soul. He shouted his rage into the wind and screamed "Why?" to the skies. Flocks of birds flew in disarray, shrieking their dismay at his pain. The roars of lions disturbed from their rest echoed his anguish. All the animals in his kingdom twisted, writhed, and groaned with his agony.

He came to a stream and allowed his winded stallion to drink deeply. Regret for his harsh treatment of the loyal steed nibbled at his conscience. He stroked the animal's flanks and apologized for his cruel behavior. The horse shook his mane and continued to drink. In the distance, Benaiah's men shouted and called his name. Solomon washed his face and hands with the cool water and sat on a rock. *What was this place?* He'd traveled the width and breadth of the land, yet this area was strange to him. Silence folded around him like a blanket and he felt the presence of God.

"Solomon." The Lord's small voice spoke to him. "Why do you despair?"

"My Lord, do you not behold my anguish? You give me soaring happiness and the depths of grief on the same day. Why do you do this to me?"

"Do you love me above all other gods?"

"Yes, you know I worship you alone."

"Then why do you build shrines to others?"

Solomon shook his head. "I'm building a Temple for you."

"What of the others? The ones in Jerusalem. The

ones your wives keep."

He covered his face with his hands. "I must marry to make alliances. I need to be tolerant of other ways, other religions. It is how I keep my borders and my people safe."

The Lord's small voice grew louder, displeasure coating each word. "Did you not listen to your father as he lay dying? Did the great King David not tell you to walk in the ways of the Lord at all times?"

"I keep the Sabbath, I observe your laws. Your priests and prophets control Israel. Isn't that enough? Let the women have their Asherahs. They are nothing more than wooden dolls. They are powerless, they are nothing like you."

"The Queen of Sheba now worships me and promised her nation will worship me, too. If the woman you say you love can do this for me, why can't you, my favorite among men?"

Solomon rubbed his knuckles into his eyes. *Did Adonai think the goddess a rival?*

"You took Makeda from me because women worshipped their own gods? I cannot think, cannot breathe, and cannot eat, for grieving over her. You gave me my greatest joy and punished me by ripping it out of my hands on my wedding day. I hungered and thirsted for this soul mate. You placed a feast before me, and then took it away. I'm a man who sees water in the desert and drinks sand, thanks to you. My God is a jealous god, indeed."

He closed his eyes and wished he'd brought his sharpest sword to fall upon.

Someone touched his shoulder. He threw his hand behind him. "Cut my throat. *Please.* You will end my sorrow and pain. I cannot bear to live another day."

"My king, I would not harm a hair on your head, nor would I allow anyone else to hurt you."

Solomon opened his eyes. Benaiah knelt beside him, his sun-bronzed face lined with sorrow.

"I bring terrible news about your mother."

Chapter Fifteen

Summertown, Present Day

Eliana decided the only good thing about the hot, humid environment of West Virginia was if they found radiation contamination victims who needed to be hosed down, they wouldn't complain about the temperature of the sixty-five degree fire hydrant water. Sweat dripped inside her bulky personal protective equipment, or PPE, and she knew it was only a matter of time before Rob Pearson, the Incident Commander, insisted Eliana and the other agents rotate out. So far, only the pregnant and the deceased werewolf girls had shown anything above normal background radiation. The deceased girl's body emitted over three-hundred rem.

Per the CDC and the Radiation Emergency Medical Management algorithms, in humans the risk of hemorrhaging commenced at one-hundred rem. A radiation induced miscarriage was not out of the question. To the best of the knowledge of the experts at the CDC, however, there were no studies on the effects of radiation exposure among werewolves. Had the radiation caused the miscarriage—or something else? At any rate, they had to prevent her from exposing more people. The deceased girl's body now sat at the local funeral home in a lead lined coffin, awaiting a memorial service and placement in the Adalwolf family crypt.

Containing the dangerous radiation in the lead-lined coffin was a rule straight out of the radiation management textbook.

Managing the surviving pregnant werewolf's condition, on the other hand, was not. Upon admission to the hospital the night before, the girl was diagnosed with dehydration, exposure, and *hyperemesis gravidarum*. Unable to keep any food or fluids down, she was on continuous intravenous fluids. Eliana surveyed the girl with her radioisotope identifier, or RID, and did a double-take.

That couldn't be right.

She keyed her helmet radio. "Novak, could you come over here for a minute? I need you to check something."

Encased in PPE, the Chief waved to an ambulatory patient to move on to the cold triage for minimal care. She lumbered over to Ellie. "What's up?"

Eliana pointed to the blonde on the gurney. "Would you survey Brigette for me please?"

Eyes wide, tears trickled down the side of Brigette's face. "What's wrong?"

"Chief Novak is just checking with her equipment to see if mine is working correctly."

Hands on her abdomen, a sheet draped across her torso over her hospital gown, Brigette's bruised and scratched arms and legs gave mute witness to her escape through the thick forest the night before. Ellie's heart went out to her. The girl had been through so much. To make matters worse, she was pregnant with her rapist's baby and suffering from debilitating nausea and vomiting. *What could be worse than that?*

Novak passed the wand over Brigette's head, down her neck to her shoulders. The instrument clicked at twice the normal rate. "Arms by your side, palms up, please."

Brigette complied and Novak continued her examination. She approached the young woman's abdomen, and the clicking increased in frequency. The noise grew louder when she placed the wand directly over the baby bump. Novak moved the wand down to the girl's legs, and the noise ebbed. The roar of angry crickets re-commenced when she moved back to the baby bump.

The girl trembled and sobbed, "What's wrong with me?"

"Brigette, you're contaminated with radioactive material. We think it might just be on the surface. We need to scrub you down." The girl attempted to sit up. Eliana placed a hand on Brigette's shoulder. "You're too sick to do it yourself. We'll do it for you."

She called for a physician to supervise the proceeding and for another female to assist them. Novak rolled the gurney into the decontamination tent and elevated her so the water would run off. The team divvied up the girl into quadrants using her waistline for demarcation of zones. They washed, rinsed, and wiped each section of the girl's body using soap, water, and soft sponges. Once wiped, the girl was showered using the same approach. After the front surfaces were cleansed, they rolled the girl onto her side and the process was repeated. Every effort was made to preserve her modesty and to assist her when bouts of vomiting overcame her. After she was completely decontaminated, and the wash water was collected for processing and disposal, Eliana surveyed her again.

Dammit. The meter showed a modest decrease, but not a significant one.

Three-hundred rem. How could that be? She should be sicker, with uncontrollable bleeding in her mouth.

She wrapped a second blanket around Brigette. The girl smiled, nodded, then stiffened. Brigette frowned, arched her back, and closed her eyes, and began to shake so hard, Eliana feared she'd fall. The blankets slid to the ground as Brigette thrashed, and Eliana struggled to keep the girl from sliding off the end of the gurney.

The PPE encased physician lumbered away and returned in a few minutes with a crash cart and a Rapid Response Team. He removed his heavy rubber gloves, beneath which were latex gloves, and injected an anticonvulsant. A nurse took her vital signs and checked her IV. Gradually, the thrashing stopped, the labored breathing slowed, and the girl appeared to sleep.

Eliana stepped back to give the team room and gasped. The baby bump was larger than it had been just thirty minutes before.

Things *could* be worse. Not only was the girl pregnant by her rapist, but the were-jinni was growing at an exponential rate. To top it all off, Brigette wasn't suffering from hyperemesis gravidarum. She was suffering from acute radiation sickness, ARS. Based on the survey readings, the girl's onset of vomiting, and the neurological involvement, a human would be given less than forty-eight hours to live. But Brigette was a werewolf.

Not only were there no studies of werewolves and radiation, she had no idea how they regenerated so quickly from wounds. At first she thought this was only an act of revenge, a blood feud from biblical times. Did the jinni know the werewolves were super-healers, resistant to the effects of radiation that would kill humans? At any rate, he acquired a double dip with Brigette—a robust breeding vessel *and* revenge.

She passed the wand over the girl's belly one more time, and the clicks of enraged crickets burst into the air. Would the baby survive or succumb to the radiation? Or was the were-jinni the *source* of the radiation?

Whatever the outcome, right now they had to get Brigette into a lead-shielded space, like an X-ray room, draw blood samples to assess the radiation dose, obtain urine and fecal samples to determine if there were other isotopes at play, and begin treatment with Prussian blue to counteract the cesium. *If* they could get the Prussian blue into her. *If* the girl lived the thirty days for the drug to attach to the radioactive isotope and drag it out of the girl's body. *If* the were-jinni didn't explode from the girl's abdomen like a scene out of a sci-fi horror movie. *If* she survived, would Brigette be able to mother a newborn were-jinni? Would she want to mother the infant?

Could anyone?

Time was of the essence. The ARS protocol had to be initiated ASAP. She took the bespectacled physician aside and briefed him on everything, including the possibility that the source of the radiation could be the baby. Eliana found his composure unnerving.

Why was he so calm?

As if in response to her unspoken question the doctor nodded and said, "Summertown is my home, has been most of my life. I'm related by marriage to the Adalwolf family. I'm also in the Navy Reserves. I treated sailors who worked in the radioactive plumes after the Fukishima disaster. I'll take charge of her care. If you find out anything else I need to know, tell the hospital operator to page Doctor Goodman."

Relieved Brigette was in his hands, Eliana sighed as she watched the gurney roll away with the girl to isolate her in an X-ray suite. Right now, she needed to inform Pearson of this latest finding. The radiocomm crackled to life.

Pearson's voice boomed. "Solomon, you're wanted at the command tent. Now. We've got a situation."

"I've got a situation, too, sir." Still in her PPE, she walked the half mile to the cold zone all the while briefing Pearson about Brigette.

A short time later in the Incident Command, or IC tent, she towered over the portly Summertown Medical Center CEO. From the soles of his expensive wingtip shoes, to the custom made suit, to the dead animal toupee lounging on his head, Joe Dowling bore out every stale stereotype of hospital administrators. Oily with sweat, his round face remained immobile even as he shouted at Eliana and Pearson.

"I'm the CEO, I give the Code Black order to evacuate, no one else. It's my job, my decision, my hospital, my patients, my staff, how dare you—"

"I tried to call you, *sir*," Eliana interjected between the man's outbursts, "but your administrative assistant said you couldn't be disturbed."

He shook his finger at her face. "I was in an *extremely* important meeting."

Eliana refused to back down. "In addition, *sir,* your assistant refused to give me any contact information for the chair of your board of trustees, who is authorized to issue a Code Black, also." She nodded at the salt-and-pepper haired Pearson. "At that point, I had no choice but to call the code and to loop in Dr. Pearson, the Director of the West Virginia Division of Homeland Security and Emergency Management. I gave your organization the courtesy of two attempts to manage this. You *chose* not to be available in an emergency."

The CEO spoke through gritted teeth. "I was in ambulatory surgery, having a *private* medical procedure."

Botox injections or hair transplants?

"I beg to differ, *sir*. You weren't *in* the hospital. The SPD and West Virginia State Troopers blockaded the streets around SMC. They called me to get permission to allow you through the blockades. The only reason you're here is because *I* cleared you."

His face flushed to the roots of his ugly hairpiece. "All these troubles started after you arrived in Summertown. I'm lodging a complaint. In fact, I'm betting you created this incident just to destroy our business, embarrass our town, and ruin the wine festival. Chief Novak should—"

"I should do what, Terry?" The tall redhead emerged from the side of the big blue tent. "Call your wife? Tell her where you *really* were?"

His mouth flapped open, and he flew into a tantrum, complete with foot stamping. "You—you—women! Always sticking up for each other, always stirring up trouble. Mayor Schaeffer serves on my board. I'll have your job."

"Mr. Dowling," Pearson interrupted. "Did you lose sight of the fact that we are in the middle of a radiation emergency? There's no time for this pissing contest. Either you help us, or you will be removed from the area. Then you can explain to your trustees and the townspeople where you were today. Your call."

The CEO glared at Eliana and Chief Novak and turned to Pearson.

"I want a status report before I help you. You may be the incident commander, but I'm still responsible for this hospital."

Pearson nodded. "As soon as Agent Solomon identified gamma rays from cesium isotopes, she ordered the SMC page operator to call a Code Black. Thanks to good training, the SMC emergency response team evacuated vertically, from the top floor down. Your staff led ambulatory patients down stairways and into the warm triage zone. As the walking patients moved through warm triage with tracking paperwork in hand, agents surveyed each person for radiation contamination, beginning with their head and neck, going down their arms, hands, torso, groin, legs, feet and shoes." Pearson took a breath and shook his head. "The sicker patients required a greater number of staff to move the bed and equipment. One ICU patient with intravenous bags, oxygen tanks, and multiple other pieces of vital machinery required three staff members to pack up and transport him in safety."

Dowling sighed. "Thank God this wasn't flu season."

"All but one of your patients is in the cold zone

now. Brigette Adalwolf is in an X-ray suite that's been converted to an isolation room. Dr. Goodman is treating her for ARS. Out here in the cold zone, your intensivist is reviewing the sickest patients to see if they need to be transferred to another hospital. Other physicians, including a psychiatrist, are seeing the ambulatory patients."

"A psychiatrist? There's no psych unit. Who is it?"

Eliana spoke up. "Dr. Arta Shahani."

Pearson continued. "Psychological and emotional decontamination is important, too. Otherwise, people worry about short and long-term effects of radiation, not realizing they're exposed to it every day."

Dowling scowled. "Sounds like you took care of everything. You don't need me to do anything."

Pearson held his hand up. "Hold on. SMC is one of the largest employers in Summertown. Add in visitors, candy-stripers, and volunteers and we're looking at about five hundred people we need to track. The head of volunteers is working on her list, plus the list of visitors, including vendors, and sales reps. The VP of Nursing said all her on-duty nurses and aides are accounted for, per unit charge nurses' tracking tools. And each department manager has a list of his or her shift personnel, too. The only department we're missing is the morgue. How many people do you normally have working there?"

"One. We don't get a lot of dead people in SMC. The morgue attendant reports to the pathologist. He's away at a medical conference." Dowling pulled a smart phone out of his pocket. "I can access the hospital intranet and get the names of everyone who logged in with their magnetic ID cards today. When her boss is out of town, Janie likes to play hooky." He shook his head. "Teenagers."

Eliana raised an eyebrow. "And she still works for you?"

"Small town. We don't get a lot of applicants who want to care for the dead."

Dowling tapped at his phone several times, squinted, tapped again. "Janie didn't swipe in today. She still lives at home." He held the phone up to his ear. "I'm calling her mother."

"Hi, Mrs. Schaeffer. It's Joe Dowling." He nodded. "Yeah, things are pretty crazy right now. Is Janie there?" His eyes grew wider. "Are you sure? Could you check her room, please? It's important. I'll hold."

She caught Dowling's gaze. "Schaeffer? As in Mayor Schaeffer?"

He nodded. "No, no need to panic, Mrs. Schaeffer. I'm sure she's around here somewhere. We'll find her." He pressed the end button. "Now what the hell do we do? It's the mayor's eighteen-year-old daughter we're talking about."

"Maybe she misunderstood the code and sheltered in place instead of evacuating. I'll lead a small team into the hot zone, looking for her and any other stragglers." Eliana picked her PPE helmet up from the table. "You, on the other hand, Mr. Dowling, get to stay here in the cold zone, safe and sound."

A look of surprise crossed the arrogant man's face. *Yeah. That's why they pay me the big bucks. Not.*

She turned to Novak. "You in or out?"

Novak grabbed her PPE gear. "Janie knows and trusts me. Let's go find her."

What if Janie wasn't in the hospital? Then what?

Where should they look for a teen-aged girl with a predator on the loose? Despite the heat, a chill slid down Ellie's back.

Oh, God, not the mine tunnels, please. Anything but that.

****

Pressed into service, Arta focused on meeting patient needs for comfort and emotional support. Anxiety and questions about the health effects of radiation exposure floated over the cold zone tents like a mushroom cloud.

"Am I going to get cancer?"

"Will my skin fall off?"

"Will my hair fall out?"

"Omigod, I'm pregnant! What about my baby?"

A gnarled hand seized his jacket as he moved down the line of cots.

"Am I going to die?"

Arta sat next to the elderly woman, took her hand in his and gazed deep into her eyes. "We are all going to die, however this incident is unlikely to contribute to your death."

"I was in the long-term care unit getting rehab for my hip replacement. At the time of the surgery, I thought sure I'd die on the table. I didn't. Then I thought I'd die in the rehab unit. I didn't die then, either. I was hoping this disaster would be the end for me. I'm tired of living." A tear slid down her wrinkled cheek. "No family, no one visits me. I'm tired of being alone."

"How long have you been unhappy?"

"A year. That's when my husband passed away. I can't go on without him, but I'm not taking my last breath, either." She sighed. "Why can't I be with him? I'm so lonely."

"God does not show us His plans. We only get glimpses." Behind the woman, an elderly man in a wheel chair leaned forward, listening to every word of the conversation. "Sometimes a disaster can be an opportunity. What is your name, my dear lady?"

"Bessie. Bessie Haverford Harris. And yours?"

"Arta Shahani. I'm a psychiatrist, doing some work in the area." He pointed to the elderly man. "What is your name, sir?"

"Carl Hogan." He waved. "Bessie, do you remember me from typing class in high school?"

"Carl Hogan! You're still alive? I thought you died in a motorcycle accident."

"Lost a leg, not my life. Or my love of life."

"You were always in trouble." She flushed. "I remember when you snapped my bra. You were very naughty."

"You didn't seem to mind."

Arta whispered in Bessie's ear, "Remember, we don't know God's plans."

He stood and said in a louder voice, "I'll let you two get reacquainted." Behind him, as he left the yellow tent, Bessie giggled and said, "Carl, you rascal!"

He wished he could charm Eliana the way Carl did Bessie. Perhaps he'd start snapping her bra. His phone buzzed in his pants pocket. *Speak of the devil.*

"I was just thinking of you. Where are you?"

"I'm in the hospital morgue, on their landline."

"Is it safe for you to be there?"

"The place shows normal background radiation now that the deceased girl is out of here."

"Why are you in there?"

"I came here looking for the morgue attendant, thought maybe she got confused and sheltered in place instead of evacuating. There are signs of a struggle. And blood."

"Damn. Shouldn't you call the police?"

"Chief Novak is with me. She's calling her crime scene techs now." Eliana paused and lowered her voice. "He's got the mayor's daughter. The place reeks of jinni stink."

Chapter Sixteen

Jerusalem, 953 B.C.E.

Solomon lay in his darkened bed chamber and prayed for the courage to kill himself. Almost nine moons ago, he lost both his love match and his mother on the same day. God could have sent cattle deaths, boils, frogs, hail, pestilence, and locusts to his land. Instead, He sent Makeda home to salvage her nation and killed Bathsheba with an earthquake that toppled rocks onto her as she went forth to prepare his wedding feast. The mountains rumbled, shook, and split down the sides. Thunder and lightning rent the sky, fires blazed in the hills, even the Dead Sea rocked. The Lord stabbed the spear of His wrath into Solomon's heart and twisted it for good measure.

He rolled over on his bed and came eye to eye with Basemath and Taphath. His daughters knelt by his bed and stared at him.

"What are you doing, my little ones?"

Taphath, the younger girl, gasped and fell over backward.

Basemath glanced back at her half-sister. "I told you he wasn't dead."

"Who said I went down to Sheol?"

The older girl sing-songed, "Rehoboam said you were dying, and he was going to be king and kick us out of the palace along with our mothers."

Solomon flopped back on the bed. *Damn that child's spiteful lies.* Naamah must be filling his head with poison. If Bathsheba were alive, she would skin the Ammonitess with her tongue.

"Abba?" Taphath whispered.

He sighed. "Yes, my little rose?"

"Why is your hair so long?"

"I'm in mourning for your grandmother. I'm forbidden to cut my hair." Truth be told, the time for remaining unshaven was long gone.

"Abba?" Taphath whispered again.

Why didn't she ask her questions all at once? "Yes, my little one?"

"Why is there a stench in here?"

He sat bolt upright, threw the blanket off the bed, and swung his legs over the edge of the platform.

Taphath's eyes grew as big as twin moons, and she backed into her big sister's knees.

"She didn't mean it, Abba." Basemath hurried to defend the tiny child.

His heart sank at his daughters' terrified expressions. At what point did he become a demon who struck fear into the hearts of children? He scrubbed his face with his hands and his seals caught in his long black beard. He could be taken for a Nazarene, one of those religious zealots who never shaved and never cut their hair. Hazarding a sniff at his clothes, he drew back in disgust. In all this time, not a single adult offered a suggestion to the king about his cleanliness—or lack thereof.

Wisdom from the mouth of a child.

"Taphath, you are correct. I'm not dead, but the

stench on my clothes is that of a corpse."

She shook her head. "No. You stink like a goat."

Basemath clapped her hand over her sister's mouth. "Please, tell Rehoboam you aren't dead. He's been pushing all the children around, telling everyone he's going to toss them out into the desert without water."

Solomon placed his hand over his heart. "As God is my witness, I promise to speak to Rehoboam." *And his snake-tongued mother.* "Thank you for saving me. Come now, give me a hug—"

The girls bolted out of the room as if an evil spirit chased them.

In the courtyard below, a shrill voice scolded the girls for bothering their father.

Naamah. No time like the present for taking care of that bad business.

He strode to the window and pulled back the blanket. The sun, long forbidden from his chamber, blinded him. He shielded his eyes, peered down into the dusty street, and searched for that liar, Naamah.

Carpenters, bricklayers, shape-shifters, and jinnis, once industrious on the temple construction, thronged the square begging for coins and food. Adoniram was in charge of labor. Why did he stop work on the temple? Soldiers marched by, swords clanging on their shields to drive the hungry crowds back.

Unemployed laborers? Soldiers patrolling the streets? In his kingdom? Adoniram and Benaiah must be mad. He'd have their heads. No, it was his fault, not theirs.

Solomon dropped the blanket and hung his head in shame. The guilt of the theft of nine moons, nine hundred sunrises he stole from his kingdom weighed on his chest like a boulder. He had been called by God to lead his kingdom to greatness. Instead, he allowed his broken heart to overcome his wisdom. He'd withdrawn from the world and left his nation without a leader. Rather than punishing the captain of his soldiers for maintaining order while the king hid away from his people, Solomon should reward him with gold and beg his forgiveness.

Nine moons he had lain in bed, rising only to eat and use the chamber pot. In all that time, no adult dared reproach him with words or looks. Neither Zadok, nor Nathan, nor Benaiah confronted him. Not even the brash Hoopoe spoke up. Where was that bird? Solomon deserved to be deserted. He abandoned his family, throne, and country as long as it took for a woman to give birth.

Birth.

If Makeda was pregnant when she left Jerusalem, as the Lord had told him, even now she could be in labor somewhere in the desert, screaming out in pain. Childbirth, a harrowing event for the hardiest of women, was the most dangerous time of a woman's life. Would she survive? Would the baby survive? Would he ever see them again?

Not if he stayed in bed like a weak old man he wouldn't.

Time for a change. He bellowed for his household administrator.

"Ahishar, get in here. Now."

The sound of sandals slapping on the rock floor reminded him of flapping wings. Yes, he needed one more aide. *Now, where was that chattering busy body bird?*

****

Makeda's swollen belly, legs, and ankles made any movement difficult, and she could no longer climb on the mare with ease. Tamrin had to cup his hands and assist her onto the horse's back. Each sunrise, when they camped and slept through the heat of the desert day, she fell exhausted onto the heap of perfumed pillows and blankets her handmaidens prepared for her. After nine moons and relentless pushing through the desert nights, they were so close to home, she could smell the moisture in the air, feel its droplets on her skin, but still could not spare precious water for a bath, not even for a queen. If only she could hold out a bit longer, if only she could reach the Blue Nile's waters, Makeda would sink into its cool depths and wash the dust of the long journey from her swollen body. The baby had taken over her life, demanding food, water, rest—and kicking her with the vigor of a young stallion.

As she leaned from side to side to ease the soreness in her lower back, Makeda closed her eyes and thought of her young stallion, the man who filled her thoughts, dreams, soul, and belly with his seed. *Solomon.* Moonrise after moonrise, she relived the pleasure of his lips on her mouth, neck, breasts, and belly. The blissful memories of his soft caresses helped her to pass the long night rides. Not only had God given him a wise and discerning mind, but also many gifts, not the least of which were his abilities to woo and bed a woman. No other king would ever compare with Solomon. No other man would ever touch her. He was her only love.

I am dark and beautiful, daughters of Jerusalem. Solomon came to me, not you.

On the night water trickled down her leg unbidden, Makeda told Tamrin they could travel no more. She called for the midwife. The gap-toothed woman placed her hands at the baby's head and dancing feet to estimate the child's size. Makeda was tall for a woman. However, even the midwife was astounded by the baby's magnitude.

Her brow furrowed with concern, the midwife spoke in low tones meant for one set of ears. "My queen, I have delivered many babies in my time. Never have I brought one this large into the world in one piece."

Fear gripped her heart. Thinking she misheard, Makeda clutched the older woman's thin arm. "What are you saying?"

"I'm sorry, but to save your life, I may need to cut the baby into pieces."

"You'll do no such thing." Rage bubbled up in her throat. "Get away from me." Makeda pushed the woman so hard she fell over backward.

The crone grabbed a tent pole to pull herself to her feet. "Everyone in the caravan agrees, it would be a good thing if the baby did not survive." Her wheedling tone was not lost on Makeda. "Instead of returning to Aksum in disgrace, you can remain the Virgin Queen. Return with honor and riches from your trip to Israel, instead of hanging your head in shame. Your country needs you. The baby, on the other hand—"

"Is the heir to two kingdoms." The queen spoke between gritted teeth to keep from screaming. "Get out of here before I have you killed."

The hag fled the tent. *Lucky for her.* Makeda always carried a hunting knife at her hip. A moment longer, she would have thrown the blade at the crone's breast. Did the woman not know betraying her country was punishable by death? Did she truly speak for others? Who among her people plotted to kill her son? *Was Tamrin part of this conspiracy?* Had his jealousy led to revenge against Solomon's unborn child or was the crone spewing her own madness? About to give birth, the Queen was vulnerable to attack by loyalists who believed her father's lies. She looked at the group of women servants huddled outside the royal tent, and wondered if they, too, planned to chop the baby into pieces. She should have accepted Solomon's offer of a bodyguard from the first born of each tribe of Israel. She hugged her belly. Who among her servants was the most trustworthy?

There was only one who had already risked her life for the Queen of Sheba.

She called Tehetena, the woman who pretended to be queen when she met Solomon. The handmaiden knelt at the Queen's feet.

Makeda glanced around and whispered the midwife's threats. "You and I must leave this place. He will not be safe until he is born. You must help me deliver this child. Alone."

Tehetena bit her lower lip and nodded. "I heard rumors, but never thought the midwife would take part. We can go into the hills, make a camp hidden from the others."

"I will pretend to sleep. You must gather up food, water, and supplies. We will slip away in the middle of the night."

The young woman's lower lip trembled. "The soldiers saw packs of red wolves circling our camp. The risk will be great to us."

"The risk is greater if we stay here. Some humans are more treacherous than wolves."

****

The camp slumbered at last. Makeda and Tehetena led the queen's faithful mare laden with food, water, blankets, and birthing tools taken from the sleeping midwife. The women made their way by the light of the full moon, careful to stay in the shadows, away from the eyes of the guards, away from rocks and hard surfaces that would betray their progress. Frantic to get away from her murderous subjects, Makeda prayed for the strength to keep walking between each cramp that gripped her abdomen.

Lord, give me time, protect my son from those who would harm him, keep him safe.

From the corner of her eye, Makeda saw one low slung shadow running alongside them, keeping pace with them, then another shadow joined the first one, then another, and another. A deep abdominal pain gripped Makeda, stealing her breath.

In a flash, a large wolf leaped up on an outcropping of rock and stared down at her. A shaft of moonlight shone on the red wolf, and Makeda locked gazes with the regal animal. It wasn't the mother wolf she'd met when she was five, but a descendant of that one. He knew the promise Makeda made and kept throughout her rule—the red wolves were protected, never hunted by her people.

Tehetena gripped the queen's arm. The whites of her eyes huge in her face, she spoke in a low voice. "The wolves are going to attack us."

Makeda shook her head, and sweat flew off her

brow. "We. Are. Safe."

The leader locked gazes with Makeda. *I will take you to a hiding place.*

The abdominal pain receded, and she pointed at the wolf. "Follow him."

Tehetena's mouth fell open. "You can speak to wolves?"

The queen merely began to walk in the direction the wolf led them.

"My queen, they are called tricksters for a reason. You cannot trust them."

Makeda stopped, turned, and regarded her terrified servant. "This was promised to me as a child when I spared the life of a mother and her pups. They will not harm you, nor will they harm me and my baby, unlike our traveling companions. You may follow me, or go back to be tortured at the hands of those who wish to find me."

Shaking her head, Tehetena followed Makeda and the wolf.

The animal led Makeda over the outcropping, through a cleft and into a large cave. The horse whinnied and ambled to the edge of an underground stream. Four wolves entered and lapped at the fresh water next to the mare. Tehetena unpacked the horse, placed bedding on the rock flooring, and filled the empty water gourds.

An iron grip seized Makeda's belly, and she doubled over in agony. "He's coming."

Tehetena lowered her to the blankets and raised Makeda's skirt.

"I know little of childbirth, my Queen. I pray my hands do the Lord's work."

Makeda pressed down and pushed. Stopped. Panted. "Is the baby here yet?"

"No. But the blood, it's heavy and bright red. I fear I will lose you."

"Bring the knife. Cut me open if you must. Save the child."

Tehetena held the gleaming blade in her hand, tears running down her face. "If I cut you open, I may hurt the child and lose you both."

"Dear Lord, I beg of you, help me in my hour of need."

A soundless explosion of light dazzled Makeda.

Tehetena gasped and slid to the floor.

When her vision adjusted to the light, Makeda was ecstatic to see her prayers had been answered. Metatron stood before her, filling the cave with his luminous presence. He stared down his prominent nose with eyes the color of the morning sky. His wings stroked Makeda's cheeks, and the pain disappeared.

She sighed. "Thank you."

"Don't thank me yet. We need to wake up your handmaiden." He touched Tehetena's cheek with a wing.

Her eyes fluttered, then opened. "My Lord."

He shook his head and sparks flew into the stream, sizzling as they hit. "Not your Lord. The Lord's scribe and messenger."

Tehetena bowed her head. "What is it you wish me to do?"

He inclined his head toward Makeda. "Catch the baby."

Tehetena scrambled to the queen's side, grabbed a silk cloth, and placed it between her thighs. Makeda burst into tears when she saw the baby slide out of her body and into Tehetena's waiting hands.

A multitude of angels in different sizes, colors, and shapes appeared in the grotto and exploded into song. "*Kadosh, kadosh, kadosh*! Holy, holy, holy, the Lord God is all mighty!"

The wolves joined in howling and yipping with joy.

Tehetena cleaned the child, tied the cord with silk thread, and placed the infant on his mother's breast. He began to suckle at once. Makeda marveled at his ten fingers and toes, his fat cheeks, perfect thighs, and adorable buttocks. When he raised his head to take in his new world, she gasped. He had his father's nose and eyes. Truly the Lord and Solomon had given her all she desired.

Metatron's voice boomed in the cave. "How will he be known?"

The host of angels stopped singing and leaned in. Even the horse and wolves drew near.

Tears blurring her vision, Makeda said, "He is the child of the union of two great nations. He will need to learn to rule with compassion and wisdom. He shall be called Menelik, the son of a wise man."

Chapter Seventeen

Summertown, Present Day

With PPE piled by her feet, Eliana stood in the cold zone tent and briefed Pearson, Dowling, and Arta on the crime scene techs' preliminary findings. "It appears the girl struggled with her assailant. I found equipment knocked over and a scalpel covered in blood in the hallway leading out the back door." She sighed and shook her head. "I don't understand why he's going after humans now. Humans aren't resistant to radiation sickness, they can't tolerate his offspring's energy."

Dowling broke his silence. "She's not human."

Eliana stared at the hospital CEO. "You told us Janie was Mayor Schaeffer's daughter."

"Legally, yes—biologically, no. Winifred Adalwolf was pregnant with her first litter when her husband died in a car crash. The stress combined with a congenital heart condition—well—doctors told her if her heart gave out, she'd lose all the babies. She needed a thallium scan, signed a waiver. Did the test. Lost two pups. Janie's the sole survivor. Schaeffer married Winifred when Janie was a baby and adopted her."

So Shifty Schaeffer wasn't all bad.

She revised her opinion of the pompous politician.

Dowling raised an eyebrow. "Of course, it didn't hurt that Winifred had millions of dollars and he needed money for his mayoral bid."

On second thought.

"What the hell's going on? Where's my daughter?"

Speak of the devil.

Mayor Schaeffer huffed and puffed and his face oozed sweat—and fear.

The reason for his terror trailed five steps behind him. Between sobs, Winifred Schaeffer squeezed Eliana's arm. "Please. I beg of you. Janie's my only child. That monster already killed two other girls."

"The police are working the scene now, Mrs. Schaeffer."

The older woman clutched her chest. "I can't bear to lose another child. Can't *you* do *something*?"

She exchanged glances with Arta. He gave her a small nod. *Okay, he was game.* "I don't want to make any promises, but we might be able to track him." She paused. "Is it true Janie was exposed to radioactive thallium *in utero*?"

The large woman's bosom heaved. "Yes." She dabbed at her eyes with a fist full of tissues. "A heart blockage. I needed a stent or I was going to die. What does this have to do with Janie?"

"She may be immune to some forms of radiation, which will protect her. If we had an idea of who we were looking for, that would give us a better idea of where to start."

Winifred looked surprised. "Didn't Lowell give you my message?"

Eliana shook her head.

"My women went house to house, business to business, conducting a town census, just like you asked. A few missing men were accounted for by their families. Out of town, on business trips, whatever." She took a deep breath and dabbed her eyes. "There was one we couldn't track down, and no one has seen for over a week. I left a message with Cousin Lowell that we needed to find out where he is. After all, he's Lowell's employee."

Eliana held her breath. "Who's missing?"

The mayor's wife shook her head. "I hate to point fingers. He's always been a loner. Reclusive, doesn't like people much. He may be off in the vineyards, doing his thing."

She bit her tongue to keep from screaming. "Who?"

"The winemaker from Livonia. Old Thiess. We can't find him anywhere."

Eliana grabbed her PPE and opened a storage locker.

"Arta, grab one of these. We're going hunting."

In the last place she wanted to be. The tunnels beneath the winery.

****

Government sedan packed to the hilt with every possible piece of survival gear she could grab along the way to the car, Eliana stood with her hand on the driver's door and stared at Arta's contributions.

"What are the book and the bottle for?"

"If Old Thiess is possessed, these will help to drive the jinni out." He re-wrapped the book and a white kufi in tissue and returned the bottle to its bubble wrap. "The Koran, the prayer cap, and the olive oil, all blessed by Imam Abdal and ten other holy men." He placed the items in a foam padded camera case. "For good measure, I packed them in a lead-lined container."

"This jinni discovered a way to harness radiation. I'm not sure prayers and sacred objects will work against him."

"Who said religion and science can't work with each other? In my practice, I've dealt with many strange experiences. You know as well as I do there are things we can't explain that people attribute to the power of prayer. Visions, miracles, impossible cures of deadly diseases. You believe in physics. I believe in medicine. Let's not rule out the power of prayer—in any form."

Eliana shook her head and stared at the ground. "Prayers didn't save my mother."

He grabbed her hand with his free one. Warmth rushed up her arm and exploded in her face. She locked gazes with him.

"Your mother's prayers saved *you*. Never forget that."

"But—"

"She died of cancer. Have you ever been so sick you were hospitalized?"

Her head spun and she tried to pull out of his grasp. "No, but—"

"Do you think that was a coincidence? Your mother dies of an acute form of cancer, so rare the doctors think she works with radiation. You, on the other hand experience *no* ill effects from that night. How is that possible?"

Lip trembling, she stared at the ground, certain she couldn't speak without bursting into tears. That night, a fire that didn't consume filled her. Except for the marks and the burning sensations, mildly annoying at best, excruciating at worst, her legacy from the confrontation with the jinni as a child was minimal. Her mother swore her to secrecy. She'd told no one, not even her father. Could she trust Arta? He was a psychiatrist. Would he think she was crazy?

She lifted her gaze to his. "I wasn't unharmed."

"What did he do to you?"

Sliding her sleeves up, Eliana revealed her inner arms. Raised serpentine scars, one black, one white, twisted in double helices like three-dimensional tattoos on her *café au lait* skin.

"I tried laser removal. They came back."

Arta traced the twin snakes with a gentle fingertip.

Her promise to her mother to remain a virgin until marriage was to protect Eliana from unwanted scrutiny and challenging questions about her scars. Now she was exposed, her secret revealed. His touch sent shockwaves through her core, making her wish she never made that promise to her dying mother. She pulled her arm away and lowered her sleeves. She broke one promise. What was one more? Time to let him know the rest.

"When I'm near a jinni, my skin feels as if I'm being eaten alive by a million fire ants. The closer I get, the hotter I burn. My mother told me to never tell anyone about those sensations, to run away when I felt the stinging. I use it as my secret weapon to find evil jinnis to avenge her death."

Arta blew out a long breath. "You're in greater danger than I thought."

"How could things be any worse for me than they are?"

He lifted her hand, pushed up a sleeve, and pointed to her scars.

"This jinni doesn't want those girls. They're bait. He wants you."

****

Eliana's expression shifted from grief to stoicism, a bravado Arta didn't share. For some reason, this jinni had branded Eliana as *his* when she was a child. Keeping his thoughts to himself, he wondered if the jinni was after Eliana that night, not her mother. The mother was an impediment, of that he was certain. Without her protection, the child would have been another missing person, ripped from this dimension into a parallel one, abducted to be the *'Ifrit's* bride. Her mother's prayers protected Eliana for a lifetime—until she made it her life's mission to be a jinni hunter. Here they were, moths to the flame of a manipulative *'Ifrit.* His fingers itched to turn into claws and rip the creature apart. "You must leave. Get as far away from here as you can. This one belongs to me."

"No way, Arta. He's mine. He killed my mother, branded me with his disgusting snakes, and, as you say, baited me. This is my fight, not yours."

"Don't be stubborn. This is your *life* we're talking about."

"You've got what, some relics and a prayer? Science and my internal jinni radar are my weapons."

In exasperation he shouted, "I don't want another incident like the one in Arizona."

She flung the car door open. "You left me for dead and disappeared, so now you think it's better for *me* to be a coward? To run away while you take this…this…*shaytan* on by yourself?"

"Satan would be a walk in the park compared to this guy. The *'Ifrit* possessing Old Thiess is more

212

powerful than any I've ever dealt with before. The one in Arizona showed up again in Chevy Chase. He wasn't dead. He came back to give me a message after he tortured a teenaged girl for months." He tried to pull her away from the car, but she shrugged him off. "Dammit, Eliana, listen to me. Old Thiess is the *body* he's taken over. We don't know his name."

She stopped and stared up at him, her green eyes wide with fury. "I don't need a name. I'm not conjuring him up. He's here already."

Her curly hair a wild black cloud around her face, she was even more beautiful than before. She took his breath away.

"Please." He tried to calm her, make her understand the risks. "I'm a psychiatrist, remember? This one is unpredictable, maybe even insane. If I can get his name out of him, it may give us a way to control him. He sees you with me, he could get the wrong idea, think we're—"

"We're *what*?"

"Involved. Better you stay behind. I can use the radioactive isotope detector. I can track him. I can confront him."

"Even if Homeland Security allowed me to deputize you, I can't send an unarmed shrink off to hunt down an *'Ifrit*." Eliana leaped into the car and the engine roared to life. Clutching the metal case, he raced to the passenger side and jumped in as she peeled away from the curb. Pedal to the metal, she forced the vehicle down the blacktop toward the winery.

She poked at his upper arm. "Unless you have some super-powers up your sleeve, you're flying on a wing and a prayer on your own."

He sighed and stared at the signet ring on her hand. Where should he begin his story? She showed him her scars. Perhaps it was time to show his.

"I need to tell you about that assignment in Arizona and about my father." He started with the explosion, then waking up naked in tribal territory, then went on to describe his experience in Chevy Chase, and his mother's revelations. He finished with the chase in the forest and his new found control of his shape-shifting ability.

Ten minutes later she pulled into the winery parking lot, turned off the engine, and stared at him in silence.

He tried another approach. "I know it sounds like I'm crazy—"

"Crazy? What's crazy is you keeping this from me for so long." She slammed her palm on the steering wheel. "Why the hell didn't you tell me this sooner? It's not as if I don't work with werewolves for heaven's sake. Why wouldn't you trust me with this information? What's *wrong* with you?"

He burst out laughing. "What's—wrong—you say?"

Her stern expression cracked, and she giggled until she gasped for air.

"Oh. My. God. We *are* like the start of a bad joke: A jinni-hunting Jew and a shape-shifting Muslim walk up to an *'Ifrit* in a cave." Shoulders shaking, she wiped tears off her face. "My poor father's going to explode."

"He already hates me for leaving you in Arizona. Is it because I'm Muslim?"

"No," she chortled. "Because he's allergic to cats." She opened the door and snickered all the way to the trunk.

He climbed out of the vehicle, and the heavy metal case banged against his thigh. "You're not going to let this go, are you?"

"All this time, I thought you ran away from *me*. Until this trip, I thought you never wanted to see me again."

"Quite the opposite." If she knew how much he wanted her, she'd probably be more afraid of him than the jinni. "How are we going to drag these PPEs with us?"

She pointed to his enormous wheeled suitcase, still in the trunk of the car. "Empty that and stuff them in there, along with the blueprints, water bottles, and protein bars. I'll warm up the radioactive isotope identifier. We'll carry our head gear, get dressed when we get into the wine cellar after we find the door in the floor plans Adalwolf gave me."

They walked toward the showroom and Arta scanned the winery for signs of life. Oddly silent, the building echoed with their footsteps and the squeak of the suitcase wheels. He glanced around and whispered, "Did Adalwolf send everyone home?"

"Why are you whispering?"

He shrugged.

"My guess is the hospital evacuation sent people into a frenzy. Small town, lots of relatives. There were crowds of people milling around beyond the yellow tape."

"I don't like it. Too quiet. Someone should be here. At least a security guard?"

"You're right about that." She stopped. Scanned the area. "Hello? Anybody here?"

Eyes wide, head cocked to one side, her concentration gave him an opportunity to admire her long, nibble-worthy neck.

She shrugged. "Let's keep moving."

Dragging their equipment, Arta found an elevator, and they took that rather than the narrow staircase down to the chilly wine cave.

"There." She pointed to a large dark tapestry framed with gold embroidery. A harvest scene in a vineyard woven in muted grays, purples, greens, with splashes of orange and yellow, contrasted with the bright white walls of the wine cellar. She motioned for him to assist her in pulling it away from a wall.

"This must weigh over two-hundred pounds." A flat baseboard kept the rug snug to the wall, but made it difficult to lift and keep elevated. "Hold on." He dragged a partially full metal wine rack over and draped the wool artwork over it. If they got out alive, Arta would gift Adalwolf with a colorful and lightweight Persian carpet instead of this dusty old rug. Tucked beneath the textile was a dark wood door.

"If the jinni came through here, why is this still in place?"

She shook her head. "Old Thiess has been working here for years. He's familiar with every nook and cranny of this property. He's gone into the tunnels some other way. This is the easiest way for us." She yanked open the suitcase and shimmied into her PPE. "I hate tunnels and caves. This is like my worst nightmare."

"It's not too late. You can still go back."

She grinned and her green eyes danced with mischief. "What? And miss watching you turn into a lion? No way."

"Be careful what you wish for."

"You too, my friend." She held her headgear up and pointed to the side. "Press this button for the radiocomm. You can leave it on, if you want. It's the only way we can communicate with each other in these suits."

He pressed the button. "I am lion, hear me roar."

"You need a new pick up line." She grabbed her instrument and the backpack. "Put on your head lamp and watch your step."

His breath rasped loud in his ears and sweat began to trickle down his back. Arta gripped his metal case with slippery rubber gloves and followed the bobbing light. Metal beams supported the wide struts overhead. Below, train tracks led the way deeper into the bowels of the abandoned mine.

"Anything?"

Eliana's voice crackled in his ear. "The instrument's just picking up normal background radiation. Nothing to write home about."

He spotted a small wagon on the tracks. "Think we can put our stuff in here and push it along?"

She lumbered over and tested it. "I don't see a hand brake. Seems to slide pretty easily." She dropped her back-pack into the cart and gave it a push. "Yay. It's moving." The cart picked up speed. "Whoa, slow down, Nellie." Eliana moved like a Sumo wrestler stomping down the track. She picked up speed, the sole indicator of her progress the bobbing light from her head lamp.

Unused to a PPE in any circumstances, much less in a cave in the dark, Arta clomped along behind her, trying to avoid falling over his own feet. He tapped the radiocomm. "Stop running. I can't keep up with you.

Aren't we supposed to be sneaking up on him?"

The round light bobbed ahead of him faster and faster. Had she climbed into the cart? No. That would be foolish.

"Can you hear me?" His heart pounded in his chest like a kettle drum. Why didn't she answer him? "Eliana?"

The light shuddered, blinked, and disappeared.

Chapter Eighteen

Northern Ethiopia, 953 B.C.E.

Baby at her breast, Makeda sat at the mouth of the cave and gazed at the full moon which marked the prince's first month of life. She closed her eyes, sighed, and enjoyed the evening breeze. One more month, and she planned to rejoin her people. *If she could trust them.* For now, her retreat gave her time to rest, regain her strength, and prevent maladies carried by evil jinnis. Red wolves stood sentry on every rock, ears pricked up and noses on high alert. The living ring of protection around the queen and her prince gave Makeda a sense of peace she had not experienced since her time in Jerusalem.

Solomon. Did he think of her as often as she thought of him? She wished he was here to share in her joy. Tears pricked her eyes. No use thinking about him. That time was in the past. Her future lay ahead in Aksum.

"*Oop-poo!*"

Makeda blinked and looked around, searching for Hoopoe. *Was he really here?*

"*Oop-poo!* My queen, there you are. I searched the entire desert for you."

A female wolf lunged at the bird, and he flew up to perch on an outcropping.

"Stop," she ordered the wolf. "He is a friend. Tell the others to grant him safety."

The red wolf tossed a hungry look over her shoulder and slunk out of the cave.

"That wolf wanted you for a tasty snack, Hoopoe."

He fluttered down to her side and spread his wings. "Does she want to choke on this bag of bones? The bugs were sparse in the desert. I had to make do with little."

She shifted the sleeping baby off her breast and swaddled him. "How is my one true love?"

"Devastated by losing his bride and his mother on the same day."

She stopped her infant care and stared at the bird. "Bathsheba? Dead?"

He nodded. "An earthquake dislodged a heavy stone and sent it down on her head."

Despite Bathsheba's constant attempts at political manipulations, Solomon loved his mother. "His heart must be broken."

"He withdrew from the world. His wives and concubines were planning his funeral and worrying about that brat, Rehoboam, becoming king." Hoopoe nipped at a worm inching its way across the floor.

"Then what?"

"Two of his little girls paid him a visit. He said they were more honest than any of his advisors. Told him he smelled like a goat."

Horrified, Makeda wondered how her beloved allowed himself to fall so far. His anguish and grief drove him to madness, of that she was certain.

Hoopoe cocked his head and stared at the infant. "What did you name the child?"

"Menelik, the son of a wise man."

The bird nodded. "Of course. I see his father in him, even at this young age."

The handmaiden, Tehetena, approached. A basket swung from her arm. "We are low on provisions, my queen."

Makeda nodded. "The wolves tried, but were unable to steal into the food stores. They lost one of the pack in the attempt."

Tehetena spoke in a hushed voice. "I hate to break our retreat and fear what we will find when we return to our caravan, but—"

"*Oop-poo!* I will bring a message to your friend, Tamrin."

"We don't know if he is loyal to us." Makeda recounted the midwife's words, leaving nothing out. "He might be part of the conspiracy."

Hoopoe cocked his head. "I found the remains of bodies staked out in the desert by the caravan. I counted five, all in women's clothes. I feasted on the beetles that burrowed into them."

She shuddered at the image. "Tamrin must have torn the camp apart when we went missing." She removed a gold ring from her pinky and placed it in the chatterbox's open beak. "He gave this to me when we were children. He will know it."

The bird began to walk to the ledge.

"Hoopoe?"

He turned.

"Try not to get killed, please?"

****

The wolves parted to allow Tamrin through on horseback. He leaped off the stallion, raced up to the cave, and fell to his knees, shouting a prayer of gratitude to God. Tears streaming down his cheeks, he alternated between sobs and laughter. At last he spoke.

"Praise God, you are alive."

"Alive and a mother, Tamrin." She lifted the silk wrapped bundle and showed her precious boy to her dearest friend. "His name is Menelik."

"My queen, I have never seen such a beautiful child. He is you and King Solomon, in one dear package." He placed his forehead on the ground. "I am, and ever will be, to the end of my life, you and your son's faithful servant."

Hoopoe strutted to Makeda's side. "*Oop-poo!* I found him weeping in his tent, praying for your soul. I had to sit on his head to get his attention. He swatted at me until I dropped the ring."

"Hoopoe tells me you were difficult to talk to."

Tamrin rocked back on his heels, his mouth open. "You speak to the animals."

Not a question, a statement.

She nodded. "How long have you known?"

"Years. I wondered how a small girl had the power to kill the lioness. I watched you. Saw you head to head with your horse, the parrots, and the beasts we brought to Jerusalem. I knew you had a bond."

"You never spoke of it to me."

"Nor to anyone else." He gave her a penetrating stare. "I feared people might call you a demon, a witch, or the worst, a jinniyah."

She shuddered. "And now?"

A silence fell between them. One. Two. Three heartbeats.

"You were never meant for me. You were meant to

love King Solomon, the greatest king of all times, who also communicates with all manner of beasts."

Makeda exhaled, and realized she had been holding her breath waiting on his answer.

"Tamrin, you honor me with your loyalty. I hope I continue to earn it."

"I must say this to you now, and I will never speak of it again. I will love you until my last breath, Makeda, Queen of Sheba. No one will ever hear of your powers from my lips. I swear this upon the heads of my children."

"Tehetena swore a similar oath. I trust you with my life, and the life of my son. We cannot leave this place for another month, lest the baby fall prey to maladies from evil jinnis. We need food. Can we trust the others?"

"I personally staked the midwife out in the desert. She and four other women confessed to planning to kill the baby."

"She cleaved to the notion I should be a virgin queen. I could not dissuade her."

He shook his head. "No."

"Then why?"

"Someone in Jerusalem paid her to make sure the child didn't make it into the world."

A chill snaked down her spine. "Did she say who?"

"Her spirit left her before she named the culprit."

Who would do such a thing? Bathsheba was dead, but that didn't mean she couldn't have paid for the assassination. Who would be so cruel as to take her child away from her? The Egyptian princess? Naamah, the jealous mother of Rehoboam? Had the Ammonitess been telling the truth about the Elders? Her heart sank.

As long as there were enemies waiting to kill her child, she could never return to Israel.

****

Solomon paced the courtyard and scanned the night sky. Two moons and still no sign of Hoopoe. He hoped the bird was alive and well. He liked the chattering creature. More importantly, he yearned for news of his love, Makeda.

Soldiers stood guard at the gate to his palace and stared straight ahead. He knew they whispered among themselves. Benaiah told him while he lay in mourning, rumors flew about his health. Was the king mad? Did the foreign queen bewitch him? Still stabbing at Solomon with the sharp tip of his tongue, the captain of the guard told him few were sad to see her go. Sickened by his venom, Solomon sent Benaiah away. Now he waited, alone and lonely. He closed his eyes, knelt, and beseeched God to send him a sign.

"*Oop-poo!*"

Solomon jumped to his feet. "The Lord answered my prayer. Tell me of my love. Is she well? How does she look? What did she say to you?"

Hoopoe strutted across the stones and bowed to his king. "I bring you good news."

"Yes?"

"Not only is the Queen of Sheba healthy and as beautiful as when you last saw her, she is also the mother of your child."

He dared not hope, but his tongue spoke before he could bite it. "Is it a boy?"

"His name is Menelik, son of a wise man."

Solomon burst into song, the one he planned to sing to Makeda on their wedding day, his song of songs. "Let him smother me with kisses from his mouth, for your love is better than wine—"

Hoopoe shrieked. Solomon stopped singing and stared at the bird. "You dare interrupt me?"

"Your son is in danger. Someone from your court plotted to kill him as he was born."

Solomon grasped the back of a chair so hard, his hands ached. "Who? What? How?"

Hoopoe shared the midwife's plot and the queen's escape. "The woman died without telling Tamrin the name of the person who paid her to kill your son."

The list of those who wished the Queen of Sheba ill scrolled before his eyes. All of the queens and concubines were jealous of the special place Makeda held in his heart. Naamah stood high on his list of suspicion. Benaiah would have to keep a sharp eye out on her.

Benaiah.

Was he behind the plot? No. Not possible. He would have been *seen* talking to the midwife. It would have been out of place for the unmarried captain of the guard to meet with someone who tended to women's needs. But the man never spoke well of Makeda. Why, even on the eve of his wedding the soldier insisted Solomon check her feet, make sure she wasn't a jinniyah. Just today, as he pined over losing his love match, Benaiah took the opportunity to say no one really missed her. Benaiah. Solomon dared not come right out and accuse him. Surrounded by his troops, the captain of the guard was powerful. The man was quick to establish a military rule when Solomon took to his bed in grief. He needed to find out for certain who would be so filled with hate she plotted to murder a newborn child. This called for waiting and watching.

Solomon glanced around and lowered his voice so the soldiers could not hear.

"Hoopoe, I need your help. In fact, I need the help of *all* the birds in my kingdom."

Chapter Nineteen

Summertown, Present Day

Encased in the clumsy PPE with its self-contained breathing apparatus, or SCBA, Arta slogged forward, desperate for a glimpse of Eliana. Sweat poured down his back and congealed in a pool of dread at the base of his spine. Fear of falling, fear of what he would find kept pounding in his brain and heart.

Why hadn't he told her he loved her? Why hadn't he confessed this truth right after he told her about his Persian lion persona? She didn't flinch. Wasn't that enough of a sign that she was the one? He was an idiot.

Lord, spare this woman, please, she is a good woman, a hard-working woman, a woman of valor. I beg of you, please keep my true love safe and sound.

He edged toward the sinkhole that swallowed his determined jinni hunter and angled his headlamp to search the void. *There, there she was.* A crumpled heap of yellow PPE lay next to the overturned wagon. He turned his head. The rails looked as if they'd buckled and fallen into the chasm, like a twisting banister in an old house. *A banister.* How many times did he slide down that polished oak railing in his house, with his mother shouting at him in Farsi that he was going to kill himself? *Time to put all that practice to use.* And, yes, he might just die trying.

There was no time for stealth. He must get to her. He removed his gloves and twisted the SCBA straps through the handle of the metal camera box. Arta pulled his gloves back on, tugged at the case on his hip, and took a deep breath of canned air. If he had a leather belt to put around the iron, he could improvise a zip line, except it was going down. *Way down.* He lay on the ledge, grasped the metal railing with his gloved hands, swung his legs around the curvature, and placed the soles of his boots on the face of the old coal bed.

Now or never. He pushed himself off and slid down, yelling as his stomach remained behind him on the ledge. The heat from the friction on the gloves began to burn his palms.

Shit, that hurts.

Distracted by his blazing hands, Arta slammed onto the ground with a thud. Momentarily stunned, he was grateful he didn't fall on his back onto the SCBA gear. That would mean broken ribs, not a bruised tailbone. He stood on watery legs and stumbled to Eliana's side.

"Eliana, I'm here." He knelt down, pressed the radiocomm again. "Speak to me, please." No response. A black terror the size of the sinkhole began to suck him down.

No, no, no. Damn the SCBA. He needed to see her face. The hand-held air quality monitor indicated the oxygen level at twenty-one percent and carbon dioxide and other noxious gases well below the threshold for concern. He turned off the flow of oxygen, and pulled his hood off. The air in the long unused coal mine was musty, but breathable. A few feet away, the slow clicking of the RID unit gave evidence of normal background radiation.

Using gentle hands, he repeated the process with Eliana's gear, and cushioned her head with her hood. Miraculously, her breathing apparatus was still functioning. Illuminated by the headlamp, her face brought tears to his eyes.

So beautiful. So brave. So headstrong. He removed his singed gloves and felt a pulse in her neck. Not bounding, but evidence of life, for sure. One at a time, he pried each eye open. Pupils equal and reactive. A good sign. Without a CAT scan or MRI, there was no way to tell if she sustained a concussion. After that fall, anything was possible.

"Eliana?"

No response.

Now or never.

"If you don't wake up, you'll never know how much I love you. From the moment we met and shook hands, I was bedazzled by you. Every time you spoke, even when you were angry, I heard poetry. Regardless of our differences, maybe even because of them, you are my beloved. You fascinate, frustrate, and infuriate me—and I love you for it with every beat of my heart."

He took a deep shaky breath. "I want to marry you, have children with you, grow old with you. I have no idea of what lies ahead, but I know I want you at my side, for all time. Please, please wake up so we can start our future together."

Tears threatening to burst into sobs, he leaned forward and kissed her lips. She tasted like cinnamon, honey, and dates. An exotic scent like frankincense or myrrh met his nose as he nuzzled her neck.

"Please wake up, my love. My life will have a dull,

aching void if you die. You will be a phantom limb, an ache I cannot touch, but a pain I feel with every breath I take."

No response. He rocked back on his heels and bowed his head. How would he get help for her if she had a brain injury? All he had was his ability to change into a lion.

Dear God, what should I do now?

****

Jolted out of the black hole of unconsciousness, Eliana stared at the back of her eyelids, her heart jack-hammering in her chest. *He loved her.* Part of her wanted to leap up and sing like a Broadway star. Another terrified part of her wanted to run and hide. Yet another, peevish part wondered why he hadn't spoken up sooner. Did she need to be at death's door to get him to confess his love? Was that safer for him? Or was it safer for her?

The last thing they needed was emotional entanglements that could threaten the mission. She needed to be cool, calm, and collected. Not hot and bothered by his kiss which left its smoldering imprint on her lips. Her neck blazed from his touch and she craved more. Good thing the PPE deterred her impulse, or she might have done something incredibly stupid, like grab him and pull his well-muscled body on top of her to finish what he so foolishly began. She blinked, stared up into darkness, and opened her mouth to respond—and the sound of crickets ricocheting off the hard walls of the tunnel interrupted.

"Arta, what the hell is going on?"

"You're awake." His face hovered over hers. In the darkness, his headlamp blinded her with its intensity.

"Where do you hurt, what can I do for you?"

"Help me up. How long has the RID unit been clicking like that?"

"That just started. It's been doing a slow click, like the background radiation noises you showed me before."

"I need to get up."

"Not a good idea. I need to examine you for breaks."

Turtled on her back, she refrained from a tart response. "If you don't help me up, we risk more than a few broken bones. I don't want to glow in the dark, do you?"

Arta moved behind her and pushed while she pulled herself up to sitting. "How's your back?"

"I won't be sleeping on it much in the future."

"Can you raise your arms? Wiggle your fingers and toes?"

Eliana slowly twirled her hands and waved her fingers. Her left ring finger throbbed. Did she smash it in the fall? The dark made it impossible to assess if the signet ring remained intact. She lifted first one, then the other leg, and flexed her ankles. "Can we get this show on the road, please? We need to cover up."

She rolled over to her knees. "They should put jet-packs in these suits." She pulled the hood on and tapped the radiocomm. *Nothing.* She lifted the headpiece. "My radiocomm broke in the fall. We'll use hand-signals."

Arta nodded.

Hood up, SCBA in working order, she made her way toward the RID on rubbery legs, her headlamp imitating the way her legs felt. She walked and searched for the shoebox sized device, and all the while her heart fought with her mind about Arta. On the one hand, he was smart, sexy, and sizzling as a sidewalk on a July day in Baltimore. On the other hand, his kisses were like caramels, sweet and addictive as a sugar rush, minus the calories.

When she'd awakened with his lips on hers, heat coiled around her core, squeezed her in an intimate embrace, and screamed for release. She shook her head and the lamp veered in erratic loops in the void. *Foxhole sex.* That's what her body craved. Fear of dying kicked her biological clock into the alarm mode. *No sex.* Not until she found her love match, "blessed by the ring," whatever that meant. She promised her mother on her deathbed. End of discussion, raging hormones. Get back into work mode and find the damn RID.

There.

Half hidden behind a boulder, the beige instrument lay on its side. She stopped and turned, pointing. Backpack over his shoulder, camera case on his hip, Arta halted and waited for her lead. She lifted the box and inspected it. *Dinged and scratched, but still intact and clicking, the needle squarely in the green zone.*

She took two steps forward. Crickets shrieked, and the needle headed for the red zone.

Eliana held the device at eye level. *Higher levels of radiation, definitely cesium.*

Hands shaking, breath rasping in her ears, she continued walking. She wondered if they would come face to face with Old Thiess, the werewolf of interest, or an *'Ifrit* in another guise.

She stopped, and Arta plowed into her.

He held his hands palms up in the universal

"What's going on?" gesture.

Eliana shook her head.

Something's off.

The RID clicked louder, urging her to move through a tunnel into a larger opening.

She stopped to peer at the dial under her head lamp, and Arta plowed into her—again. She really needed to work on this hand signal thing. Next time she'd put her hand up. Her slow, careful gait warred with her urge to run. But, then, that was how she'd fallen off the ledge, into the sinkhole. She wasn't doing *that* again. Her jinni sense had pulled her along like a magnetic tractor beam. Her legs took over and her body and mind had followed—right over a cliff.

That's it.

Her jinni radar wasn't working. No prickling sensations, not a single nettle sting.

Nothing.

Either her homing beacon had been knocked out of her when she fell, or they weren't following a jinni. What the hell was it? Cesium for sure, but what source?

The needle buried itself in the red zone, and a million crickets raged.

Eliana stopped and stared around the small cave, seeking the source of the radiation. She pointed to her eyes and motioned to Arta to examine the space. The shaft of light from the headlamp snagged on something out of place.

What the hell? She took a step back, grabbed Arta's arm and pointed.

Two dead snakes, one white, one black, both practically glowing with cesium gamma radiation lay intertwined on a rock shelf, like offerings on an altar.

Beneath her PPE, the snakes on her arms writhed. This was a trap. They had to get out. *Now.*

Tremors shook her entire body, and rumbles echoed in her chest. She turned toward the tunnel they had just walked through. Rocks crashed down, throwing up pebbles that dinged off their suits, and a cloud that blocked even the piercing halogen light beams of their headlamps.

They were going to die, and she hadn't told Arta she loved him, too.

She was an idiot.

She clutched Arta's arm until the rumbling subsided, and her legs stopped shaking. When the dust cleared, she could see a rockslide blocked their only exit. *Do not panic.* Think through all the options. How could they get the hell out of this hellhole? What did they have on hand they could use to save their lives? She weighed the good, bad, and ugly in her mind.

On the good side of the column, she wasn't *alone.* She was with Arta, a guy she loved, and she was going to let him know. *Somehow.* On the good side, they had air in their tanks—for now. On the bad side, they were exposed to three hundred rem of cesium, and would begin to bleed internally if they couldn't block the radiation. Plus, they were on their own, no one knew where they were, or where to look for them.

In fact, it was highly unlikely anyone would look here for them. They would run out of clean air in less than an hour and choke to death on coal dust. That was better than hemorrhaging to death. *Maybe.* Her dream of finding a love match had come true at the same time as her worst nightmare. They were running out of air, sealed in a small cave with radioactive snakes. And no way out.

****

The clicking racket of the RID piercing his ears, Arta lumbered in front of Eliana and pulled her away from the jinni's taunting altar. The monster toyed with her, crawled under her skin, and played with her mind. As a psychiatrist he specialized in head games. The jinni, wherever he lurked, drew pleasure and energy from Ellie's fear. Arta wanted to protect her, in any way he could, from physical and mental intimidation. Yes, they were trapped in a cave, yes their air was limited, but the snakes presented an *immediate* psychological threat. He needed to break the *'Ifrit's* hold on Ellie's psyche. How? He turned around in a slow circle, searching the cave for something. The camera case banged on his thigh. Had he been able to reach his forehead through his headgear, he would have smacked himself.

Of course.

He unstrapped the lead-lined case from his hip, removed the relics, and approached the serpents with care. Yes, he wore gloves, but the radiation levels posed major safety risks. Using a flat rock as a spatula, he scraped the floppy snakes into the metal box, snapped the lid shut, and fastened the clasps. The din of a million raging crickets ceased. He took a deep breath, started to turn, and was almost knocked down when she wrapped him in a clumsy embrace.

Their head gear touching, he shouted, "We're going to be okay."

She raised her head, gave him a weak smile through the scratched plastic, and shouted back, "From your lips to God's ears."

He clutched her as best he could through the bulky PPE and pondered their fate. He disposed of the radioactive snakes, but the clock continued to tick on their oxygen supply. With luck, there might be thirty minutes of air left in their tanks. Due to the hospital evacuation and ensuing chaos, the winery was empty when they arrived. Would anyone notice they were missing in time to find them? They needed to find a way out of the cave before they were forced to remove their headgear and breathe the dusty air filled with God only knew what. He didn't want to die in this hole in the ground without knowing if she returned his love. *No.* They didn't fight this hard and come this far to give up.

He tapped her helmet, pointed to the pile of rubble, and pantomimed digging.

Eliana looked at him with a "you're crazy" expression.

Nothing to lose.

He slogged his way over to the rockslide and pounded on the wall of rubble. A few rocks tumbled down, a large one landing next to his foot.

That wasn't good.

If he wasn't careful, he'd give himself a concussion—or worse.

A hard tap on his shoulder startled him. He turned and looked to where Eliana pointed at the ceiling of the entryway. A gap appeared in the wall of rock. He motioned for her to stand off to the side while he readied himself for another run at the wall.

She stepped back—and crumpled to the ground.

Heart jack-hammering in his chest, he lumbered to her side and knelt down. Her eyes were closed, her lips blue. Her SCBA gear. Did it spring a leak in the fall? No matter. He ripped her head gear off. *Shallow rapid breaths. Not a good sign.* He needed to get her out. In his human form, he was only as good as his two arms. In his lion form, he had four big paws and claws made for killing—and digging. He took a deep breath. Every other shift was involuntary. A bad time to test-drive his abilities, but what choice did he have?

God give me the wisdom and strength to do the right thing.

He crouched down on all fours and prepared for the change. His hands grew larger and the claws began to tear through his skin of his right hand. He grunted in pain.

Good, this was good.

A few more moments, and he'd be out of this suit and in his lion form.

Jump up on the ledge, enlarge the opening. Get Eliana out. Focus.

His left hand prickled and throbbed. He took a deep breath and bore down.

Now. He needed his lion form *now.*

The radio crackled in his ear. "Yo, Arta, can you hear me?"

Astonished, he raised his paw and touched the comm button. "Hong Feng? Is that really you?"

"Man, you were not easy to track down. Lucky for you, the FINDER detected your heartbeats and breathing in the rubble. You okay?"

His claws retracted and his paws became hands. "Eliana's unconscious."

"Get as far away from this pile of crap as you can. We're coming through."

Arta dragged Eliana behind a large boulder. "Hang in there, Eliana. We're getting out of here." He covered her body with his, and an explosion shook him and left him with ringing ears. Dust and small stones rained down. The radio screeched and crackled.

"Move it, Arta. You gotta get out before everything caves in."

Lights bright enough to land a plane shone through the now open entrance to the cave. Putting his hands under Eliana's armpits, he dragged her backward, even as the walls shuddered and shook around them. He spotted the camera case and relics. For a split second he paused—and a coffee table sized boulder dropped on top of the outcropping with a thunderous bang. He'd apologize to the Imam when he saw him—if he survived.

A man in a PPE climbed over the rubble and pulled Eliana out of the space. Arta cleared the entrance, and another quake shook the mine.

Four men in hazmat suits, one of them pulling the suitcase sized FINDER, rushed at him, dragging him away from the entrance. One man put an oxygen mask on Eliana's face, another snapped her into an airlift rescue vest and tucked the green oxygen tank under her arm, and a third hooked the vest up to a winch.

Hong Feng shouted in his ear. "She goes first, then you, then the rest of us. We have to get out of here fast. The guys up top will lead you out. Just follow them."

The winch seemed to take forever pulling Eliana to safety. Eyes glued to her limp form, Arta prayed for a miracle. If only he hadn't waited so long to tell her he loved her. If only he had said something sooner. If only—

"Go."

A rescue net dropped at his feet. He sat down, wrapped his arms through the ropes, and swung through space. When he arrived at the top where the wagon had run off the rails, the winch deposited him alongside Eliana. Still wrapped in the rescue vest, face covered with the green plastic mask, she gestured like a wild woman until she spotted Arta. She stopped, stared at him, and began to cry. Between sobs, he thought she said, "I love you."

He leaned in to hear her better, and Hong Feng grabbed his shoulder.

"Time to go, man."

Arta tapped his comm. "What about Janie?"

"You mean the Adalwolf girl?"

"Yes, she's the whole reason we came down here."

"She escaped by speed shifting into her werewolf form when Old Thiess was distracted by causing the cave-in. She's with her family. She's safe."

Something wasn't right. The girl got away on her own? That was easy. *Too* easy.

Chapter Twenty

Aksum and Jerusalem, 932-930 B.C.E.

Makeda stood at the side of the circle and watched her handsome son practice with his sparring partner. Long-limbed and light on his feet, Prince Menelik had the reflexes of a cat—and the ability to communicate with them, too. Like her, the gift appeared early in life. Unlike her father, she did not respond harshly to the five-year-old boy's tale of meeting a black-maned lion named Shirzad in the jungle and sharing a drink in a stream. Tamrin confirmed the event. Ever since that day, Shirzad served as his sentinel on the outskirts of the palace grounds. She was certain Solomon sent the lion-shifter to protect the boy. Much as she tried to induce Shirzad to join the court, he stood firm in the distance, away from the Queen, eyes on the Prince.

Tamrin also kept watch over him, protecting him since birth. No one had ever been able to determine the name of the enemy in Jerusalem who paid the mid-wife to kill Menelik as he was born. Each day, whenever he went out, wherever he rode, Uncle Tamrin escorted him.

He turned to grin at his mother and wave, and her heart skipped a beat. For a moment, her love match, Solomon, stood before her in all his manly glory. Her boy had grown into a golden-skinned, dark-haired man with a noble profile and hazel eyes. He, too, strode among the common people and asked probing questions, not to abuse the workers, but to learn from them. Like his father, Menelik's thirst for all manner of knowledge was that of a camel at the end of a long desert trek.

Makeda loved the boy and showered him with kisses, as well as lessons learned at her father's knee. Over twenty Rosh Hashanahs, Yom Kippurs, and Feasts of the Tabernacles had passed since she left Jerusalem and returned to Aksum.

Twenty years ago, the Queen of Sheba rode into the capitol with her son in her arms and triumph in her heart. Her country-men and -women had celebrated her return and rejoiced at the birth of a Prince, a new beginning for Shebans. The future was bright for all. Everyone was happy. Only *one* individual had pestered her to know the name of the father of the child.

Her son.

She closed her eyes and thought back to years of battling with her offspring about his father's identity. Every day, every week, every month, every year, the boy drove her mad with the same questions. It had become a ritual between them.

"Who is my father? Everyone says he's a wise king."

"Why do you believe gossip?"

"What is his name?"

"You will find out in good time."

"Why haven't I met him?"

"He lives a long way away."

"Will he come to visit?"

"His work keeps him busy. He can't leave his

241

country."

"Do I look like him?"

"Yes."

"Why aren't you with him?"

"Because I'm a queen.

"Why don't we go visit him?"

"I can't leave my country, again. No one is left to rule in my stead."

"Can he talk to cats, like you and me?"

"Yes. He commands all animals, men, and jinnis."

"Is he dark-skinned?"

"He is like you, golden and burnished by the sun."

"Is he strong?"

"You ask the wrong question."

"Is he a good man?"

"He is the wisest of all men."

On and on, the boy would beleaguer her until she would shout, "Am I not enough for you? Am I not your mother *and* your father? Leave me, or I will make you practice your writing."

That threat always made him fly away, Tamrin right behind him.

Until he turned twelve years old.

On his birthday, Menelik folded his arms over his chest and said, "Mother. I will sit here day and night and practice my writing and learn your father's lessons. I will not run. Next year I will be a man. It is time you told me who my father is."

She sighed. He was right. So she sat down and told him the whole story, leaving out the conspiracy to kill him at childbirth. He didn't need to know that—yet.

A wolf yipped. She blinked and the past disappeared. Her sweaty, dust covered grown son stood before her, a wide grin on his face.

"Hello, my beautiful mother. How are you today?"

"Happy to celebrate your birthday with you, my handsome son."

"Are you ready for the party?"

"Yes, and for the feast. Everyone will be complaining tomorrow they feel like bloated pigs, but tonight they will drink and eat."

They strolled toward the palace, and a red wolf trotted alongside them. He had been in the shadows while the Prince sparred. Attached to the boy from birth, the red wolves had tasked one of the pack to be at his side at all times. Pups followed Menelik wherever he went, begging to be his next protector.

She stopped and put her hand on his arm, despite the dust. "I made an important decision, my son."

He scratched the wolf behind the ears and waited.

Makeda removed the Seal of Solomon from her finger, took her son's hand, and placed the ring in his palm. "It is time for you to meet your father. Take this and your best men and go to Jerusalem. When you meet him, show him the seal. That way, he will know you are his son."

His eyes gleamed with unshed tears. "Mother, I have waited years to hear these words. I am so happy. I will make you proud, I promise."

"You always make me proud. But you must temper your joy with caution. Trust your men and your father *only*. Before we feast, I must tell you another story. It involves the Hoopoe bird—" her mouth went dry "—the red wolves, and your birth."

****

Solomon reviewed the accounts of his governors of

the twelve regions of Israel. Each official was required to make provisions for the king and his household for one month in the year. While he always welcomed the tributes of flour, meal, oxen, cattle, sheep, deer, gazelles, roebuck, and fatted fowl, the ones that gave him most pleasure were the offerings from his daughter's husbands. When it was their time to provide food for the king and his court, his girls came along with the tribute and stayed for the month. Of course, they weren't children anymore, but in his mind, they would always be the little ones who raised him from his torpor of grief and brought him back to life. To these daughters, he and Israel owed much. Even if Taphath had said he smelled like a goat. He guffawed at the memory, startling his court scribe.

"Is there something amiss, my King?"

Solomon shook his head. "No, merely thinking back to my younger days. Where have twenty years gone?"

The scribe, a stooped man with a long gray beard shrugged. "The river of time sweeps us away, leaving no one untouched, not even the wisest man of all time. Hang on to the memories of your loved ones, my King. More than blankets and a fire, they will warm your heart as your bones grow stiff and cold."

"That is poetry. You should write those words down."

"I am no poet. Merely an observer of life," he sighed, "and lost loves."

With those words, Solomon's heart ached and hearkened back to the one year, twelve scant moons, he spent with Makeda. He closed his eyes, and she sprang up before him, young, full of life, laughing. Twenty years had passed since she left. Was she gray-haired now, like him, or did her hair retain its rich blackness and curls? Was her body still lithe and supple? His loins stirred at the memory of their one night of passion. Had she stayed, he would have spent every night with her for the last twenty years, ignoring all the other wives and concubines.

"King Solomon, I bring news."

He blinked and Makeda dissolved into a messenger coated in dust.

"What is it?"

"A man who looks just like you, only younger, approaches Jerusalem. He arrived in Gaza, and the governor thought he was you."

Solomon leaped to his feet. "When was this report?"

"From yesterday. I rode hard, nearly killed my steed. The ruler of Gaza sent me ahead to warn you an imposter might be on route to attempt to take over your throne. He said to warn you so you could prepare for an attack."

Solomon laughed. "Would you call your child a fraud?"

The messenger shook his head. "I don't understand."

"This is not time to raise the troops." He leaped to his feet. "Scribe, take good notes from this day forward. You and I spoke of lost loves, and the warmth of good memories. Come, let us go forth and meet the seed of my greatest love which has taken shape and grown into a man. Let us prepare to welcome my son."

****

Once again, Solomon stood in his courtyard

surrounded by musicians, soldiers, and priests and awaited the arrival of a Sheban. This time, however, instead of dancing with anticipation for his love match, he twitched with impatience for his love child. Did his son truly favor him, or was it just another rumor created by a kingdom that loved royal watching? Even as well fed as they were, Israel's people hungered and thirsted after gossip. Today would give them many tales to tell over food and wine for years to come. On this day, they would say, the king's son arrived after a long journey from Sheba. Accompanied only by his best men, the young man had traversed the desert and taken a ship across the Red Sea, then traveled across yet another desert to make his way to Jerusalem.

What had Makeda told her son about Solomon? Had she been kind and loving in her words? Did he come to Solomon in love—or in anger for abandoning his mother? How could he explain to his son, Menelik, that his father and mother had been in correspondence for twenty years and that each letter was signed with love and longing?

"*Oo-poo!*" The bird fluttered and landed at his feet. "He comes up the hill with his men. His steed is white as the sands of the beach of the Salt Sea. Your son sits high on the saddle, his shoulders back, eyes forward. He craves a glimpse of you."

"And I of him." The first Hoopoe had passed away when it was his time. His offspring, the mirror image of his father was just as talkative as the original. Solomon turned to the crowd. "Let us go forth and greet my son with joy." He hoped Menelik would be happy to see him. Twenty years of a father's absence could fill a boy—no, a young man's head with doubts and fears.

The moment to wipe away those concerns had come, at last.

Musicians played the lute and lyre, songs of joy filled the air. Crowds filled the streets outside the palace. Children perched on parents' shoulders craning for a better look. People jostled one another for a good spot on the king's route. Soldiers stood at attention, legs splayed, blocking the throng from surging into the street in their frenzy to touch and be touched by him. Solomon hated to keep the people away, but Benaiah insisted on protecting him from would-be attackers.

On one occasion, a rag covered subject, scrawny and filthy from over long fasts and wanderings in the desert, had attempted to kill Solomon. The mad man babbled about how Solomon enslaved nations and lunged at him with a knife. The guard dispatched him in short order. How could the man say such things? Yes, he demanded tribute and workers, but not for his own glory, but for the glory of God. He shuddered at the recollection of the demonic look in his eyes, and mentally thanked Benaiah for taking precautions.

A prancing steed crested the hill. Solomon raised his eyes and the sun blinded him. Before he could blink and shake away tendrils of apprehension, a strapping man, built with legs like small tree trunks leaped off his horse and knelt at his feet, head bowed.

"Abba. Baba. Father. I am Prince Menelik. I bring you greetings from my beloved mother, Makeda, Queen of Sheba. She sends you her respect and wishes for your long life. The entire nation of Sheba now worships the one true God as she was taught here in Jerusalem. She bade me give you this seal so you would recognize me."

"Rise my son. I need no ring to prove you are mine. I see my father, King David, in you and your mother's teachings are in your voice."

Solomon's son embraced him, and grief and joy rushed through him in a torrent. Would Menelik ever forgive him for all the missed years? Tamrin guided him, but did he love him like his own child? He must prove his love for his child, now a man, and a prince in his own right.

That was it.

Releasing his son from his embrace with reluctance, King Solomon called for his mule. The groom arrived with the sluggish animal, and Solomon urged the puzzled looking Menelik to mount the beast. The music stopped and a hush fell upon the crowd. Some of the elders had seen this before, when he was but a boy and the old king lay dying. He motioned for Benaiah and Zadok to come to him.

"It is time to announce my heir to the throne. You shall lead the mule with Menelik through the streets of Jerusalem shouting to all, 'This is the son of King Solomon. On this day, he shall be anointed king.'"

Benaiah protested. "My friend, *please.* You are besotted with joy at seeing your offspring from the Queen of Sheba. How can you say he is fit to rule your kingdom? What of Rehoboam's claim as next in line?"

Solomon spoke through gritted teeth. "In the words of my beloved mother, may she rest in peace, 'Cease your braying, my stubborn one.' Your king has spoken. My word is law and the one and only God has given me wisdom beyond that of any man. Now, go with Zadok and proclaim Menelik to be my son and heir. You must bring him to me at the Temple at sunset. There he shall be anointed in the presence of the Lord before all of Israel."

Upon hearing his father's words, Menelik, his eyes wide, tried to dismount from the mule. "Father, I did not come to usurp your throne. My father still lives and is in good health before me. I came to meet the wisest man in all the world, the man whom my mother loves still. Please do not do this from a sense of guilt. You owe me nothing. Your fatherly love is all I desire."

Makeda still loved him and spoke of him to their wonderful, humble son. How unlike Rehoboam this young man was. Menelik's objections only served to strengthen his resolve. He had chosen wisely. This one was the true inheritor of his kingdom, not that covetous offspring from Naamah.

Solomon grabbed his son's strong young hands in his weaker, older ones, and kissed Menelik's knuckles. "You have the best of both your parents. Your mother's deep and abiding sense of honor and my wisdom. You are already the king in my heart. Tonight, all the world will know you will become the ruler of Israel upon my death."

Menelik bowed his head and wept. "My father, may our Lord grant you a long life, full of joy and blessings. I pray I shall never disappoint you."

"Already you make me proud. Let every ear hear and every eye see you. You, my son, are my blessing." Solomon waved to Benaiah and Zadok. "Take him forth with cymbals and lutes, lyres and horns. Let his men follow you and rejoice in the Lord's name for this day of wonders."

Embarrassed by his show of emotion, Solomon covered his face with his hands. Amid the jubilant sounds of his son's progress, the still small voice of the Lord spoke to him. *Your wisdom serves you well. He will illuminate nations with his faith.*

Face still covered, Solomon laughed until he became short of breath. Wondrous are the ways of the Lord, indeed. He turned to go into his palace to bathe and prepare for the evening's ritual and froze at the sound of a woman screeching his name.

"Solomon! Have you become possessed by demons like Saul? Is it a jinni who has taken over your body and forced you to do this to your child? Who should we call to exorcise it? King David is gone, his lyre silenced these many years. Shall we raise him from the dead like Saul raised Samuel to cast out this foreign influence?"

"Naamah, stop. This is not your decision." The woman tormented him as badly as any demon. She did not know her place. "The Lord blessed this choice."

Rehoboam fell on his knees before him. "Father, tell me this isn't true. Make them stop saying he's the next king of Israel."

"I smell the wine on you from here, my useless son." Disgust clogged his throat. "It's always a holiday for you, isn't it, Rehoboam? You never listened to a word I've said. You never took any interest in the running of the kingdom. Your whole life you have been spoiled by your mother."

Naamah gasped and sputtered. "You dare call *me* a bad mother—"

"Not once did this woman listen to Bathsheba, my blessed mother, may she rest in peace, about your upbringing. You were mean to other children and servants. Look at you now, a grown man, still a brat. Your robe is filthy, covered in wine stains, food, and the perfume of harlots."

Bleary-eyed, Rehoboam brushed at his clothing in a useless attempt to remove the blemishes. "Father," he whimpered.

"Silence! I am ashamed to call you my son. You and your mother are reaping what you sowed. Your brother—yes, he's your brother—Menelik will be the next king. You will bow your head and bend your knee to him, just as you must to me. Go now. Bother me no more, lest I call upon the Lord to release His wrath upon you."

Fists on her hips, Naamah refused to budge. Her eyes wild, gray hair flying around her face like dancing snakes, the woman shrieked, "The Council of Elders won't agree to this. Rehoboam is your oldest son. The Queen of Sheba seeks to conquer Israel. Mark my words. They will not allow this foreigner to reign over this kingdom. Only a true Israelite has that right. I will see to it that Rehoboam gets his birthright. The Lord is on my side in this, not yours."

"Go. Now. Before I order you to be stoned for blasphemy." He motioned to two guards standing by the door to the palace. "The family squabble is over. Get them out of here." He turned back to Naamah. "If you or your foolish son ever step foot in my palace again, you will be punished."

The soldiers stepped between the king and his unruly wife and son and ushered them out of the courtyard. Her tongue silenced at last, Solomon took a deep breath and shook his head.

God, give me strength. If only he had paid more attention to the child, not been so obsessed with the Temple, perhaps, Rehoboam would not be such a disappointment as a man. But the Lord commanded him to build, and he did as directed. What a magnificent sanctuary God had ordered for His worship.

The Temple boasted a wide porch in front and narrow windows that allowed the sun to come in, yet kept the interior cool. Built of prepared stone, no hammers nor axes nor iron tools of any sort rent the air with their din during construction. When the Temple was completed, Solomon covered the outside of the house with timbers of cedar carved into flowers. Everywhere the eye rested gold sparkled. Overlaid in gold, the oracle and cedar altar gleamed like mirrors. Inside the oracle, two gold covered cherubims made from olive trees, each fifteen feet tall, stretched forth their seven and a half foot wings, one touching the other in the middle of the house. All around, the walls of the Temple were covered with carved figures of cherubims, palm trees, and open flowers, all overlaid with gold. Even the floor of the Temple was overlaid with gold.

The Temple was finished after seven years of construction. The elders of Israel came, and the priests took up the Ark of the Lord, the tabernacle of the people, and all the holy vessels that were in the tabernacle. King Solomon and the people of Israel assembled with him before the Ark and sacrificed multitudes of sheep and oxen, so many they lost count. The Ark of the Covenant held only the two tablets of stone that Moses placed into the Ark at Horeb. Upon completing the sacrifices to the Lord, the priests carried the Ark into the oracle, the most holy of places, and set it beneath the watchful gaze and protective wings of the cherubim.

The priests departed the holy of holies, and a dense cloud filled the house of the Lord, so thick they could not minister. Kneeling before the altar, Solomon heard God's small voice speak to him.

Here I will dwell.

Now, a new King would be declared. The nation would rejoice and feast as it had when the Temple was accepted by the Lord. That evening, as the sky turned red with the setting sun, Solomon stood on the entryway of the Temple. Head bowed, Menelik stood before the holy of holies in white linen, his arms at his side, palms up. As Samuel had done for David, and as Zadok had done for Solomon, the old priest now poured oil over Menelik's dark curls and recited the blessings.

When Zadok finished the ritual, Solomon held his son's right hand on high. "Behold, I give you your next king, who shall now be called David, after my father the great king. All hail, King David!" The hills of Jerusalem rang with the sounds of rams' horns, flutes, pipes, and shouts of joy. His people were grateful for his wisdom in choosing David/Menelik as his successor, of that he was certain.

Chapter Twenty-One

Summertown, Present Day

Dressed in the traditional butt-in-the-breeze hospital gown, Eliana perched on the edge of a gurney behind a gray curtain in a private ER room and pleaded with a stone-faced nurse. "I'm fine. I was a little dehydrated, that's all. You gave me the IV—" she waved her left arm "—and I'm back to a hundred percent."

The gray haired, green-eyed woman wasn't budging. "I may just be an agency nurse, but I know what my orders are. Your blood work isn't back, and that big ring is covering a nasty burn. Doctor says we're keeping you for observation. I suggest you sit back and relax."

"I know you're swamped since the hospital re-opened. Why not give my spot to someone who needs it?"

Clad in blue scrubs, Arta stood in the door and smirked at her. "Do I need to post a security guard on you?"

The nurse shook her head. "See if you can talk some sense into her. She's all yours, doc." She pulled the door behind her with a thunk.

"Yes, she is." He grinned and strode over to her side and grabbed her free hand. "Outside you might be a special agent, but in here—" he gestured around the room "—I call the shots."

She groaned. "Bad puns this early in our relationship?"

He pressed his forehead to hers. "Yes, now and forever, my dearly beloved, you will be subjected to all my terrible Persian puns. You can thank my mother for her love of words."

Dearly beloved. Her heart thundered so loud, he must have heard it thump. Breathless, afraid to ask, she forced herself to ask the question. "Speaking of parents, what are we going to say to them?"

"As Rumi said, 'Love is the water of life.' Without you, I would be a man in a loveless desert dying of thirst."

A warm flush washed over her. "You and your poet leave me breathless."

"I am going to tell my mother *Dostash Daram— Ghesmat man bood.* I love her—she is my destiny. And you will tell your father we are, how do you say it? *Beshert.* I am *your* destiny. We are meant to be together." He leaned in for a kiss, and a thrill of anticipation feathered down her spine. She reached up and ran her fingers through his thick hair and pulled him closer. His soft lips met hers and opened. A heady mixture of caramel, cinnamon, dates, honey, and wine, met her tongue.

His hand slid beneath the loose gown, pressed against her unencumbered breast, and circled her nipple. She gasped in pleasure and pulled him between her legs. The hardness of his cotton-covered flesh rubbed against her, teasing her with the promise of even greater pleasure. She arched her back, and he slid his hands under her buttocks, pulling her closer.

He paused and whispered against the tender skin at the base of her neck. "Are sure you want this? Your promise to your mother—"

"Was to protect me from being hurt. My mother told me the ring would let me know when it was the right man. The burn on my finger tells me our union is blessed. You're never getting away from me." She pulled him tighter, the thin layer of underwear barely containing her longing "Don't stop until I tell you to."

A chuckle rumbled in his chest, and he ground his hips against hers. "Better?"

"Yes, oh, yes." She rose up again and again, every fiber of her core on fire with the need to be one with this man.

He breathed into her ear as his nimble fingers danced across her nipples in feathery touches. "I wish our first time together could be more special, in a bedroom, with silk curtains, satin sheets, and the scent of roses and lilies filling the air."

"You are my heart's desire. I don't need finery or flowers. Wherever you are, I'm home."

Arta lifted her gown and suckled at her breast, his tongue flicking, teeth nipping. A hiss escaped her lips. His finger glided under the thin material, found her frantic bundle of nerves, and stroked all around her nub, never touching it directly. He was driving her mad with desire.

"I want you." The words were scarcely out of her mouth when he slid two fingers inside her. Goosebumps erupted on her arms, and she quivered with anticipation.

"You like?"

"Yes, I like, but—" She scooted back on the gurney, disengaged from him, and in an instant missed the connection. "I want this—" she undid the tie of his scrubs, reached inside, and slid her fingers across the slick tip of his erection "—more than that." She slid her hand up and down his hardness and he moaned.

Pupils dilated, irises now a dark shade of gold, Arta allowed her to push his pants down.

She stared at his groin. "Big. Bold. Beautiful." She slid out of her panties and pulled him tight, thigh to thigh, groin to groin. "Hurry."

"Yes, ma'am." Grinning, he slid inside her, and she gasped with pleasure. He stopped. "This is your first time. Are you okay?"

"Never better." Eliana gazed deep into his eyes and saw devotion. Devotion to his profession, his family, his beliefs—and to her. "I love you. No matter what happens, no matter what our families think, I'm never letting you go."

"Sometimes the smartest people can ignore the most obvious signs. I've loved you from the first moment we met. When we parted, I was afraid to tell you who or what I truly was. Yet, here you are completely accepting of something I can hardly understand. Too bad it took a brush with death and a jinni to see we're meant to be together."

"Should we write him a thank you note? Stop talking." She rose up to meet him with a deep kiss and arched upward. He filled her with his flesh and soul. Fast and frenzied, again and again, each stroke bringing greater pleasure. She ached with the need for release. Fingers threaded through his hair, she pulled his head closer, urging him on. He nuzzled her neck and bit her nipples through the thin cotton. She swallowed a scream, whimpered, and fell back on the gurney.

Heavy lidded, face flushed, Arta moaned and fell on top of her, whispering, "Hail to thee, O Love, sweet madness!"

Breathing heavy, she murmured, "A bedtime poem and a nap would be good, but—"

"Code Pink, Code Pink." The PA system shrieked overhead. "All employees to their designated stations. Code Pink, Code Pink."

Arta jumped to his feet, pulling his pants up while Eliana scrambled back into her underwear. "The baby abduction code. We'd better find out what's—"

The nurse slammed into the room, ripped the curtain back, and pulled out Ellie's IV. "You're back on duty, Special Agent Solomon. The nurse with the pregnant werewolf in the X-ray suite hit the inter-com, shouted Code Pink, and was cut off. There was a guard with her. We haven't heard from him, don't know if he's alive or dead." She tossed a set of scrubs at her. "PPE gear and radios are waiting for you in the hospital basement, right where you get off the elevator. The Prussian blue capsules we gave you and Dr. Shahani should protect you from cesium poisoning. We'll be monitoring your radio channel."

Eliana stared at the nurse. "Who *are* you?"

She grinned. "Didn't I tell you I was an *agency* nurse? Your boss has your back, never forget that. Now get going."

Bert was going to hear from her about this. *If she survived.*

"Wait." Arta grabbed her shoulders. "He's using the pregnant werewolf girl as bait, playing games. He wants *you*. That's why he branded you. He thinks you belong to him. The trip into the mine was to try to capture you. Janie didn't escape. He let her go. It's always been about you. I can't let you do this. I'll go."

The agency nurse snorted. "Dr. Shahani, she's under orders."

Eliana twisted her snake branded arms to the full fluorescent light. "Beyond following commands, it's time for me to confront my tormentor. The *'Ifrit* took my mother away from me and scarred me for life. You can come with me, but don't expect me to hide behind you. This is *my* battle."

He pulled her into a violent embrace. "I'm never letting you go, is that clear? Never."

She nodded, her chin rubbing his broad shoulder. "You can come—if you follow my instructions."

****

Eliana and Arta moved slowly toward the X-ray suite, following the trail of radioactivity with a fresh RID, since hers had been lost in the mine. Listening to the steady clicking, her jinni radar buzzing faintly on her skin, they moved forward with caution. They rounded the corner to the suite, and Ellie's heart lodged in her throat. A uniformed police officer, sidearm still in his hand, lay next to a nurse in pink scrubs, each surrounded by a pool of blood.

She keyed the radiocomm. "Arta?"

"Right behind you." He removed his bulky gloves, knelt by the cop, felt his neck for a pulse and shook his head. He followed up with the nurse. "She's alive. He barely missed her carotid. Call for help while I put pressure on her wound."

Again Eliana keyed the radiocomm and shouted for

help, then spoke to Arta. "Stay here. Take care of the nurse. I can't stop now, not while he has the girl."

Blood oozing between his fingers, he gazed at her with stricken eyes. She turned and walked away before she lost her nerve. The pregnant werewolf carrying a were-jinni was missing. *Find the girl, save the baby.*

Skin itching with the sting of a thousand nettles, she followed the radiation trail deeper into the bowels of the hospital. Pipes with giant valves vied with mops, storage units, and buckets for space. The dark corners, side corridors, and metal doors each called for a quick once over to see if the clicks increased. Everything seemed to be chirping, as if the jinni had sprayed the tunnels with cesium. *The possessed Old Thiess could be anywhere.* She turned yet another corner, and the needle buried itself in the red zone. A million crickets raged, and her skin burned as if on fire. Another door, this one labeled "Boiler Room," stood at the end of the hallway.

He must be in there.

She took a deep breath, marched forward, and slammed the door open.

Show no fear.

Drool dripping from his fangs, the enormous brown wolf, the same one she saw in the woods, sat on the floor, claws poised over the pregnant girl's belly. He grinned at Eliana—and laughed.

Mesmerized and horrified, she raised her hands to show she was unarmed. She needed to confront the *'Ifrit* who destroyed her family. Encased in the PPE, Eliana couldn't communicate with anyone except her team. She *must* know why he hated her. Slowly, she removed her headgear, leaving the radiocomm switched on. She stripped out of her bulky yellow suit and stood before her nemesis clad only in blue scrubs, bare feet, and latex gloves.

"Why did you—"

"Ahhh, my lovely Eliana. You've grown up to be a beautiful woman. Just like your mother, her mother, and her mother's mother and beyond."

Her skin screamed with pain, and to her horror, the snakes began to move on her arm. "What did we ever do to you? Why do you hate my family?"

"We go back many centuries, Eliana Solomon, or should I say, my Queen?"

"I have no idea what you're talking about."

His yellow eyes flashed, and he shifted his weight.

"Once upon a time, a white snake and a black snake fought in a desert."

The snakes on her arms battled with one another.

"A stupid man came across this battle and wounded the black snake with his spear."

He locked gazes with her. "I was the black snake. Before I shifted to the jinni realm to save my life, the white snake appeared before your ancestor in human form and promised him his sister as a reward. She was pledged to *me*! Her brother and I battled because he decided to go back on his word. I deserved the *jinniyah*, not that filthy human. I was too weak to battle him right then, but I never forgot."

Eliana felt light-headed and woozy. "I need to sit down." She stepped back, and her foot hit something. A large toolbox, big enough to serve as a seat, gave her respite.

He grinned and chortled. "I'm sure this all comes as a shock to you."

Stall for time and hope the others would come

soon. Keep him talking.

"I can understand your sense of betrayal. But why come after my mother and me after so many years?"

"You're all alike, you *jinniyahs*."

She shook her head. He was mad. "I'm not a female jinni. I'm an Ethiopian Moroccan American Jew."

His eyes flashed gold, and his fangs grew larger. "SILENCE!"

She bit her lip. How much longer did she have? Her radiocomm was wide open. Why wasn't anyone coming? Where were the back-ups? Couldn't they hear this raving *'Ifrit*?

"You are just like your great-grandmother many times over, Makeda, the Queen of Sheba. Why do you think your middle name is Dameka? It's an anagram. You come from King David/Menelik, the child born to King Solomon and the Queen of Sheba." He stroked the werewolf girl's forehead with his paw. "Her kind, all the wolves, are loyal to you and your house. King Solomon commanded me with his seal, made me a slave."

Beneath the latex covering, her ring pulsed with heat.

Could it be true?

"The *great* king." He spat the words out. "Forced me to work on his Temple. When the Queen of Sheba came to Jerusalem, I knew she was my *jinniyah*'s daughter. Makeda was rightfully mine. She was *owed* to me. She teased me with her eyes and body, led me on, and made me want her, just like her mother. She coerced Solomon into forcing me into an iron bottle, trapping me at the bottom of the Dead Sea for centuries.

She *betrayed* me."

Stall for time. "I'm not my ancestor."

"You have her blood. You and your mother."

Her heart wrenched in her chest. The truth. At last. "You killed my mother."

"Makeda and Solomon thought they were done with me. I swore I would avenge myself on their descendents. Little did I know their treachery would give me greater powers. As I raged within my iron chamber, an earthquake split the floor of the sea open, and the container fell into a crevice that glowed and pulsed so hot, I could see through the walls of the bottle."

A natural nuclear fission reactor? Could it be? Rare, but real, it sounded as if the underwater gulch his bottle fell into was a uranium deposit with self-sustaining nuclear reactions.

"Made from smokeless fire, my *jinni* form was impervious to destruction. Instead, I became more powerful and learned to harness the destructive force given to me." He shook his head. "Still the bottle held me."

"How did you escape?"

"Twenty human years ago, another earthquake sent the jar flying to the surface of the salt sea. A stupid American tourist found it and smuggled the container into the United States." He guffawed. "He got quite a surprise when he opened the bottle. I destroyed him and went looking for the descendants of Makeda and Solomon. I found your mother and her pretty little daughter."

She closed her eyes. *That night in Baltimore.* The wind whipping a frenzy around them. The stinging of a million wasps. Her mother drove him off with her ring and prayers, but not before he focused his power on her blood cells. Intense exposure to radiation in such a short time caused her mother's sudden onset of leukemia.

"You belong to me. I marked you that night. This time the black snake wins. This time, the jinniyah comes with me to the jinni realm, never to return." He turned his attention to the werewolf on his lap. "Your job protecting humans and werewolves from jinnis served me well. I have no need for this girl or her baby now."

He raised a huge paw with razor sharp claws, and the girl moaned as her stomach writhed with contractions. Startled, the possessed werewolf dropped her.

It was just the distraction she needed. *Now or never.* Eliana pulled off her glove and held up her left hand. "I order you to obey the Seal of Solomon."

He roared, leaped at Ellie, and knocked the loose ring off. It clanked as it hit the concrete floor.

He wrapped his front paws around her waist. "You're mine and you're coming with me to the world of the jinnis." He sniffed her neck. "You've been with a man. Did you think losing your virginity would protect you from me?" He whispered. "He is nothing. I will take you over and over again, until you die from exhaustion."

She struggled, elbowing his gut and stomping on his foot with her bare feet. *Where the hell was her back up?* If they didn't get here soon, she'd be trapped in another dimension. He put a paw over her eyes and chortled, "Hang on, we're going now."

A lion roared.

The *'Ifrit* shouted, "Shirzad! You will not defeat me this time!" He shoved Eliana away and charged at the black-maned lion.

She spotted the ring under a pipe and grabbed it. Turning to the toolbox, she fought with the clasps and flipped the top open. She placed the ring back on her hand, and as the lion roared, she shouted, "I command you into this container."

The jinni swirled out of the huge werewolf's mouth, shrieking. The old werewolf dropped like an empty gunny sack. Arta roared over and over and leaped at the evil one. Eliana commanded him again, this time calling on higher power. "In the name of the Lord, by the power of Solomon's Seal, I command you into this iron box."

The jinni clung to the sides, howling, "Noooooooo!" until Eliana slammed the lid shut and snapped the clasps closed. The toolbox rocked, shuddered, and fell over, but remained sealed. He was contained. For now.

Where the huge brown werewolf had been, now lay a shriveled up elderly man with a ragged ear. Non-responsive to her attempts to revive him, Old Thiess did not survive the jinni possession. Eliana turned to assist the werewolf girl. She, too, wasn't breathing. No pulse. Blue lips. *The baby, she had to try to save the baby.* She pumped on the girl's chest, breathed into her mouth, and attempted CPR for ten minutes, to no avail. The girl and the baby were gone. Exhausted, Eliana wrapped her arms around the lion's neck, threaded her fingers through his mane, and sobbed. At last, she wiped her eyes, cleared her throat, and pressed the radiocomm.

"Didn't you hear us down here? Where the hell is

everyone?"

The undercover nurse, whatever her name was, responded. "We had nothing but static. All the access routes to the basement were locked. We just got the elevators to work."

She shook her head. The jinni had thought of everything. "We have five dead down here. The guard, a nurse, Old Thiess, the girl, and the baby. You'd better send two lead-lined coffins."

Arta pawed at the toolbox. He was right. They had to do something with that.

"And, we're going to need to transport a radioactive container to a water cooled reactor for decontamination."

"Good God."

"Exactly." The werewolf girls had been pawns in the jinni's game, a tool to draw Eliana into an elaborate chase. She'd been the real target all along. The *'Ifrit* loved playing mind games, just like Arta said. Eliana knelt beside the lifeless werewolf girl. "I'm so sorry you gave your life because of me. I wish I could do something to make it up to you." She reached over to stroke the girl's hair. Something moved beneath the hospital gown—and wailed.

Chapter Twenty-Two

Jerusalem and Aksum, 930-929 B.C.E.

Solomon sat in his private chambers carefully applying ink strokes to the scroll before him. This was to be his final version of this proverb, perfect for the past year he'd spent with his wise son, David/Menelik, and his foolish son, Rehoboam. *A wise son maketh a glad father: but a foolish son is the heaviness of his mother.* The heaviness of his mother, indeed. He'd never been able to prove Naamah had hired the midwife to murder David/Menelik at birth, but in his heart, he knew she was guilty.

Never an easy woman, his bitter wife had been filled with the venom of jealousy. Each person she spoke to, it seemed, became infected by her snake bite. The rumbles were not kept secret. In fact, one of the Elders had come to him to entreat him to reconsider David's kingship. How would it look, they asked, if you continue to reject your first born? At least give Rehoboam co-regency with his half-brother. That would be the fair thing, he argued.

"Co-regency does not work. Ask my dead brother, Adonijah."

"That's not a fair comparison. Your brother sought to be king without your father's blessing."

"He sought to undermine my rule like a colony of

termites. The surface intact, the plague of insects would suck the life out of my royal house."

"You are alive and healthy. You can give Rehoboam your blessing, bring him to your side to learn to be a great ruler like you."

"My foolish son does not follow God's laws, except in his talk. He swills wine, eats like a swine, visits harlots every day. Is that what you want for your next king?"

The Elder looked down. "David is—foreign. Not born here, not been raised with the congregation of Israel. His ways are—"

"The same as ours. His mother converted to our ways before she returned to Sheba. David became a man in the way of all our men. He is circumcised, of that I can attest. He attends services and celebrates the holidays more earnestly than many born here in Israel."

"But—"

"Enough. Just because you do not understand my decision, or because Naamah bent your ear for the past year, does not mean my wisdom left me. Were Rehoboam to become ruler, all would suffer and the kingdom of Israel would be destroyed. I will not speak of this with you any longer. Leave."

"Ooo-poo!" The garrulous descendant of his first feathered companion interrupted his train of thoughts. "Trouble comes this way."

"It cannot be Naamah. She is forbidden to approach me."

"No, it's worse. The entire Council of Elders is in the courtyard. They are arguing with Benaiah, they want to meet with you and David."

"David is busy. The scribe is teaching him how to

write in our language."

A hoarse shout traveled through the window. "We demand to meet with the king now."

If he did not allow them to approach the throne, they would only grow angrier. Solomon threw down his brush in disgust. "Hoopoe, tell David to meet me in the courtroom."

This had gone far enough; he would put a stop to this nonsense today. Had they no respect for the throne? His word was law.

"Father." David/Menelik bent his knee and bowed his head. His son's red wolf lay down on the floor and covered his face with his paws.

A rush of affection filled Solomon's chest. How much he loved this young man. Respectful, compassionate, smart, industrious, a good listener. Makeda had prepared him well to be a king. "Arise, my son—and companion. I wish to put my arms around you." He pulled David to his chest and hugged his son's rock hard muscles with all his strength. "You are like a great cedar of Lebanon."

"My mother insisted I be able to hunt and fight, as she did and her father before her. She bested me in many a competition until I became a man. I must confess, she is still better at conquering a predator without raising a spear. Her gift is stronger than mine."

"Sometimes age is a good thing. You learn what works and does not work. You've learned about how I distribute justice here. I suspect your mother's approach is like mine."

David laughed. "Yes, but every now and again, she must kill someone to make sure they know she's still in charge. I haven't seen you do that."

Solomon lowered his voice. "That is where my old friend, Benaiah, takes over."

"Ah." David glanced at the captain. "He knows you well."

"Yes, he even understands why and when I allow those unruly Elders to come see me." He nodded at Benaiah. "Let them in." He motioned to David to sit in a throne at his side. It wasn't as elaborate as the one the Queen of Sheba had graced, but it was gold and ivory, encrusted with jewels, suitable for the next king of Israel.

The Council of Elders straggled into the throne room and bent their knees, some with more difficulty than others. To his surprise, Zadok was among them. What was his game? Enough. "You wished to see me. What is your purpose?"

Zadok pushed to the front. "We are concerned about a revolution."

"What treachery is this?"

The high priest, his eyes filmy with age, gazed at Solomon, a look of pity on his face. "Your people are not happy with your choice of a new king. They say he is a foreigner, bent on destroying Israel, taking it over so Shebans can steal its riches."

Solomon glanced at his son. White knuckled, David gripped the arms of his throne and glared at the priest.

"My son is here. You speak as if he is not present. Where is your respect?"

"Did I not anoint him? Would I have done that if I did not respect you and him? It is not I who bear these grudges. Your actions opened old wounds and resurrected fears. At this moment, I serve only as your people's mouthpiece."

"I serve as God's voice. Did you forget?"

"Never. Your people need assurances."

"Go back to your tents and tend to your business. I shall tend to mine and that of the kingdom."

"Father—" David inclined his head. "May I speak?"

Solomon leaned back in his seat. This should prove interesting. "Please."

"Father, High Priest Zadok, Council of Elders. I heard great things of my father and his kingdom and they were all true. As an honored guest in Israel for twelve moons, I learned much, grew to love my father and his country like my own." He paused. "I miss my home. I long to see my countrymen." He smiled. "I miss my mother. With your permission, Father, I wish to return home to Sheba. My heart is already there. Let my body follow."

Solomon locked gazes with his son. Never had he been so proud in his life. David read the situation and salvaged everyone's pride. He showed his respect for his father and rescued the nation of Israel from turmoil and strife. He wished he could keep this young man at his side. It was not meant to be. He would suffer the loss of his son, but not lightly. His vision blurred with unshed tears, he spoke in a soft voice. "You are as honorable and as wise as your mother."

David inclined his head. "Thank you."

"I will allow you to return to Sheba, under one condition." Solomon turned to the assembled group before him and raised his voice. "As it is in Israel, so shall it be in Sheba. On my right and left stand the leading men of Israel. Therefore, each of you shall send your first born sons to return to Sheba with my son and remain there with him as his Governors."

A collective gasp told Solomon his spear had hit the mark. *Good. They shall suffer, too.*

"Scribe, bring me the names of the first born of these honored families."

The stooped over scribe rose and rummaged in the wall of scrolls. He pulled out a large one bound in leather and brought it to Solomon.

Staring straight at the high priest, he announced the first name. "Azariah, son of Zadok, the high priest, shall go and be David's high priest."

The old man clutched his chest and cried out. "No, not my son."

Solomon continued down the list. "Elias, son of the Archdeacon, shall serve the same role as his father, in Sheba. Adam, son of Arderones, leader of the people; Fankera, the son of Soba, scribe of the oxen; Aknohel, son of Tofel; Samneyas, son of..." As he intoned each name, men wailed and protested. *Justice is mine, sayeth the Lord—and the Lord's servant.* In all, the list numbered twenty-one young men, all tasked to serve their new king, David, in Sheba.

Too soon, the time drew near for farewells. Solomon dragged himself out of bed and prepared for the dreaded day ahead of him. The preparations for his son's departure tore at Solomon's heart, just as his mother's leaving had years before. Lest his son return to Sheba empty-handed, he gifted David with chariots, horses, riding-camels, and mules. Wagons filled with gold, silver, jewels, pearls, tents, clothing, and splendid attire stood waiting for the long trip south.

David's men joked among themselves and talked

about all they planned upon their return home. The firstborn sons of Israel and their families, however, wept and cursed Solomon. Mothers, fathers, and kinsmen of the new Council of Sheba assembled before him, begging him to reconsider. Solomon saw their sorrow and compassion filled him. He, too, was losing a child. "Fear not for your sons. Instead know it is the Lord's will for them to spread the word of the one true God."

Although some still muttered, the parents ceased to tear at their clothing. In the back of the crowd, Solomon spotted two people with the grins of hyenas. Naamah and Rehoboam. Let them gloat. Never would he anoint that sinner king.

He raised his hands for silence and asked Zadok to bless the caravan. As the high priest intoned the ritual prayers, Solomon said his own.

Dear Lord, please watch over my son. Keep him safe. Give him the strength to rule with wisdom, justice, and compassion. Let your love protect him from those who would do him harm, especially those who pretend to be friends.

David asked to make one last sacrifice at the Temple before he left and would never be able to bask in the glory of the Ark of the Covenant again. "One request, since Zadok's son is the new high priest for me, could Azariah offer it on my behalf, so he knows what to do in Sheba?"

Solomon agreed this was a good plan and gave one hundred bulls, one hundred oxen, ten thousand sheep, ten thousand goats, and ten of every kind of animal that could be eaten, along with fine white flour and forty baskets of bread. After they offered up the sacrifices,

Solomon returned to the palace and slept, albeit poorly knowing the next day would be the last he would spend with his son.

The next morning, David came to Solomon and asked for his blessings. Solomon clutched David to his heart. "Blessed be the Lord my God, who blessed my father, David. May He be with you always, may your seed be blessed, and may you multiply and may your children and grandchildren be as numerous as the stars in the sky." He paused. "May all the birds and beasts and fish be your subjects. Be gracious, kind, generous, and wise. May you find a love match as true as I did with your mother, who will always be in my heart. I love you son. I always will."

Red-eyed, David could barely choke out the words. "And I you."

"Give your mother my love."

David nodded, turned and mounted his steed. Hundreds of ram's horns sounded. Accompanied by a cloud of dust, the caravan marched out of Jerusalem. Solomon stood on the roof of his palace and listened to his city mourn. Dogs howled, goats bleated, and the cries of his people ripped at his heart. He gazed into the horizon until the sun set in a blaze of red glory. Hoopoe perched on the wall, awaiting his orders.

"My friend, you know me well. Report back to me tomorrow morning, let me know my son is safe."

"Ooo-poo! I'm on my way." The striped bird lifted off and flew high above. Solomon wished he could have that bird's eye view. He sighed and thought of his father's poetry. *"How long shall I take counsel in my soul, having sorrow in my heart daily? How long shall mine enemy be exalted before me?"* He had to trust in the Lord. Naamah and her foolish son would be dealt with by Him in His own time.

****

The next morning, Solomon arose with a sick feeling in his gut. Grief, his old friend, came back to visit him. Unlike the time Makeda left, however, he would not sink into an abyss of despair. His country needed him awake and alert, firmly in charge of his realm, especially now that Rehoboam and his mother circled the throne like vultures. *I'm not dead, yet, Naamah.* His heart surged at the sound of flapping wings.

"Ooo-poo!" The bird fell from the ledge. "I flew as fast as I could. Terrible news."

Alarmed, King Solomon knelt at Hoopoe's side and lifted him with gentle hands. "What happened?" He brought the bird to a basin of water.

Revived, but still unsteady, Hoopoe rested in Solomon's arms. "I followed the caravan, as you instructed, but they traveled so fast, I couldn't keep up. I swear I saw a wagon covered with dirty clothes lift into the air and fly, taking the procession along with it. The entire caravan was over the river, in Gaza, by noon." The bird shook himself. "Impossible. A mirage fooled me. I'm sorry I let you down."

Solomon's stomach, already in knots, swooped and fell at Hoopoe's words. He recalled his strange dream of a brilliant sun, which shone on Israel for years. The sun flew away to Sheba and stayed there in all its brightness forever. When he was with Makeda, he thought the dream was about her. Was the dream about David? Or something even more ominous?

Benaiah appeared in his doorway.

"My king, there is treachery. A forgery of the Ark of the Covenant was placed beneath the wings of the cherubim."

Solomon's mouth went dry and his legs turned to water.

"Call out your soldiers, go after my son's retinue. Someone amongst them stole the Ark of the Covenant."

Benaiah raced out the door and shouted for his men to mount up. The chase was fruitless, but he must send them.

"Ooo-poo!" The bird sagged in Solomon's embrace. "Too late, my King. It is gone." Hoopoe closed his eyes and his spirit left him. His little friend had given his life in service to his king. Solomon bowed his head. Tears of sorrow, frustration, and anger poured down his cheeks. How could God allow the Ark to be stolen? Why did God forsake them? Why did the Lord choose Sheba over Israel? Whatever the reason, he prayed Makeda and David would give the Ark a good home and keep it safe forever.

****

Makeda rejoiced at Menelik/David's return—and gasped at the miraculous arrival of the Ark of the Covenant. David told her the chest containing the stone tablets from Moses *wanted* to come with him. The Ark was to be revered and feared. If the Ark didn't want to be with him, it would have never allowed itself to be hidden. She knew the Lord chose her nation for great things. Now Sheba's job was to protect the Ark and keep it safe from those who would wish to steal it for its power, not for its covenant with the Lord. Just as she foretold at his birth, David/Menelik was now King of two countries. It was time for her to step down, hand the throne and her nation to her son. Like Bathsheba, she would advise him. Unlike Bathsheba, she wouldn't choose his brides.

Two years after his return from Israel, King David/Menelik appeared in her chamber door. He bowed his head and asked to enter.

"You need not stand on ritual with me, my son. You are always welcome. What do you seek?"

"Your blessings, Mother."

She smiled. "Another marriage, my son? This will be what? The sixth? Is she pretty?"

He beamed. "Beautiful, long-limbed, large brown eyes, big baby bearing hips. She will give you many grandchildren."

"Which family will she align you with? Are they north or south?"

"She comes from humble people, has no worldly wealth—except in the children she will bear."

Makeda frowned. "That is a bad precedent, my son."

"I love her."

Her breath lodged in her throat. "You've never said that before."

"Your love match was with the greatest king of all time. Who says my love match cannot be a commoner?"

Makeda sighed. "What did the ring tell you?"

"When we kissed, I felt as if I was struck by lightning. The ring burned my finger." He pulled the seal off his left hand. Blisters seared his flesh.

"You cannot marry a commoner." Makeda held her hand up. "I know you love her. I see the ring approves. There is another way."

"How?"

"Make her your concubine."

Chapter Twenty-Three

Summertown, Present Day

Eliana lifted the dead girl's hospital gown and gasped. Somehow, despite the mother's death, the baby had survived. The baby's tiny *human* head emerged from the birth canal. Mouth sucking for air, the newborn fought for life. "Arta, I could use a hand—or paw—over here." She threw a glance over her shoulder. Nude, her beloved rose from all fours and strode to her side.

He knelt beside her. "He's alive?"

"Yes, and in need of a doctor. You'll do, even in your birthday suit."

"Give me the belt to your scrubs."

She pulled the thin blue tie out of the waistband and handed it to him.

"There may be a pair of bandage scissors on the dead nurse. Get me those and some blankets and towels. And, grab whatever lead aprons you can find."

Bare-footed, pants falling, she sprinted back to the X-ray suite, avoided the congealing pool of blood around the nurse, and rummaged in the dead woman's pockets. "Sorry." In addition to the scissors, she found a pair of forceps. She rolled the top of her waistband and clamped it in place. The suite had a stack of bedding. "Blankets and towels. Bonus find—scrubs for Arta."

The lead aprons hung over the machines in a dark corner. She lifted one. The damn things were heavy. How was she supposed to get two of them back to Arta? Her gaze snagged on a stainless steel cart laden with papers. That would do. She knocked the documents onto the concrete floor and piled everything on the top shelf. Unlocking the casters, she raced back to the boiler room and found Arta cradling a blood-slicked baby.

"He couldn't wait." Arta grabbed a towel and wiped the boy down. "Scissors."

Umbilical cord tied off in two places, he snipped between the blue knots.

"Blanket."

She handed him the thin bath blanket and watched as he swaddled the pink infant with care. "He's so quiet. Is he okay?"

Footsteps echoed in the distant hallway.

"Seems to be. Hold him while I get dressed." He handed the child to Eliana and hurried into the scrubs.

The baby turned and rooted at her breast. "He's hungry. We need to get him some formula."

"Yes, and we need to take care of ourselves, too. Prussian blue won't protect us completely. Wrap him in one of the lead vests. I'll put the other one around the tool box."

A PPE clad team of four shuffled into the room. The lead person tapped his helmet. Eliana lifted her head gear and keyed the radiocomm.

"Find some formula for this child."

"What's that?" The leader pointed to the lead-apron draped toolbox.

"A radiation hazard with the potential to become a

weapon."

The team shuffled backward in unison, as if choreographed.

"We need an armored car to take us to the closest university with a water cooled research reactor, we need a bomb disposal robot waiting for us at the reactor, and we need to do it NOW."

Arta said in a low voice, "You know we need to neutralize the child, too. He's as much a risk as that jinni, maybe more because he has no control of his power."

"Yes, there's only one way to take care of both of them at the same time." She gazed down into the baby's perfect face and her chest tightened. "It's the only choice."

****

Arta admired Eliana as they sat in the back of the armored truck and rumbled toward Maryland. As best she could with the heavy vest, she fed, burped, and cuddled the baby as if he were her own.

"Where'd you learn to do that?"

"What?"

"Take care of a baby. More secrets?"

She laughed. "In high school, when I wasn't studying, I used to volunteer at the NICU at Harvey Medical Center. A lot of parents came to visit and spend time with their kids, but not all the babies had *competent* parents. Drug addicts' babies needed to be held, rocked, fed. The nursing staff had their hands full. I felt bad for the babies. It wasn't their fault their mommies were addicts." She nodded at the lead vest covered infant in her arms. "Just like this little guy. He can't help who his father is. The sins of his father shouldn't be held against him." She locked gazes with him. "Unlike the *'Ifrit*, I don't hold this baby responsible for what happened to my family."

He nodded and flexed his fists. "What about me? Do you forgive me for the time in the desert?"

Surprise crossed her face. "How could I hold you responsible for turning into a Persian lion? That would be like me trying to control the color of my skin. It's who you are. I love you. All of you. Whatever form you take. Just do me a favor and don't shapeshift in bed."

He burst out laughing. "It took me a while, but I'm not the Incredible Hulk anymore. I'm getting better control of when and where I shift."

The truck rumbled to a stop and a voice called overhead. "College Park. We're almost at the reactor. The bomb disposal robot is in place."

He took a deep breath. "Now or never." Clutching the weighty toolbox with one hand and his beloved's elbow with the other, Arta led the way into the cinder block and lead lined building. The Cherenkov blue water that cooled the nuclear reactor seemed innocent, unless you knew it was just as radioactive as the baby and the metal container he carried.

He set the toolbox down just inside the door, and Eliana placed the naked, wailing child in the basket they'd requested. Pushing the heavy door closed, a scientist in white lab coat led them to the viewing room. Arta squeezed Ellie's hand.

"He'll be okay. He comes from hardy stock."

She gave him a weak smile. "I hope you're right."

They stared at a computer screen with multiple views as a seasoned bomb squad expert guided the small, tank-like robot to the toolbox first. Pincers extended, the machine reached for the handle, and then lifted the box over the edge of the cobalt blue colored pool and dropped it in with a splash. The box glowed, pulsed, and turned black. Thanks to the radioactive water neutralizing him, the *'Ifrit* wasn't radioactive anymore. Once the case was retrieved, Homeland Security would keep the jinni in a vault in perpetuity.

The robot turned toward the basket where the infant rested. Eliana clutched Arta's hand so hard her nails dug into his palm. He squeezed back and stared at the computer screen. The baby howled like a tiny werewolf, and the hairs on the back of his neck stood up. If they didn't neutralize the child soon, his tiny tantrum could mushroom into something much more dangerous. The miniature tank lifted the handle of the loosely woven basket and slowly made its way to the side of the pool. Arta glanced at the ordnance expert remote controlling the robot. A rivulet of sweat trickled down the side of the man's face.

"Eliana, let us pray for the baby's safety, for everyone's safety." She nodded, closed her eyes, and bowed her head on her fists, the Seal of Solomon facing outward. The two of them, she whispering in Hebrew, he in Farsi, begged for the Lord's blessings on the child and his safe return. When she opened her eyes, the robot had crawled forward and inched the basket down into the water. The cameras caught every movement as the basket bobbed on the surface, and then began to sink. If the baby's swimming reflex didn't kick in, he'd drown and they'd have no way to rescue him without endangering their own lives. The water lapped over the baby's legs, belly, and arms. His neck and chin turned blue in the cobalt water, which began to creep over his mouth and nose.

Ellie's breathing grew rapid and shallow. Tears filled her eyes. "I can't watch."

"You have been called for a higher purpose. Do not despair. He is with you. Use your power to command the were-jinni." *Where did that come from?* The expression on his face must have matched the astonished one on hers.

The water covered the infant's forehead, inching toward his crown. Tears streaming down her face, Eliana screamed, "Baby, for the love of God, kick your little feet and swim."

The newborn shot up in the water, threw his head back, and gasped for air.

"Get him out, get the basket under him and get him out," she shouted.

The robot arm swung the container under the child and lifted him free of the water.

"He's safe, he's safe!" Arta reached down to kiss his beloved, but she was already out of the room. He flew after her. The scientist snatched the door open and the robot brought the basket with the baby to Ellie. He was safe and so was the world now, thank God.

Outside in the rising sun, the swaddled baby in her arms, Arta laughed with joy. Cooing and humming, she hugged and kissed his little face a million times. "You're in love with that baby, aren't you?"

"Is that bad?"

"No. But we have to call him something other than baby all the time. What shall we name him?"

She locked gazes with him and smiled. "Isn't it obvious?"

Of course. He laughed out loud. "The baby in the

basket, rescued by a princess. He shall be called Moses."

She held the baby out to him. Arta gasped. "Your arms."

The black and white snakes were gone.

Eliana shrieked with joy and startled Moses. He wailed and howled.

"Poor baby, hush, I'm sorry, I didn't mean to scare you." She hugged and rocked him, but the child was inconsolable. "I'm sorry, so sorry." She turned a stricken face to Arta. "What shall we do? He has no mother or father." The baby screamed so hard he turned deep red. "He's a new breed of supernatural creature, unlike any other before him. His mother died giving birth to him. If the werewolves won't keep him, we can't hand him over to the jinnis, even the good ones. They hate wolves. Who can teach him right from wrong and how to control his powers? Who will accept him and raise him as a normal child?"

The baby and Eliana sobbed.

Arta wrapped his arms around her and the baby ceased crying. Open-mouthed, eyes wide, his beloved gazed at him in awe. He knew what they needed to do.

Sharon Buchbinder

Epilogue

Washington, D.C., One Year Later

A plethora of colors and scents of the national flower surrounded the couple in the U.S. Botanic Gardens in Washington, D.C. Standing in the center of an octagonal parterre, Eliana, dressed in a simple ivory white suit, held a bouquet of red roses and Arta, wore a navy blue blazer with a red rose boutonniere in his lapel. The retired African-American judge known for his civil rights activism beamed at the couple as he read a Rumi poem provided by Arta's mother.

"May these vows and this marriage be blessed.
May it be sweet milk,
this marriage, like wine and halvah.
May this marriage offer fruit and shade
like the date palm.
May this marriage be full of laughter,
our every day a day in paradise.
May this marriage be a sign of compassion,
a seal of happiness here and hereafter.
May this marriage have a fair face and a good
name, an omen as welcomes the moon in a clear
blue sky. I am out of words to describe
how spirit mingles in this marriage."

The judge cleared his throat. "I am out of words—almost. This union is special not just because you love

286

one another, but because you love this baby enough to take care of him when others might not. Your differences make you strong. Others may see it as a weakness, a place where a wedge goes. I'm betting right now, your parents, Eliana's father, Arta's mother, are worried about your future, how others will treat you. I grew up in a time when a black man and a white woman could not love one another in public. We are now in a time when Jews, Muslims, Christians, and many others may question your choice of mates. Do not allow narrow minds and mean hearts to dictate your decisions. True love knows no color, no religion, and no creed. May you and your blended family be blessed and may you grow and prosper in a country free from prejudice and terror. You may kiss the bride."

Arta tipped Eliana back for a passionate kiss. Their families and friends, including her boss, burst into applause and shouts. "Congratulations! *Mazel tov*! *Tabrik Meegam*!"

Eliana gazed at her husband. Truly they were a blended family. The Adalwolf pack, still in mourning over the loss of their young women, refused to take Moses into the family. Lowell Adalwolf, speaking for the clan, had said, "We would do him a disservice if we attempted to raise him as a normal member of our pack. We have no way of controlling his jinni powers—or our memories. We cannot forgive and forget." She and Arta agreed to keep the infant and raise him as their own child.

Moses Joshua Solomon-Shahani sat on her boss's lap, playing with a large black and white feather. Bert had given it to the child and told Eliana since he was the baby's honorary uncle, Moses was now a member of his tribe.

When they had given Arta's mother and sister the news they were engaged, the women welcomed her with open arms and promises of Persian cooking lessons. Her father, on the other hand, had required some convincing. He was worried about how the world would treat them, yes, but more importantly he wondered if the man who left his daughter to die in the desert could be trusted. After a very difficult conversation, a lengthy description of Arta's family history, and an on the spot demonstration of Arta's shape shifting ability, the astonished rabbi had come around. Today, he clutched his new son-in-law to his chest with tears in his eyes. "Take good care of her. She's all I have."

She loved the contemporary house they found halfway between the new grandparents' homes. With a home office, Arta was able to continue to practice psychiatry, specializing in jinni possession. He also consulted for Homeland on difficult cases, some involving shape-shifters. Her job still meant a lot to her, but was no longer her entire world. Eliana served as a consultant for the Science and Technology Directorate Anomaly Defense Division and was training her successor.

The new jinni hunter's grandmother had worked for the O.S.S., the Office of Strategic Services, the predecessor of the Central Intelligence Agency, in the China-Burma-India theatre during World War II. When Jane Holloway disappeared, everyone assumed she was dead. A year later, she reappeared in the O.S.S. station in Calcutta with a wild story of meeting a jinni who rescued and took her to his realm. The O.S.S. provided the AWOL woman with a Section Eight discharge and a one-way ticket to St. Elizabeth's Hospital in Washington, D.C. Released to her worried family after three months of treatment that included electro-shock therapy, Jane never spoke of her time in Burma again. Two generations later, her granddaughter found her grandmother's journals in a trunk in the attic of the family farmhouse and realized her "crazy" grandmother may not have been hallucinating.

Eliana thought the new girl would grow into the job, just as she had. When not consulting, Eliana was content to stay home and raise her little were-jinni while teaching him how to control his temper tantrums, which could destroy a room. In addition, she was preparing the nursery for his little sister, another shape-shifter.

After all, girls were easier to raise than boys—right?

A word about the author...

After working in health care delivery for years, Sharon Buchbinder became an association executive, a health care researcher, and an academic in higher education.

She had it all—a terrific, supportive husband, an amazing son and a wonderful job. But that itch to write (some call it an obsession) kept beckoning her to "come on back" to writing fiction. Thanks to the kindness of family, friends, critique partners, and beta readers, she is now published in contemporary, erotic, paranormal, and romantic suspense.

When not attempting to make students, colleagues, and babies laugh, she can be found herding cats, walking dogs, fishing, dining with good friends, or writing.

You can find her at www.sharonbuchbinder.com

~*~

Paranormal Romance Guild Winner
Best Mystery/Thriller, 2012
EPIC's eBook Award Finalist
Romantic Suspense, 2014

~*~

Other Sharon Buchbinder titles
available from The Wild Rose Press, Inc.
KISS OF THE SILVER WOLF
OBSESSION
SOME OTHER CHILD

Coming Soon
KISS OF THE BURMESE PRINCE

Thank you for purchasing
this publication of The Wild Rose Press, Inc.

If you enjoyed the story, we would appreciate your
letting others know by leaving a review.

For other wonderful stories,
please visit our on-line bookstore at
www.thewildrosepress.com.

For questions or more information
contact us at
info@thewildrosepress.com.

The Wild Rose Press, Inc.
www.thewildrosepress.com

Stay current with The Wild Rose Press, Inc.

Like us on Facebook

https://www.facebook.com/TheWildRosePress

And Follow us on Twitter
https://twitter.com/WildRosePress